Marry Me Mad

THE ROUSSEAUS, BOOK #2
THE BLUEBERRY LANE SERIES

KATY REGNERY

SPENCER
HILL
PRESS

Excerpts from "La Vie en rose," original French lyrics by Édith Piaf and English lyrics by Mack David.

Please visit www.katyregnery.com

First Edition: October 2016
Katy Regnery

Marry Me Mad: a novel / by Katy Regnery—1st ed.
ISBN: 978-1-63392-093-4
Library of Congress Cataloging-in-Publication Data available upon request

Published in the United States by Spencer Hill Press
This is a Spencer Hill Contemporary Romance.
Spencer Hill Contemporary is an imprint of Spencer Hill Press.
For more information on our titles visit www.spencerhillpress.com

Distributed by Midpoint Trade Books
www.midpointtrade.com

Cover design by: Marianne Nowicki
Interior layout by: Scribe Inc.
The World of Blueberry Lane Map designed by: Paul Siegel

Printed in the United States of America

The Blueberry Lane Series

THE ENGLISH BROTHERS
Breaking Up with Barrett
Falling for Fitz
Anyone but Alex
Seduced by Stratton
Wild about Weston
Kiss Me Kate
Marrying Mr. English

THE WINSLOW BROTHERS
Bidding on Brooks
Proposing to Preston
Crazy about Cameron
Campaigning for Christopher

THE ROUSSEAUS
Jonquils for Jax
Marry Me Mad
J.C. and the Bijoux Jolis

THE STORY SISTERS
(coming 2017)
The Bohemian and the Businessman
The Director and Don Juan
The Flirt and the Fox
The Saint and the Scoundrel

THE AMBLERS
(coming 2018)
Belonging to Bree
Surrendering to Sloane

THE ATWELLS
(coming 2019)
Blueberry Lane Books #21–24

Based on the bestselling series by Katy Regnery,

The World of...

The Rousseaus of Chateau Nouvelle
Jax, Mad, J.C.
Jonquils for Jax • Marry Me Mad
J.C. and the Bijoux Jolis

The Story Sisters of Forrester
Priscilla, Alice, Elizabeth, Jane
Coming Summer 2017
The Bohemian and the Businessman
The Director and Don Juan
The Flirt and the Fox
The Saint and the Scoundrel

The Winslow Brothers of Westerly
Brooks, Preston, Cameron, Christopher
Bidding on Brooks • Proposing to Preston
Crazy About Cameron • Campaigning for Christopher

The Amblers of Greens Farms
Bree, Sloane
Coming Summer 2018
Belonging to Bree
Surrendering to Sloane

The English Brothers of Haverford Park
Barrett, Fitz, Alex, Stratton, Weston, Kate
Breaking up with Barrett • Falling for Fitz
Anyone but Alex • Seduced by Stratton
Wild about Weston • Kiss Me Kate
Marrying Mr. English

For my #WonderTwinsOfWien, Selma and Sejla, with thanks for their kindness, enthusiasm, support, love, and friendship.

A note to readers of
The Rousseaus books

Marry Me Mad shares the same time frame as *Jonquils for Jax*, beginning a week after the wedding of Étienne Rousseau to Kate English.

CONTENTS

Chapter 1

"Hilton Downtown Houston Center—how may I direct your call?"

Madeleine Rousseau bit her bottom lip. Her boyfriend disliked it when she called his hotel while he was working, but she'd already tried his cell phone twice, and he wasn't picking up. Besides, this was big news! She wanted to share it with him as soon as possible.

"Dr. Thatcher Worthington, please? He's a hotel guest."

"Yes, of course. Hold the line, please. I'll connect your call."

Mad reached down to open the bottom drawer of her credenza and pulled out a vintage black Chanel bag, which she placed on her desk. She unzipped the side compartment, then took off her glasses, tucking them into a quilted case before zipping the pocket shut.

The phone in Thatcher's room rang twice before a woman's voice, low and smooth, answered the phone.

"Hello? Room service?"

"No. I, um . . ." About to power down her computer for the day, Mad's fingers froze as she looked over at the framed picture of Thatcher on her desk. "I think I have the wrong room."

"No worries," said the woman. "Bye, now."

The line went dead, and Mad sat up straighter in her desk chair, refusing to let the sinking feeling in her heart take over. This was Thatcher, whom she'd been with for years, whom she was planning to marry . . . as soon as he got off his duff and asked her. She glanced at the picture of them on her desk, taken last New Year's Eve at midnight, and a small, hopeful smile pulled on the corners of her lips as she touched the phone app and scrolled back to her recent calls so she could redial the hotel.

"Hilton Downtown Houston Center—how may I direct your call?"

"Thatcher Worthington," she overarticulated. "*Doctor* Thatcher Worthington, please."

"Yes, of course. Hold the line, please. I'll connect your call."

"Burning the midnight oil, eh, Mad?"

She looked up to see the director of fundraising, Chad Stephens, leaning over her cubicle. Grinning back at him, she shrugged. "You know me."

Chad glanced at his watch. "It's almost nine. How about a celebratory drink? Big day for you!"

Although Chad knew full well that Mad had a boyfriend, he'd been relentless in his pursuit of her since he'd started working at the Free Library of Philadelphia six months ago, asking her out at least once a week. There was nothing wrong with Chad—he was handsome and affable, funny and kind—but Mad had been dating Thatcher for almost three years now, and she hadn't invested that much time in her relationship with him to give up on him now. A marriage proposal was coming soon. She could feel it.

"Sorry, Chad. I can't."

He cocked his head to the side. "Are you sure? Just a drink? We should celebrate!"

"Hello? Room service?"

The same woman who'd answered the phone before answered it again, and there was no room for doubt this time: she was in Thatcher's room.

"Yes," she whispered to Chad, heat crawling up her throat to her cheeks, which flushed uncomfortably.

"Oh, great!" said the woman as Chad mumbled something about "another time" before giving Mad a friendly wave good-bye. "We want a bottle of your coldest and best champagne, two glasses, chocolate-covered strawberries, and—"

"I mean, *no*! No, I'm not—I'm *not* room service!"

"Oh. Sorry. They said they'd call right back."

"Well, I'm . . . I'm not—Who are *you*?" she demanded, feeling flustered, standing up at her desk with her free hand on her hip. Over the wall of her cubical, she watched Chad stroll away from her desk toward the glass double doors that led to the elevator that would take him down to the lobby. She was alone in the office now and raised her voice. "Why are you in Thatcher's room?"

"Who are *you*?" asked the woman, a hint of pique in her tone.

"Madeleine."

There was a long pause, during which she could almost *feel* the other woman's discomfort through the phone line like a living, breathing thing. When she spoke again, her voice wasn't as confident as before. She sounded more like an uncertain teenager than a femme fatale. "Madeleine. Right. Okay. Thatcher's, um, mentioned you. I'm Chloe."

"Chloe?"

Chloe.

Chloe.

Who the hell was—

Ohhhhh, *Chloe*. Thatcher's latest intern. Mad vaguely remembered him mentioning that the university had assigned him a student to give him a hand working this conference. A hand. Of course. And after an order of champagne and chocolate, Mad had a pretty clear idea of where Chloe's hand planned to be "working" tonight.

"His intern. Right," said Mad through clenched teeth.

"We were, um, working, and we got . . . I mean, we were hungry, so I thought I would just order some—"

"Put Thatcher on the phone," said Mad in the voice she reserved for the most unruly of her elementary school readers. "Now."

"Well, he's just—"

"Now!"

"I can't!"

"Why not?" Mad screeched, the phone slipping from her sweating palms.

"He's in the shower!" blurted out Chloe.

Mad gasped, then winced, an inhuman sound of pain issuing from her throat before she could hold it back. Thatcher was in the shower . . . while his "intern" waited for a callback from room service so she could order romantic snacks. Hot tears bit at Mad's eyes, and she closed them, squeezing them shut, shaking her head with frustration and sorrow as the fragile glass case holding her dreams shattered around her.

Taking a deep breath, she recovered as best she could.

"Tell him I called," she said with as much composure as possible, refusing to let Thatcher's little slut hear the tears in her voice. "And then tell him not to call me ever again. We're over. For good this time."

"But Mad—"

"Don't you *dare* call me Mad," she growled. "Only my *friends* call me Mad."

She dropped the phone from her ear, pressed "End," then plopped down in her chair, leaning forward to rest her head in her hands, feeling stupid and naïve and way too trust-ing. Her tears fell freely in the semidarkness of the empty administration office until she'd cried them all. Reaching for a tissue, Mad wiped her eyes, tucked her phone into her bag, then swung it onto her shoulder. She powered down her computer, turned off her desk lamp, and headed for the exit.

Her phone rang several times as she locked the doors of the administrative office of the Philadelphia Free Library and somberly waved good-night to Fred, the security guard working the evening shift. It rang again as her high heels clicked down the marble steps of the library and as she stood on the sidewalk, dumb struck and disoriented, look-ing blankly across the road at a street vendor selling chees-esteaks in front of the Shakespeare Memorial.

Looking forlornly down Vine Street for a taxi, she started walking south on the mostly empty sidewalk, breathing in the hot, thick, brink-of-rain air of downtown Philadelphia. With showers imminent, no taxis passed her with their roof lights on, so her feet headed by rote toward her condo in Rittenhouse Square.

When her phone rang again, she reached into her bag, took it out without looking at the screen, and turned it off. She didn't need to look at the caller's name. She knew in her gut it was Thatcher.

He was calling to explain Chloe's presence in his room, to explain it away with indignant words about Mad jump-ing to conclusions with no evidence. She knew his psychia-trist brain well. He'd remind her of her insecurities, which were the fault of her absentee parents. He'd talk about her father's occasional mistresses and the way it had affected Madame Rousseau's trust in the institution of marriage. He'd tell Mad to give him a chance to explain in person, when he knew that her defenses were weakest. And if she somehow managed to remain strong, he'd apologize to her for "putting her through a scare" and tenderly assure her that she was wrong in her suspicions. He wasn't the one with *fidelity* problems. Oh, no. She was the one with *trust* issues. She could hear him now in her head:

You're it for me, Mad. You know *that. You're wrecking all our plans for a happy forever with your outrageous mistrust and misguided jealousy. I like champagne better than water. You know that. I love the fiber offered in fresh strawberries. Putting them together doesn't equal some squalid affair. It equals hydration and nourishment. Nothing more. And certainly nothing untoward manufactured solely in your head, darling. Stop being absurd. Would I risk you, Madeleine Rousseau—my love, my future—for one night's diversion with some silly intern? Of course not. Why do you look for wrongdoing when all that exists is innocence? My innocence. It hurts me, darling.*

She knew exactly what he'd say. She'd heard versions of it twice before in the three years they'd been together. And despite the fact that she'd chosen to believe him both times, she'd turned the words over and over in her head since— the overconfident tone in the beginning, the accusatory wheedling by the end. Did she have proof he was lying? No. Not exactly. She'd never walked in on him with someone else. She had no photographs of him cheating on her, only suspicions and hearsay. And yet, she knew. Like anything else that a woman knew through instinct and intuition, she *knew*.

Thatcher was cheating on her.

And she was a fool, like her mother, if she put up with it any longer.

Despite the warmth of the evening, a cold chill shot through Mad with the finality of the thought. They'd been together for three years. *Three years*, and lately—more and more—Thatcher spoke about "forever." A romantic, beautiful, cookie-cutter-perfect forever.

Though they didn't live together, he regularly alluded to a home and children with Mad, the doting doctor's wife, at his side. And how she'd cherished the fantasy, dreaming of a lovely life as Dr. and Mrs. Thatcher Worthington with a grand home in the suburbs and a gaggle of happy children. Except in her fantasy . . . Thatcher was faithful, and she wasn't walking home alone in the dark with tears in her eyes.

She had long since passed her condo in tony Rittenhouse Square, but her feet still moved forward. Kicking a crumpled can out of her path as the pregnant skies opened and the rain started to fall, she considered packing a bag and driving out to nearby Haverford for the weekend. Her twin sister, Jax, had been staying at their childhood estate, Le Chateau, since their brother's wedding last weekend. But Jax would know something was wrong, and Mad absolutely couldn't stomach the idea of sharing the reason. Jax didn't know about Thatcher's occasional philandering, and Mad was ashamed that she'd stayed with him despite it, stupidly allowing him back into her heart and bed. She couldn't bear Jax's judgment *or* her fury when Mad felt more than enough of her own.

As she walked farther, the gentrified neighborhood in which she'd been strolling turned, little by little, into a grittier place. Metal trash cans were chained to the rusty wrought-iron bannisters of crumbling brownstone stoops, and groups of men communing in the rain catcalled and whistled at her as she passed. The rain continued to pour, soaking her thin white blouse, and Mad was about to turn around when the sound of music—melancholic piano music not too far away—propelled her forward a few more steps to the doorway of a dingy-looking corner bar.

Notes overlapped notes as a pianist's nimble fingers traveled effortlessly up and down the keys in a Debussy-like cascade of aching melody accompanied by the low strains of a cello. Was it Debussy? Mad closed her eyes. *No.* It was Camille Saint-Saëns. "Le Cygne"—"The Swan."

She remembered the piece well from a record her mother used to play when she was a little girl: *Le carnaval des animaux.* Mad and Jax would sit side by side on the divan in the corner of the ballroom and watch as her mother, a former ballerina, pirouetted and écartéd through the long, passionate strains, maintaining an impossibly perfect arabesque as the music held its last longing notes.

After demonstrating the routine twice, she would turn to the twins and demand they replicate her steps perfectly, which was impossible for two poorly coordinated eight-year-olds. Invariably, the lesson would end with their mother calling them *"plus d'éléphant que de cygne"*—*more elephant than swan*—before flouncing from the room in her stiff pink tutu, her face sour with disappointment.

Opening her eyes to find them burning with more useless tears, Mad stepped down the three concrete steps and through the propped-open door that led to a surprisingly upscale-looking bar, reminding her that neighborhoods like Point Breeze were trying to gentrify, to attract a wealthier clientele. Old French ads covered the walls, and maps of Paris had been shellacked onto the bar and tabletops. Making her way through the smattering of patrons by the bar, she found an empty table for two and sat down by herself, letting the music soothe her raw feelings like a balm.

"What can I get you?"

A new boyfriend who doesn't cheat on me?

A fresh dream for the future that has a happy ending?

Mad looked up to find a server dressed in a white button-down shirt and a short black cocktail skirt.

"Oh, um . . ." Mad shrugged.

She didn't generally drink liquor—some champagne now and then on a special occasion when Thatcher insisted, but for the most part, she didn't like the way alcohol made her feel.

As the cello and piano duo segued into the final movement of "Le Cygne," however, she realized she didn't want to feel much of anything tonight. She just wanted to be numb.

"Tequila," she said, saying the name of the first liquor that passed through her mind. "Two of them."

"Two shots?"

"Y-Yes. Two shots."

"Salt and lime?"

"Sure."

"Two shots, salt and lime, coming right up."

"Make it three," she said.

"Three?"

"No. Four."

"You want *four* shots of tequila? All at once?"

Mad nodded, pulling her wallet from her purse and plucking her American Express card from a neat row of cards. "Here. Start a tab."

The waitress flinched, and a look of sympathy flitted over her hard features as she took the card and shrugged. "Whatever you want, honey."

The thing is? It *wasn't* what she wanted. What she *wanted* was for Thatcher and Chloe not to be fucking in a Houston hotel room. What she *wanted* was to be enough for Thatcher. What she *wanted* was a faithful boyfriend who one day became her devoted husband. What she *wanted* was a custom-made happily ever after.

But all dreams of a happy ending with Thatcher had been blown to kingdom come tonight. She may as well start smaller this time. Getting drunk. Getting drunk was her immediate new dream, and four tequila shots on an empty stomach sounded like a quick way to make it come true.

"Le Cygne" ended with the tinkling notes of the piano, and Mad sighed deeply with melancholy, clapping softly with the other patrons. Looking up at the pianist who sat on a stool facing the piano, about ten feet away, her gaze lingered on the back of his head. After playing a piece of classical music so perfectly, she expected to see a concert pianist before her. Maybe not in a tuxedo, given the venue, but she still would have expected him to look posh and uptight, his hair carefully and neatly coiffed and his clothes conservative. No such image greeted her.

His hair, which looked to be a dark-blond color in the dim light, was scruffy and long, brushing the collar of a gray T-shirt that bore the words "Bach Off My Strings" in a graffiti-style font with a Rolling Stones tongue sticking out underneath and a tiny grand piano perched on the tip of the tongue. His shirt rode up a little, revealing a two-inch strip of skin, which was tan behind the loose threads hanging out of the worn denim waistband of his jeans. Flicking a glance to his feet, her eyes widened when she realized that they rested on the pedals completely bare, but most shocking of all were his arms, which were covered from shirt sleeve to wrist in tattoos. Swirling up both arms recklessly in garish color, they were indecipherable from where she sat, but they seemed totally at odds with the music he was playing.

Without turning around or acknowledging the applause of the small crowd, the musicians started playing again—this time "Méditation" from *Thaïs* by Massenet, another French composer to whom Madame Rousseau had been partial.

The waitress returned with the shots, and Mad looked up at her, feeling annoyed with the world. "What's with the French classical music tonight?"

"It's a French bar," she answered, giving Mad a sassy look as she lined up the four shot glasses on the table with a small saucer of limes and a shaker of salt. She cocked her hip to the side. "Need anything else, princess?"

"No."

"Happy drinking."

Staring at the glasses of clear liquid before her, Mad wasn't certain what she was supposed to do with the accoutrements, so she squeezed a few drops of lime into each of the shots and dusted the tops with salt, then lifted the first to her lips and tilted the small glass cup back.

"Gah!" she yelled as a trail of fire burned down her throat and made tears slip from her eyes. Sputtering and coughing hard enough to draw the attention of the musicians, who briefly stopped playing to check out the source of the commotion, Mad colored with humiliation as waitress returned to whack her on the back.

"Watch that first one, honey. It's a doozy."

"You're telling me," sputtered Mad, picking up the next shot glass and pinching her nose with her fingers before throwing it back like a pro.

"Now you're getting the hang of it."

"I'm a quick learner," she managed through a wince.

"But you might want to—" Mad picked up the third shot and swallowed it like mother's milk *without* holding her nose. "—slow down a little."

Shaking her head, the waitress turned and walked away.

Mad turned to the musicians, whose faces swam slightly due to a mix of fast-moving liquor and some leftover tears. She waved at them, holding up the fourth shot glass as though toasting their good health.

"All good now. Sorry for choking. Please . . . keep playing."

Then she threw back the fourth shot, savored the burn, and grinned.

Chapter 2

What the hell is Madeleine Rousseau doing in a Point Breeze dive bar . . . doing shots of tequila . . . alone?

It had been a long time since he'd seen her. Maybe he was mistaken. Maybe it wasn't her.

Cortlandt Ambler squinted to get a better look at her through a haze of illegal cigarette smoke and dim lighting. Uh, yeah. Roger that. Madeleine Rousseau in the flesh. Sitting at *Voulez-Vous* in designer threads, including a damp white blouse that was clinging way too tightly to her tits, drinking tequila like a champ.

And in related news: What the fuck?

He stared at her for a long moment, and his body swiveled on the piano stool to face her until Victoria nudged him. "Are we playing or what?"

"Playing? Uh. Yeah."

"The Massenet? From the top?"

"Yeah." He paused, unable to look away from Madeleine. "No."

"No?"

"I mean . . ." His fingers moved on the keys, an old melody in his head making them twitch. "How about, uh, 'Smooth'?"

"Huh?" Victoria muttered, leaning closer, as if she hadn't heard him correctly.

Mad sat ramrod straight in her chair, staring down at her clasped hands, with something that looked a lot like misery pulling down the corners of her lips. She was downing tequila like the world supply was in danger, her face the picture of dejection. *What*, he wondered, *has led to this?*

"They're waiting. The Massenet," hissed Vic. "Now."

"Santana," he shot back, a memory surfacing with alarming speed and clarity, suddenly tethering him to Mad even though he hadn't seen her more than once or twice in ten years.

"Cort, what the *fuck* are you talking about?"

Snapped back to reality by the pissed-off timbre in Vic's voice, he looked up at her. "'Smooth' by Santana. You know it?"

"The pop song?"

He nodded. It had been playing that night on the shitty CD player his younger sister, Sloane, always kept by the pool. Jax's tears. Mad's eyes flashing with fury. The soundtrack had been "Smooth."

Ironically, however, he'd felt anything but smooth that hot summer night. He'd felt *relief* after breaking up with Jax . . . but *guilt* over why and wishing like hell that he hadn't hurt her. The touchstone moment, however, was when Mad had nailed him with her eyes, hands in fists by her sides, little breasts heaving with rage. With all her attention focused on him, his heart had throbbed in his chest, his cock stiffening under his swimsuit with teenage lust. It had been such a fucking mistake to date her sister when what he had really wanted all along was—

"Cort!"

"'Smooth,'" he said again.

"Forgive me, *douche*, but it's French classical night."

"Can you play it or not, Vic?"

His partner pursed her lips in annoyance. "I can play anything you can play."

"Then stop being a bitch and do it."

Vic shrugged, her fingers moving to tighten the strings of her cello. "Fine. But if we don't get asked back for another gig, you owe me, shithead. Green. Lots."

"You know I'm good for it," he said absentmindedly, taking one last look at Mad before turning back to the piano to face the keys. "It was written in 1/15. Can you keep up with 1/10?"

"If you can, I can." Vic gave him a dry look before repositioning the cello between her legs. "And it was written in 1/13. It was *recorded* in 1/15. A-flat minor good for you, superstar?"

Cort chuckled softly, nodding because she was right. As usual.

For as much as he and Vic squabbled almost constantly, trading insults like it was their job, he loved her like a sister—a very gay sister who dated some of the hottest women in Philly, a circumstance that eliminated all potential romantic bullshit from their relationship, thank God. After his last two girlfriends, he'd officially sworn off drama. He was too fucking old for it. All he really wanted was something real, something good, something that felt like it had legs and could go the distance.

"Yeah," he said. "I'll give you three."

Laying his fingers lightly on the keys, he counted three slowly, then started playing the Latin-influenced intro originally covered by Carlos Santana's electric guitar, closing his eyes as Vic came in on command with a strong melody line on the strings.

His right knee bounced slightly to the rhythm as his left foot pressed down on the brass pedals below, his mind racing back to *that night* like it was yesterday.

Why, Cort? Why? Because I won't sleep with you?

He'd gritted his teeth, saying the words he knew she expected. *Not because of that. I'm just not into it anymore, Jax.*

You mean you're not into me!

I'm sorry.

So that's it? You're dumping me? Just like that? Because I won't put out? You're a total asshole, Cort Ambler! Jax had covered her eyes with her palms and sobbed pitifully.

As he and Vic segued into the iconic guitar solo, Cort heard Mad's voice in his memory, like an avenging angel, words spitting from her mouth, fists balled at her sides, as she suddenly appeared beside her sister.

He's a DISGUSTING USER! Shallow and shameful and . . . and . . . he's just a . . . a . . . a MOTHERFUCKER!

Her eyes had flashed like chartreuse lightning, fury spitting bright-green sparks of fire from her eyes as she put her arm around her weeping twin and quickly ushered her home.

He'd been shocked that a word so filthy could issue from the sweet, soft lips of Madeleine Rousseau. But seeing the fire explode from her in volcanic force had added a whole new facet to his quiet adoration of her. It had shifted, in an instant, from chivalrous admiration to something altogether hotter, deeper, and more intense.

She wasn't just sweet Mad Rousseau singing in the choir, with her nose in a book, all blushing smiles and lowered lashes when he gave her a compliment. No. Inside of her was also this hot little demon who could curse like a sailor—like a righteous avenging angel spitting fire.

As he watched the sisters walk away, Mad had looked back at him with narrowed eyes, and he'd felt it like an electric shock to the system, like a shot to the balls, like a Taser to the heart, and his fascination with her had increased a hundredfold. There was a fuckload more to Mad Rousseau than anyone probably noticed. And now, with Jax's version of their breakup on full display for public record, she had an excellent reason to hate him forever.

As though Vic felt the passion that was pouring from Cort's performance, she ramped up her own playing, setting her strings on fire to keep up with him during the solo while beads of sweat rolled down their faces.

And when they finished? Letting that epic solo taper off into nothing? The bar was utterly quiet. For a moment. Before breaking into enthusiastic, whooping applause.

He turned around on his stool to find most of *Voulez-Vous'* patrons on their feet, clapping their approval.

Just about everyone, in fact, except for Madeleine Rousseau.

Her cheek rested on her forearms, which were flattened on the small cocktail table. Cort frowned. Was she fucking asleep? He'd just played the duet of his life, and she'd fallen asleep?

Straining his neck and taking a closer look, however, he realized her eyes were open and she was wincing in pain or—

Fuck. She wasn't sleeping. If he wasn't mistaken, she was about to be sick.

"Play a solo, Vic," said Cort, jumping up from his stool.

"A solo? We're a duo!"

"Just do it, huh? You're a Juilliard virtuoso. And make it something soothing."

"Asshole," muttered Vic, drawing back her bow to launch into some furious Stravinsky.

Cort threw his partner a dirty look as he approached Mad's table carefully.

"Madeleine?"

"Mm?" Her eyelids fluttered closed. "Oh, no."

He squatted by the table to speak closer to her ear. "Are you okay?"

With an extravagant effort, she picked up her head and looked at him, running her bleary eyes over his face. "Cort Ambler."

"Yeah." He offered her a small smile. "You okay?"

"Nope."

"You gonna be sick?"

She seemed to consider this for a second. "Yup."

"Shit." He bounced up and moved behind her, putting his hands under her arms and pulling her up into a standing position. "Come on. Let's get you some air."

But the motion of being pulled upright was too much for her, because her whole body tensed before she groaned and heaved. And suddenly, four shots of tequila and whatever she'd had for lunch came up with gusto, splashing down onto the tabletop like a foul-smelling waterfall.

"Oh, God," she muttered, slumping back against him. "Oh, my God. I'm so . . . sorry."

"Aw, fuck! Come on!" exclaimed Darla, rushing over to the table with a rag, a look of disgust plastered on her weathered face. "Are you fucking kidding me?"

"I'm sorry," wailed Mad as Cort wrapped his arms under her breasts and pulled her flush against his chest, stepping back from the mess on the table.

"I'll cover it," said Cort to Darla. "Give yourself a big tip on my tab. Hundred bucks."

Darla sneered at him, shaking her head as she started sopping up the mess.

Repositioning Mad against his side with his arm still holding her up, he walked her carefully through the tables between them and the door, helped her up the stairs to the sidewalk, and led her a few feet down the block to the empty stairs in front of a dark brownstone.

"I just threw up," she said with tears in her shaking voice, flattening her palm on the stoop step before sitting down. "I just threw up . . . in a bar."

"Yes, you did," he confirmed, standing in front of her at the foot of the stairs. "Spectacularly."

"Oh, God," she muttered, leaning her forehead on her knees.

"The good news is that most of the alcohol probably wasn't absorbed into your system yet, so you'll probably feel much better in a little while."

She sobbed softly, then sniffled. "No lady would throw up at a bar."

"You're clearly not a lady," he teased.

"And you're just as horrible as you were at seventeen," she said, picking up her head to glare at him.

"When did you recognize me?"

"You were playing 'Smooth,' Cort."

"So?"

"So . . . it was playing the night you broke up with Jax. I can't hear that song without . . ."

"Remembering," he finished.

She took a deep breath and nodded.

Why this pleased him was beyond simple comprehension. Maybe because he suddenly knew that any time "Smooth" had played at a party or in a taxi or while she was working out over the past ten years, she'd been forced to remember him the same way he'd been forced to remember her. It mattered to him because that thread that tethered him to her the moment he'd seen her in *Voulez-Vous* wasn't a figment of his imagination, because it meant she hadn't forgotten him. Positive or negative, she'd maintained a connection to him as he had to her. And for whatever reason, it made his heart leap with momentary gladness.

The bad news? Her foremost memory of him was the night he broke her sister's heart.

"Long time ago."

She pursed her lips. "I still remember every detail."

"We were just kids."

She considered this for a moment, staring off into the distance before meeting his eyes. "But old enough to know better."

"Know *what* exactly?" he asked, crossing his arms over his chest.

"Right and wrong."

He sighed, the sound long-suffering in his ears. "Jax and I weren't right for each other."

"Maybe," she said softly, evenly. "But the way you broke it off? Half-drunk at one of Sloane's pool parties? Superclassy."

"That wasn't my choice, Mad."

Her eyes narrowed at him for a split second before she looked away, shaking her head with annoyance. "Whatever, Cort. It sucked."

Okay. She was right. It had sucked.

He'd never meant to date Jax.

In fact, he'd been so drunk the spring evening he'd kissed her, he could have sworn she was Mad. He was positive she was Mad. So much so that when Jax arrived on his doorstep the next morning, assuming they were an item, he initially thought it was a prank the twins were playing on him. He quickly realized it wasn't. He hadn't made out with Mad for an hour under the stars, but Jax. And Cort, who was a chickenshit seventeen-year-old who didn't want to hurt his neighbor's feelings, had gone along with it.

He liked Jax. He'd always liked Jax. She certainly had never held the fascination for him that Mad did, but Mad seemed so untouchable, so perfect. In a weird sort of way, being with Jax felt like the next best thing, and they'd managed to keep things pretty casual. They'd been one another's date to all the senior-year festivities—spring fling, prom, and skip day—their status only solidified by the fact that they shared the same group of friends. He was going to break it off the day after graduation so the drama wouldn't spill over into the last week of school, but something had happened on prom night. Something significant that he couldn't reverse. Something that had put all the cards in Jax's hand, and Cort had promised to go along with any story she chose to fabricate as means of breaking up.

"I never meant to hurt her, Mad. I promise." *I was just a dumb teenager with the wrong girl.*

"You know what?" Mad shrugged, leaning her forehead back on her knees. "Let's not talk about it."

Phew. He cleared his throat, staring at the back of her neck, which was long and swanlike in the misty evening. "So . . . you seemed pretty miserable tonight."

She nodded but didn't say anything.

"I'll beat him up for you if you give me a name."

"Promise?" She chuckled softly, humorlessly, looking up at him before glancing down the block at *Voulez-Vous*, where Vic had started her final piece. "Don't you have to go back and play?"

"Nope." He looked at his watch. "It's almost ten. Vic's finishing up."

"Vic?"

"Victoria. The cellist."

She sighed again, a sound of pure weariness that affected him. He didn't like this new, grown-up, beaten-down version of Mad Rousseau. Where was the innocent, elegant young woman with unexpected fire in her eyes? He longed to see *her* again.

"Are you okay?"

"I have to get home," she said, looking up at him and taking a deep breath. She grimaced, placing a hand over her stomach and scrunching her eyes shut for a moment.

"How's the stomach?"

"Woozy."

"You need water. And food. Where's home?" he asked.

"Rittenhouse Square."

"Well, you're not going to find a taxi here," he said, gesturing to the empty street. "How about I walk you? This neighborhood sucks."

She looked around, and he had a sense that she'd prefer to say no, to be alone, or just not to be forced to walk with him, but common sense won out, and she nodded. "Okay. Thanks."

Without thinking, he offered her his hands, which she surprised him by taking. His hands were calloused from playing piano and guitar, tough and rough, but he could feel the softness of hers, so different from his, so . . . feminine. Like her. Like her now-dry white silk blouse and simple hot-pink skirt. Like her pink pearls, which she wore tight against the base of her neck, and her black hair twisted up so gracefully. She was all class. Class with a touch of sass that had always intrigued him, living never-forgotten in his memory.

Fighting a strong instinct to lace his fingers through hers as he helped her down the steps, he forced himself to drop them and gave her a small grin. "Come on, Mad. It can't be *that* bad."

She sighed yet again before turning north to start their walk. "It is."

Though Mad had seen Cort now and then over the past ten years, she hadn't spoken to him since that night by the

Amblers' pool, preferring to hate him for breaking Jax's heart so long ago. Preferring it to . . . to what?

Well, if she was honest, she preferred it to the look he always seemed to get in his eyes when he saw her. It was a look she didn't understand, like there was something between them—or, no, not that exactly, but like he wanted to tell her something, or like they shared a secret that she couldn't remember. It was troublesome because she didn't want to share a secret—or anything else—with her twin's ex-boyfriend. Even letting him walk her home tonight made her feel uncomfortable, but looking around the seedy neighborhood, between thirty minutes of discomfort and the possibility of assault, an awkward walk with her sister's very-ex-boyfriend was certainly the lesser of the two evils.

"Tell me what's going on with you. I'm a good listener," he said, his voice warm, laced with a mix of humor and concern.

Tell me what's going on with you.

She considered it. Truly she did. But she'd already vomited the contents of her stomach. Adding emotional vomit to the situation didn't seem fair.

Besides, she didn't want to think about Thatcher. She'd have to deal with his betrayal at some point, of course, and decide if they were truly broken up for good, but not now. And one thing Mad was very good at was compartmentalizing her feelings. With a mental broom and dustpan, she swept up everything having to do with Thatcher, put it all in a box, covered it, and placed it on the top shelf of the closet in her mind. That he had cheated on her hurt, but it hurt even more that she had wasted three years of her life on someone who didn't love her enough to be faithful. But it wasn't just his cheating that overwhelmed her. The consequence of his cheating—a nasty breakup that would require them disentangling their lives from each other after three years together—was too overwhelming, too disappointing, too painful, and too exhausting to think about tonight. She couldn't. She just . . . couldn't. It would have to wait until tomorrow. Or the next day. Or the next day after that, when she finally felt strong enough to deal with it. Until then, she didn't want to think about it at all.

"Don't worry about it," she said, listening to the sound of her heels click on the slick, uneven pavement. She glanced at him, her eyes lingering on the intricate tattoos adorning the arm closest to her. "So . . . you've changed since we were kids. Is this what you do now? Get tattoos and play piano in bars?"

"You make it sound so glamorous, Mad."

Mad. Since when did he call her "Mad"? When they were younger, he'd always called her *Chevreau.*

"*Chevreau.*"

"Huh?"

"N-nothing." Her cheeks flushed. She hadn't meant to remind him of a nickname he'd probably long since forgotten, and she didn't like it that mentioning it somehow made it seem important to her. She pursed her lips, feeling annoyed with herself, but when he didn't say anything, she felt compelled to explain. "It's nothing. It's just—you always used to call me *Chevreau.*"

Cort chuckled softly. "Yeah, I guess I did. I'm surprised you remember that."

She was too. "It's hard to forget someone calling you a baby goat throughout your childhood."

"I thought I was being clever," he said. "Your brother was my friend, and you were his kid sister. 'Kid' in French was *chevreau,* so . . ."

"Wrong kid," she said, looking up at his profile beside her.

"Right kid," he said softly, his eyes kind. "Wrong word."

Cort had always been handsome. Dirty-blond hair. Soft gray-blue eyes. Full lips that she'd dreamed about kissing after listening to Jax rhapsodize about how well Cort kissed. As she walked beside him, Mad felt a very old and very unwelcome pang in her chest, and she cut her eyes away from him quickly. She'd had no right to those hidden feelings *then* and certainly had no use for them *now*.

"Yes, this is what I do now," he said, answering her question. "I get tattoos and play piano in bars . . . *Chevreau.*"

"But you went to . . ."

"Curtis," he supplied, giving her the name of the second-best conservatory in the country and the very best in Philadelphia. "Yeah. I went to Curtis, and all I got was this crummy T-shirt."

Mad couldn't help grinning as she checked out the front of the T-shirt, which read, "CURTIS INSTITUTE OF MUSIC: The Bach Festival, 2009."

"Do you play anywhere else?" she asked.

"Besides the sacred halls of *Voulez-Vous*?" He laughed. "Yeah. Of course. Small concert venues. Clubs. Vic and I may be going on the road soon, in fact. I was just doing a favor for a friend tonight. My friend Merit Atwell owns *Voulez-Vous.*"

"Why do I know that name?" asked Mad.

"Atwell? I'm guessing you know his cousins, Felicity, Hope, and Constance?"

"Oh, right." Mad groaned. "The Awful Atwells."

"Fair enough. Those three are trouble, but Merit and his brothers are good guys," said Cort. "Merit moved down here from Boston. He led an urban renewal project in a neighborhood on the South Side of Boston, and he's trying to do the same thing here in Philly."

"An Atwell do-gooder? Well, that apple fell far from the tree."

"Actually, I think Felicity, Hope, and Constance are the bad apples of the family."

"Says an Ambler."

She hadn't thought before speaking, but now her unspoken words about the way he'd dumped Jax filled the silence between them, and it made her feel a little bad. Since she'd run into him tonight, he'd been nothing but kind. It's just that she had a decade's worth of potshots waiting for him, and it was hard to hold them back.

"People change, *Chevreau*." He elbowed her gently in the side and added meaningfully, "Are you the same person you were at seventeen? Thank God I'm not." When she didn't say anything, he spoke again, his voice deeper and more measured. "I didn't mean to hurt her. I swear it."

And that stupid box on the top of her mental closet rocked and rumbled, making her spit out a thought that should have remained silent, that maybe *would have* remained silent had she not experienced her own betrayal earlier this evening. "What a crock. You dumped her because she wouldn't sleep with you. That's pretty goddamned hurtful."

He reached for her arm, stopping her, making her look at him.

"That's not true," said Cort. "That's *not* the reason we broke up."

"I was *there*," she reminded him acidly.

"I agreed to let her say that, Mad. But I swear to you, it wasn't true."

Anger boiled up inside of her. "You're saying my sister lied?"

His face tightened, and he stared down at the pavement for a moment before looking back up at Mad, his fingers still grasping her arm. "I'm saying that I didn't break up with her because she wouldn't sleep with me. We broke up for . . . well, for a different reason, but I told Jax she could say whatever she wanted to."

"Why?"

He bit his bottom lip as though considering something. Finally, he sighed. "That's Jax's story to tell."

She stared at him, into his eyes, at the calm, guileless expression on his face. He wasn't hiding anything.

He's telling the truth.

She knew it. She could feel it. Maybe she'd even known it at the time because it didn't feel right then either: Jax had claimed that Cort had pressured her to sleep with him after the prom. Jax had refused. Cort had broken up with her the following weekend. She hadn't questioned it at the time because Jax had been so obviously distraught, but she'd gotten over Cort so quickly . . . Mad had always suspected there was more to the story than Jax had shared.

She looked into his eyes again, scanning them carefully and finding no hesitation, no deception, no wheedling defensiveness in them. Just the truth.

"I don't understand."

He looked down at his hand on her arm, releasing her gently. "I may have been an asshole, but I wasn't a . . . a . . ." He nailed her with an uncompromising look. "A *motherfucker*."

Mad gulped, her words from that night returning in a rush and making her feel ashamed.

"I shouldn't have called you that," she whispered.

"Looking at things from your perspective, I understand why you did." Cort took a deep breath, searching her face before shrugging and resuming their walk. "But if I really cared about someone—if we'd been right for each other—I would have waited. I wouldn't have pressured Jax, and I wouldn't have broken up with her for saying no. I would have respected her wishes and been patient. Jax and I weren't right for each other. That's the simple truth."

She fell into step beside him. "I—I know."

The words came from somewhere deep inside, and she recognized them, approved of them, and believed in them. Teenage Cort had been a brooding and intense musician, totally out of step with Jax's universal *joie de vivre*. They'd been a striking couple, yes, but Cort didn't seem to love the parties and events that Jax did, and Jax was bored by Cort's pool-house jam sessions. He seemed to tolerate her interests from quiet corners, wishing he was somewhere, *anywhere*, else. She'd show up for the first song in his set at a local club, then skip out on a flimsy excuse, leaving Mad alone to stay until the end. Cort and her sister weren't an organic match. She remembered that well.

Plus, it had never made sense to Mad that Cort broke up with Jax just because she wouldn't put out. She'd known him since he was a little kid, and that wasn't who he was. Never had been. He was more sensitive than that. Gentler and more patient. It hadn't made sense then, but Mad hadn't allowed herself to examine it, blinded by her twin's tears and furious accusations. She'd assumed that his asshole teenage hormones had gotten the better of him. She'd made a lot of assumptions, in fact—she'd certainly never confronted Cort or given him a chance to explain. It was just easier to make herself believe the worst of him for Jax's sake.

And for hers. It was easier to hate him, since she could never, ever have him.

"Do you?"

"When you two first got together, I thought maybe opposites had attracted, you know? But if I'm being honest, I'd have to say that you two didn't seem like an organic match." She shrugged, a slight feeling of betrayal gnawing at her for admitting as much. "But she's my sister, and I love her.

You two were over, and she was hurt, and I wasn't going to question the specifics of why."

She paused in the conversation, waiting for him to say more, half-wondering if he'd tell her what actually happened the night of the prom, but he didn't. And Mad knew that if she wanted answers, she'd need to find them out from Jax. Now, like then, Cort was discreet about whatever had happened between him and Jax and had, in fact, protected her by taking the fall for their breakup. It reassured Mad in the strangest way to know that this man who looked so tough and unpredictable on the outside still bore the heart of a gentleman. What was even nicer was that she wasn't as surprised as she should have been, as if she'd known it all along, despite her sister's claims.

"How's the stomach?" asked Cort, elbowing her gently.

"Okay," she said. "Not great."

"What did you have for dinner?" he asked as they turned right onto Federal Street.

"Nothing," she said. *I got some good news today and wanted to share it with my . . . Don't talk about it. Don't talk about it. Keep the box closed.* "I just worked late. I didn't have time for dinner."

"Hm. I think we should remedy that. How do you feel about sardines?"

Chapter 3

When Mad said that shit about him dumping Jax for not putting out? Damn, but he'd gotten hot. Yeah, he'd given Jax permission to say whatever she wanted to because he felt guilty about what had gone down between them, but it had still shocked him, standing next to her at the pool where they'd agreed to have their "staged" breakup, when she suddenly went for the jugular like that. And yeah, he'd stood there and gone along with it because he felt he owed it to her to have the last word. But that *wasn't* what happened. Not at all. Not even close. And while it was up to Jax to share the truth if she ever cared to, he wasn't paying for a stupid teenage mistake anymore by letting Mad think it was true. It felt damn good to clear his name with Mad. It felt important, somehow. Vital even. Vital that Madeleine Rousseau knew that he wasn't a "motherfucker" after all.

She made a gagging noise beside him. "*Sar-sardines*? Are you serious? That's what you suggest for someone with an upset stomach? Are you the *devil*?"

He couldn't help chuckling. "They have other stuff too. Best restaurant in Point Breeze. I promise."

"I'm *not* eating sardines," she said, placing her hand over her stomach, "but I *could* eat."

He got the feeling that she was throwing him a bone—accepting his invitation as a peace offering for accusing him of something he didn't do. But he didn't care. He couldn't give a crap why she said yes . . . he was just happy he'd bought more time with her.

Putting his hand on the small of her back, he led her into the American Sardine Bar and asked the hostess for a table. She grabbed two menus and told them to follow her, leading them out onto a funky patio area where the tables were lime green and the chairs were those blue-and-white woven beach chairs favored by housewives in the 1970s. Cheerful flower boxes of hot-pink and yellow tulips rounded out the eclectic décor, and Cort grinned as the song playing faded out, and Ben Folds' "The Luckiest" started playing from some speakers over the door.

The hostess wiped down the table and chairs with a towel, and Mad sat down in a beach chair, accepting a menu and placing an order for club soda with lime. And Cort, who said he'd have a glass of whatever IPA was on tap, realized that he was in the middle of a moment.

I am. I am. I am the luckiest.

A *perfect* moment with a woman he'd never been able to forget.

It's not that he had pined for her actively or yearned for her with any real desperation. Mad had lived in a sort of dull, aching silence in the deepest recesses of his mind—someone who had caught and captured his imagination once upon a time, with whom he'd never had a real chance, but about whom he could quietly dream. And so he had. He'd even used her for a muse now and then, remembering the almost-woman she'd been, standing by the pool, cursing at him with every drop of passion in her small body. Nothing left on the table. Nothing held back. Everything laid bare in defense and protection of her twin. And that was the solid and inextricable basis for Cort's fascination with Mad: not before and never since had he met one human being who loved another so effortlessly, with such epic totality. Something in Cort's soul longed for the force of that love to be focused, with searing concentration, on him.

"What?" she asked, peeking at him over the top of her menu.

Jolted from his thoughts, he smiled at her as Ben Folds sang the chorus again: *I am. I am the luckiest.* He shrugged. "I love this song."

She took a deep breath, her eyes rising to the speakers over the door as she listened to the tender words about a man who loved a woman with all his heart. But instead of a smile growing at the corners of her mouth, her lips wobbled, and her eyes glistened, filling with tears.

"It's nice." She sniffled softly. "It's *so* nice."

Cort sat down across from her, wincing from the sadness in her voice. "I wish you'd tell me what happened today." . . . *and let me kill him, slowly and painfully, in front of you.* He cracked his knuckles, waiting for her to say something.

She sniffled again, but her lips tilted up a little as she gave him a small smile. "Maybe you're *not* as terrible as you were at seventeen."

"I promise I'm not." He sighed after a moment of silence. "But you're not going to tell me, are you?"

"I don't want to talk about it." She wiped her eyes, then glanced down at his arms, crossed on the table before him. "You have a lot of tattoos."

He nodded, pushing his menu aside. He already knew what he wanted. "Do you have any?"

Her eyes widened, and a sound halfway between a scoff and a giggle issued from her lips. "Me?"

He took a moment to trace the lines of her tan, clean skin: her face and neck, a small V of exposed flesh at the base of her throat, and her tanned, toned tennis arms. He shrugged. "Maybe you have one hidden somewhere."

"Ha!" she said, her smile brightening. "Do I *look* like the kind of girl who has a tattoo hidden somewhere?"

"You *look* like someone who isn't exactly what she seems, and never was."

Her eyes lit up unexpectedly at these words, and she placed her menu on top of his, folded her hands on the table, and stared at him. "Now you can't just say something like that without an explanation."

"Okay . . . um, let's see. You're wearing a silk blouse with a trendy pencil skirt and carrying a Chanel bag, but I found you drinking shots of tequila all alone in a dive bar."

"What do you know about pencil skirts and Chanel bags?"

"Maybe I'm not what I seem either," he said, then chuckled. "Or maybe I just have two sisters."

"Maybe I always look like this. And maybe I always do tequila shots at the end of a long day."

"Maybe . . ." he said, taking his beer from the waitress and holding it to his lips. "But if that was true, you probably wouldn't choke on them . . . or puke after shooting them."

She laughed, then nodded. "Fair point."

The waitress returned, and Cort watched Mad carefully as she ordered a roasted veggie flatbread sandwich and two whole pickles. Without looking away from her, he told the waitress to bring him the same.

"Really? Exactly the same?" she asked.

"Who doesn't like extra pickles?"

She blushed a little, looking down at the straw wrapper she was winding around her finger. "So how else am I not exactly what I seem?"

"You never seemed big on parties, but you were nice to my mom and dad when they had that weird Christmas party every year."

"I loved that Christmas party!"

"See what I mean? You were the only one." He leaned forward. "And as I recall, you wore one-pieces and sang in the choir but cursed like a sailor when someone pissed you off."

She took a long sip of her club soda, watching him over the glass and wiping her mouth delicately before placing it on the table.

"That was a long time ago."

"Listen, I . . ." He searched her face, wishing he had more to go on than a shared childhood and a decade of hunches and dreams about her. "I don't know how I know, but I'm right, aren't I? You look one way, but it's not the accurate packaging for what's inside."

She was staring back at him, as though seeing him for the first time, her green eyes tracing his face, caressing his features, and making him want things from her he'd never wanted so badly from anyone else.

"It's on my inner thigh," she said softly, in a rush, like she was confessing a secret. "Up high. M-my tattoo."

While Cort had always had a feeling about her—a *strong* one—finding out that Madeleine Rousseau's pristine, ladylike, delectable body was inked right near her pussy was enough to make him hard. He adjusted in his chair as all his blood surged to his dick, and he gulped softly as he waited for her to say more.

"I don't know why I told you that," she said, giggling nervously. "I—I mean, no one's ever seen it. Not even Jax."

"*No one?*" he asked, narrowing his eyes, wondering about the person who had made her so unhappy tonight. Wondering why he'd never had his eyes close enough to her pussy to take a good, long look at it.

"No one," she said again, though her eyes instantly lost their sparkle. "It's tiny and hidden, and he . . . he never—I mean, just no. No one."

"Well, now," said Cort, leaning his elbows on the table to draw closer to her, "that is a fucking shame for more reasons than I have a right to imagine."

Two spots of pink appeared on the apples of her cheeks, and she pulled her soda closer, taking a long sip and avoiding his eyes. He didn't blame her. He knew his eyes were hot. They burned in his skull as he wondered why the asshole who made her cry hadn't gotten a good look at her inner thigh, and what a travesty that was, and how fucking much he wanted to be the one to remedy the situation. Fuck, he'd stay there all day. He'd camp out with his tongue tracing every inch of her skin until she begged him for mercy. He'd be the foremost expert on that tattoo by the time she passed out—sleepy, satisfied, and boneless—in his arms.

His dick pulsed at the thought of his face between her thighs, and he took a deep breath. *Cool off.*

Gulping down half of his beer, he never took his eyes off her, waiting until she looked up at him. When she did, her eyes were darker, and he couldn't help but wonder if her thoughts had followed the same path as his. And fuck, that was a hot thought.

"You can't just leave me hanging," he said, his voice low and gravelly. "What is it?"

"*It?*" she murmured.

"The tattoo."

"Oh." She looked down, still blushing. "Just some numbers."

"Numbers? Like a birth date?"

"What about yours?" she asked without answering his question. "You're covered with them. What do they mean?"

Okay. She didn't want to talk about her mysterious numerical ink, but that didn't mean Cort was giving up. On the tattoo or the fantasy. He just wouldn't pursue either right now.

He laid one arm flat on the table and traced a branch that started at his wrist and wound up his arm, then backtracked to point out four apples: a Red Delicious, a Honeycrisp, a Pink Lady, and finally, a Cortland.

"Apples?" she asked, her brow crinkling for a moment before it smoothed out in understanding. "Greens Farms. You, Dash, Bree, and Sloane."

He grinned at her, nodding. His family's estate on Blueberry Lane in Haverford was called Greens Farms and had once been a working farm. There were acres and acres of apple orchards that were now sadly overgrown.

"I bet that one's yours. It's a Cortland," she said, brushing her fingers over the one closest to his wrist.

"You guessed right," he said.

Her fingers trailed softly up his arm, making him shiver lightly.

"Bree is definitely the Pink Lady."

He nodded. "How about the Honeycrisp?"

"Dash," said Mad. "Sweet and sharp."

"Damn, woman." His eyes widened. "You're good."

She grinned. "And that means the Red Delicious is Sloane."

"Why do you think I chose that one for her?"

"Is Sloane's hair still platinum blonde?"

"As of last week, yes."

Mad pulled her finger away from his arm. "The evil witch offered a Red Delicious to Snow White."

Generally, Cort was more protective of his little sister, but Mad had grown up with Sloane and knew her wily ways. He looked at her. "Just curious . . . In that scenario, who's Sloane?"

Mad laughed. "You tell me."

"She's a handful," he said, thinking of Sloane, who had a special knack for pissing people off. "Except when I played 'The Swan.' When she was little, she'd fall asleep under the piano after making me play it over and over again."

Mad was biting her lower lip when he looked up at her. He cocked his head to the side in curiosity, and her tempting red lip slipped from between her teeth, making his breath hitch, then hiss.

"It was what drew me to *Voulez-Vous* today," she said softly. "You. Playing 'Le Cygne'."

"Then I'm fucking glad it was on the lineup tonight," he shot back.

She met his eyes for a moment, and he watched with satisfaction as her cheeks pinkened all over again. And man, it was fucking satisfying because it meant he affected her, and he *wanted* to affect her. He wanted it bad.

"How, um—how *is* Sloane? I haven't seen her in years."

"Still trouble—"

"—unless she's asleep under the piano," joked Mad.

"Something like that," he conceded, grinning at her as he finished off his beer and set the glass back on the table. "But she's doing okay. She owns an antique store."

"Here in Philly?"

He nodded. "The Painted Pony."

"I know it!" said Mad, smiling with surprise. "It's not far from where I live, but I've never stopped in. I had no idea it was hers! It's got some great stuff in the window."

"Sloane's got a great eye for pretty things," he said.

"And Bree?" she asked. "How's she?"

"She's in Manhattan. She works on Wall Street."

Mad nodded. "I'm not surprised. She always held her own with Brooks Winslow, Alice Story, and Barrett English."

"The overachieving eldests of Blueberry Lane," joked Cort. "Speaking of . . . I heard that J.C. is opening a gallery."

"He is. Jessica Winslow—er, *English*—is helping him curate it. Mostly modern art, but some traditional pieces too. The space is amazing."

"I'd love to see it," said Cort.

"Would you?"

"Definitely."

"Because the opening is—" She cut herself off and shook her head like she'd said more than she intended. Her voice was flat when she finished, "—next week."

"And . . . ?" he prompted.

"It's sold out."

"Huh. For a minute there, I thought you were going to invite me to go with you." He searched her face, but she wasn't giving anything away. "And for the record, I would have said yes."

She groaned softly, reaching to push a flyaway strand of pitch-black hair behind the pink shell of her ear, her face indecisive.

"I can't—I mean, I don't . . ." She dropped her eyes, staring down at the table for a long moment before looking up at him again. "My life is *really* complicated right now."

"Well, maybe I'll call J.C. and ask him to squeeze me in so I can check it out on my own."

She looked surprised. "Are you that interested in art?"

No. I'm that interested in you. I'm not going to let you stumble into my life and just as quickly stumble out.

"I like music, theater . . . art." He shrugged. "I'm interested in *all* the arts."

"Hmm," she hummed like she wasn't sure she believed him. Unsurprisingly, she changed the subject again. Happily, it wasn't giving him whiplash anymore. He was getting used to it. "How's Dash?"

Cort turned his arm over to show Mad an intricate design of Ganesh, the Hindu god of good fortune and new beginnings, that he got a year ago while visiting his older brother in India. "Dashie. I miss him like hell. He's in Calcutta."

"What's he doing there?"

"He *was* in the Peace Corps, but he got recruited by the State Department to help them with something local. He couldn't go into details, but he signed a temporary confidentiality contract with them and said he'd be back in the spring."

Her eyes sparkled. "Wow! So mysterious!"

"Yeah, I guess," he said, chuckling softly as the waitress reappeared with their dinners and fresh drinks.

But neither of them looked up as she placed the plates and glasses on the table. Neither of them murmured more than a hushed "No, thanks" when she asked if they wanted anything else. Their conversation about tattoos and art, siblings and neighbors, drifted away, and when the server disappeared back into the restaurant, they were left alone in intimate silence, staring at each other across the lime-colored table.

Cort's heart throbbed as the twinkle-lights overhead cast Mad in a soft glow, and he was helpless to look away as long as her eyes held his. He was a romantic and a firm believer in fate—in signs and luck and taking chances. He didn't believe that Mad had wandered into *Voulez-Vous* tonight for no reason at all. In the depths of his heart, he felt—no, he *knew*—that the universe had preordained their reunion: that Madeleine Rousseau was meant for him, and he was meant for her, and tonight was just the beginning, the first page of their love story.

Her tongue darted out to lick her lips, and he wondered, for just a split second, if it was lust or nerves. He hoped it was lust. But he'd bide his time if it wasn't.

You are impossibly beautiful, he thought, lost in the unique light green of her eyes and not realizing until she squeaked "Me?" that he'd actually said the words aloud.

You are impossibly beautiful.

You are impossibly beautiful.

Cort had whispered the words, like they were sacred, or a secret, or a sacred secret, and Mad stared at him in awe, wondering where they'd come from.

"Me?"

He looked surprised for a moment, a large goofy smile covering the lower real estate of his face as he nodded. "You, Madeleine Rousseau."

And that's all it took to make Mad's life, which was already pretty complicated, *very* complicated . . . because what he said, coupled with the way he was looking at her, made her heart flip over. It fluttered first, but then suddenly, out of nowhere, it flipped, the movement rippling through the fabric of her being and shocking her to the core. She wet her lips again as her heart raced into a gallop. Her eyelids felt heavy. And her muscles—the ones deep inside that barely came alive anymore? They clenched, then released, making her skin flush and soaking her panties.

She'd forgotten this feeling of falling for someone—of feeling admired. Alive. Electric. Aroused. With a sudden flare of white-hot anger toward "he-who-shall-not-be-named," she realized that it was something she hadn't actually experienced in more than a year. Somewhere along the way, Thatcher had started taking her for granted, and their sex life, which had been hot in the very beginning, had tapered off to predictable weekly sex that both of them treated more like a chore than a treat. Was that when the cheating had started? When their relationship had become as dull as their sex life? And had she, in her own way, been complicit in its demise, since she knew it had happened and looked the other way? Why had she stayed with him? Was she so desperate not to be alone? Just to be with someone, even if that someone was—

"Mad?"

Her neck snapped up, and she met Cort Ambler's eyes, which were soft and warm at first but cooled suddenly as he scanned her face, pausing at her lips, which were closed tightly.

He sighed, shaking his head back and forth. "I swear, you'd feel better if you talked about it."

Mad reached for the box in her head, squashed down all those painful questions and memories, placed the top firmly back on, placed it *back* up on the high shelf of her mental closet, and then slammed the door.

"No. I wouldn't."

He stared at her for a long moment, then shrugged, reaching for his pickle and taking a bite.

Mad felt bad that she'd ruined such a lovely moment by allowing thoughts of Thatcher to kill the mood. She promised herself she wouldn't let it happen again tonight and took a bite of her own pickle, bright-green and crispy. She crunched happily as a zing of garlicky cucumber juice exploded in her mouth.

"Oh, my God! These are amazing!" she managed through chews.

"I told you the food here was good."

"But the garlic. Whew! Good thing I don't have a room-mate, or she'd hate me!"

"No kissing anyone but each other tonight, huh?"

He'd said the words lightly, but Mad's eyes shot to his in surprise, and she could tell from one look that he was just as surprised by his comment as she. It was probably just some-thing he said playfully when he ate something with garlic in it, but it made her stomach flutter again, made her nipples tighten behind her thin blouse as a rush of memories—Jax's voice talking about Cort's kisses—flooded her mind.

"Fuck. I mean . . ." He stared at her, his lips twitching with merriment. Suddenly, he narrowed his eyes a touch, though they still sparkled. "No. You know what? I'm not taking it back. I'm going to leave it right there." He said it again, this time with less innocence and more intent: "No kissing anyone but each other tonight."

She felt it all over her body—the full measure of his words, the weight of his intent—in the way her skin flushed and her breath caught. No matter how good it felt, the timing was terrible. This was no good.

"I told you, Cort," she said, leaning away from the table and using her most sensible voice, "my life is complicated. And I'm really grateful for your help tonight, but . . ."

He leaned closer, planting his elbows on the table, nailing her with his eyes. "But what?"

"I'm not kissing you."

"You want to, though."

"*Merde*, you're cocky."

He nodded, his eyes slipping deliberately to her breasts. She didn't need to follow his purposeful glance to know that they were like headlights against the flimsy silk of her sleeveless top. She felt her nipples throbbing behind the lace of her bra, beaded and firm, desperate for his touch.

"Maybe you even *need* to," he said, his voice low and sexy and dangerous.

It was that whiff of danger that made Mad lift her chin, cloaking herself in common sense, because yes, it was dull, but it felt so much safer.

"No, Cort," she said primly. "What I really *need* is a friend."

Chapter 4

A friend.

A friend.

Were there worse words in the English language? It was the verbal equivalent of castration.

And the tone of voice she'd used pissed him off. It was condescending and patronizing, like he was being a naughty little boy and not a fully grown man, completely ready to back up his words with actions that would leave them both breathless and wanting more.

She's lying.

The thought appeared in his head unbidden, but taking one look at her, he knew it was true. He checked out the pink flush on her cheeks and neck, the telltale eraser-hard points of her nipples under her blouse, and the way her breasts heaved with every shallow breath she took. She was obviously attracted to him. And he was hard as a rock under the table. But she didn't want anything to happen between them . . . or if she did, she wasn't going to *let* it. Hmm. Why not? Because of the mystery man she was trying so desperately not to think about? Because of someone who'd recently hurt her? Goddamnit, was she still *with* him?

He took a closer look at her eyes, and though she'd raised her chin in a gesture of overconfidence, her eyes were uncertain. Tired. Even a little afraid.

What the fuck had this asswipe done to her? Lied to her? Cheated on her? *Fuck no.* He'd have to be the biggest fucking moron on the face of the planet if he'd had Mad Rousseau in his life and done something to jeopardize it. So what? What had happened?

She obviously wasn't going to tell him. He'd already asked her four or five times, and he refused to ask again.

"Fine. Friends." He reached for his beer. "But did it even occur to you that maybe I was *trying* to be your friend by letting you know that I'm available for revenge sex?"

She gasped lightly, but Cort didn't look at her. He picked up his sandwich and took a satisfying bite that filled his mouth. It took a while to chew and swallow it down, and only then did he make eye contact with her.

"You're dirty," she said, sitting back in her chair and crossing her arms self-consciously over her chest.

"I just know what I want," he said, leaning back in his own seat and challenging her with his eyes.

"So let me get this straight . . . we haven't seen one another in—what? Ten years? Let's say ten years. Since the night you dumped my sister. Now, suddenly, out of the blue, we bump into each other at a shitty dive bar in the middle of—of fucking *nowhere* Philadelphia. I drink too much tequila and puke all over the place, and you walk me to a sardine bar. And based on that charming, memorable interlude, you want to *sleep* with me?"

She'd said *shitty.*

And *fucking.*

Cort couldn't help himself. She looked so annoyed with him, he grinned at her. "I love it when you cuss, *Chevreau* . . . and to answer your question, yes."

"Oh! You're infuriating."

"And you're not the prissy, pristine lady you want everyone to think you are," he said, adding a little steel to his voice. "Underneath that perfect exterior, I think you're a little dirty too."

Her eyes narrowed, and for just a split second, he saw shades of Madame Rousseau in her icy glare. She cleared her throat. "Is that a compliment in your world? Because in mine, you're being insulting."

He tilted his head to the side, razing his bottom lip with his thumb. "Dirty *and* complicated. What a woman."

She took her napkin from her lap and folded it carefully, then placed it on the table next to her partially eaten sandwich. "Thanks for dinner. I can walk the rest of the way home on my own."

"Like hell," he growled softly.

"Excuse me?" she asked, pulling her bag from the floor onto her lap.

He leaned forward so he could take his wallet out of his back pocket and plucked a one-hundred-dollar bill from the fold, placing it under his half-finished beer. "I'll walk you to your door like I fucking said I would."

Her eyes burned with indignation, and she stood up in a huff, swinging her bag over her shoulder and heading for the exit. Cort followed her, part of him feeling like a jerk for overplaying his hand and the other part of him glad that he'd just put his cards on the table.

He'd thought about her for years.

He wasn't about to let her walk away without acknowledging the attraction between them. He couldn't. Good timing or shitty timing, this was his chance.

That said? She wasn't *walking* away. She was running. And that was his fault.

"Mad," he said, almost tripping down the steps of the restaurant and back out onto the sidewalk, "slow down."

But her heels click-clacked on the pavement angrily as she sped up.

"Hey," he said, reaching for her arm as it swung back. "Slow down."

She whipped around to face him, and her free hand connected with his cheek with lightning speed, the sharp crack of skin against skin reverberating off the brick building beside them as his head jerked back. His fingers dug into her arm as he righted himself, but his *"what the fuck?!"* eyes cooled when he got a good look at her face. Her eyes weren't furious any longer. They were shattered. She gasped softly, her face crumbling as she lurched forward against him, *into* him. Almost knocked off balance, Cort stumbled back against the brick as he wrapped his arms around her, his chest a shock absorber for the force of her sobs. Her whole body shook and trembled against him, her tears soaking the front of his T-shirt as she wept uncontrollably.

Seconds turned into minutes.

And all the while, Cort held her.

Alternately resting his cheek or lips on the top of her head as she cried, he held her tightly, whispering gentle, meaningless words like "It'll be all right" and "I've got you."

Suddenly, his stupid banter and playful come-ons at dinner felt cheap and dirty because this girl—this woman—was wrecked over whatever had happened to her today. And what she needed, really and truly, was someone who wouldn't be a grabby dick. She'd said that she needed a friend. Well, Cort could be that for her. For her, he could be anything.

Little by little, her tears subsided, but Cort still held her in his arms, resting his cheek against her head as the showers started up again, sprinkling them with warm summer rain. He hummed something soothing, with the lilt of an Irish ballad that he didn't recognize, and words appeared in his head as though summoned:

Miss Mad, Miss Mad,
A heart so sad,
And shattered glass for eyes.
I'll stay, you know,
Miss Mad Rousseau,
'Til you say otherwise.

She took a shaking, ragged breath and repositioned her head to rest her cheek against his chest, rocking with him, back and forth, back and forth, to the rhythm of his new song.

Sniffling softly, she whispered, "I'm sorry, Cort."

"I'm not," he said, pausing between stanzas to kiss her head before humming again.

"I hit you. I had no right to hit you."

"Maybe you did. Anyway, I don't care."

She took a deep breath and sighed, and though he couldn't see her eyes, he imagined they were closed as she rocked against him in the rain.

"What is that?" she asked. "What song?"

"I have no idea."

"I don't recognize it."

"It hasn't been written yet," he murmured between bars.

"You're writing it now? Right now?" she asked, and he felt her fingers, which had been flat on his chest, curl just a little into his T-shirt, lightly razing his skin.

"Something like that."

He hummed a little more, lacing his fingers together on her lower back like they might just stay there for a while.

"Keep going," she said, the tension of her grip easing as her fingers flattened again.

Resting his cheek on top of her head, he closed his eyes and lost himself in the sweetness of the music, of the words, of the woman he held tightly against his body, as though protecting her from an enemy he'd never known.

Miss Mad, Miss Mad,
Mi caridad,
My arms were made for you.
Stay or go,
Miss Mad Rousseau,
To you I will be true.

Cort had no idea how long they stood there in the rain, rocking gently, dancing to the song in his head, which passed lightly over his lips in soft, hot breaths as he held her. He only knew that she needed this, that she needed *him*, and it had nothing to do with sex but everything to do with tenderness. And he gave it to her, because he had to, he felt *compelled* to—because the second he'd looked into her eyes through the smoke at *Voulez-Vous*, he'd continued a fall that had started a decade before.

Because she didn't like making a spectacle of herself, it should have made Mad uncomfortable, dancing on the sidewalk in the rain as people walked briskly past with umbrellas. But it didn't. Not at all. Quite the contrary: she couldn't remember when she'd felt such bone-deep peace, and had she had her way, she would have stayed there with Cort forever.

She rested her head against the solid wall of his chest, closed her eyes, breathed in the scent of Cort—soap and cedar and a bit of cigarette smoke from *Voulez-Vous*—and let her feet move oh-so-slightly to the melody he was humming, losing herself in the soothing, lilting song he was writing.

She hadn't been held in a very long time. Thatcher wasn't one to put his arms around her and pull her against him, and gradually she'd forgotten that couples in love do this—hold tightly to one another, swaying to real or imagined music—just because it felt so goddamn nice.

When he whispered, "Mad . . . Mad . . . so sad . . ." at one point, she wondered if he was singing about her, if maybe he was writing a song about tonight. And it touched her deeply that something as terrible as Thatcher's betrayal could give life to something as beautiful as Cort's song. It made her feel hopeful for no good reason at all. Like maybe this was the plan all along . . . to see Thatcher for the cheat he was and to run into Cort Ambler, someone about whom she'd thought, with quiet, forbidden longing, for years.

She didn't believe in fate—or would have said she didn't earlier tonight—but the wishful, wistful part of herself that had chosen the numbers on the crease of her thigh years before now examined the idea cautiously. It comforted her to believe that she was supposed to be here with Cort, so she leaned into it, into *him*, biting back a wince of disappointment when his song finally tapered off. His arms loosened as he pulled away to look down at her.

"You okay?"

She nodded. "Better."

His hands trailed gently down her bare arms until he reached her hands. One of his hands drifted away. With the other, he laced his fingers through hers.

"We're soaked," he said.

"I don't mind."

"I don't want you to catch cold."

"You know that's an old wives' tale, don't you?"

He chuckled softly. "If you say so."

Gazing deeply into his dark-blue eyes, she whispered, "Thank you, Cort."

His jaw tightened, and his eyes dropped to her lips, where they lingered, staring longingly at her mouth as she held her breath, the words *kiss me, kiss me, kiss me* circling in her mind in a hypnotic rhythm. She was so lost in her own desire, she started when he jerked his head up and asked gruffly, "Ready to go home?"

"Home?"

"I'm walking you home, remember?"

"Oh! Right. Home. Yeah, okay."

Her cheeks burned as he cut his eyes away, pulling her along behind him until she fell into step, grateful that the darkness hid her deep blush.

She had no business thinking about Cort like that.

One, she and Thatcher needed to formally end their relationship.

Two, once they ended their relationship, the sensible thing would be for her to spend a year or two alone—to process Thatcher's betrayal, bid adieu to their failed relationship, and figure out what she wanted.

And three? Three was the coup de grace: the death blow that couldn't be denied or ignored. Cort was her twin sister's ex-boyfriend, which made him the most off-limits man in the galaxy.

So it was a good thing he hadn't kissed her, she decided, sighing softly as they walked on in silence. Sure, she was grateful to him for his kindness tonight, and yes, he was distracting. He was, as he'd always been, incredibly hot, and the edgy musician, bad-boy thing he had going on was in such terrific and welcome contrast to Thatcher's buttoned-up doctor persona. But kissing Cort would have been an unmitigated disaster—how would she have lived with the guilt?

That said, there was no harm in appreciating his company tonight, was there? It had been a very bad day, and he was making it a little bit better. She'd say good-night to him soon enough when she got home. Home, where all that waited for her was a dark apartment with framed pictures of her and Thatcher everywhere, his slippers by the easy chair in her living room, his blue toothbrush next to her pink, his favorite wine in the fridge. No, they didn't live together, but parts of their lives had found their way into each other's apartments organically, in a way that used to comfort her.

Hmm. Maybe she'd have a bonfire later. Yes. A bonfire sounded like an excellent idea.

But before she torched her old life, she owed Cort an explanation. After vomiting at his friend's nightclub, slapping his cheek, and sobbing all over his shirt, the least she could do was tell him why she was such a mess tonight. She took a deep breath and looked askance at Cort, gathering her courage.

"My boyfriend . . ." She paused, hating the word "boyfriend" with an intensity that surprised her. Lifting her chin, she started again. "My *ex*-boyfriend cheated on me."

Cort's fingers tightened around hers, but he didn't say anything. When she looked up at him, his eyes stared straight ahead, but his jaw was squared, his lips tight and angry.

"It wasn't the first time, but it *will* be the last," she said, squeezing his fingers back. "I've had enough."

She looked up again, and Cort didn't return her gaze, but when he felt her eyes on him, he nodded in acknowledgment of her words.

Was she supposed to keep talking? By and large, Mad was a listener, an empath, a pleaser, so it felt unusual for her to be the one talking, the one needing to be heard and comforted. Part of her wasn't totally sure what to do next, which made her nervous enough to start babbling.

"We, um, we started dating three years ago when he came to a benefit at the library—the Free Library of Philadelphia. That's where I work. He was one of the benefit sponsors because he's, well, he's a world-renowned psychotherapist.

He asked me to dance. He was smooth. And sweet. And so funny. He would look at two people across the room and tell me exactly what was going on between them solely by interpreting their body language. I—oh, I don't know. He was smart. He *is* smart. He's brilliant." She glanced up again, and Cort cut his eyes to hers, nodding again, his eyes giving away very little. "At first, everything was great. Beautiful dinners. Ski trips. You know. We fell in love. But . . ." She took a shaky breath and sighed. "He has to go to a lot of . . . *conferences.* For work. And one time, I decided to surprise him in New York because it was close and I could take the train, and . . . well, I got the front desk to give me his room number. I took the elevator up to his floor, and I was excited, you know? To surprise him? But when I got to his door, I could hear him. *With* someone." She paused, recalling the loud sounds of lovemaking that had come from the other side of the hotel room door. "I never even knocked. I burst into tears, took a cab to Penn Station, and caught the first train home. But on the train, I decided I'd been hasty. What if the concierge had given me the wrong room number? What if it wasn't him? By the time I got home, I'd convinced myself that I'd totally overreacted. And when he got home, he was so . . . normal. Not a hint of cheating. No guilty eyes or extravagant gifts. Nothing amiss. It was easy to pretend I'd been mistaken."

Cort squeezed her hand again as they paused at a street corner. She looked up at him, and his eyes were strange and full of contradictions when he met hers: tender but furious, patient but burning with a hundred unanswered questions. He didn't say a word; he only raised his eyebrows, indicating she should continue, and Mad realized that he was making good on his promise: he was being a good listener.

"Cort," she said, "you're allowed to talk."

He shook his head and whispered tightly, "Not until you're finished."

She took a deep breath as they crossed the street. "The next time it happened—no, scratch that. It probably happened a hundred times. The next time I *caught* him, a few months later, he was in Beverly Hills. Another conference. My cousin Francine is a psychologist in LA, and she'd met him earlier in the year at a Christmas party here in Philadelphia. She was attending the conference and swore she saw him in an elevator, making out with a young woman, kissing her neck, and whispering dirty things on the way to his room. Before he and the blonde left the elevator, Francine leaned over to check out his nametag. It . . . it was him." Mad bit her lip, her brow creasing. "When she called me to tell me, I got angry with her, denying it was him even though she was calling from the hotel where he was staying, but when I hung up with her, I immediately called him. He picked up on the first ring, and his voice was totally normal. Even. Good-natured. Nothing out of the ordinary. But I was upset, and I blurted out what Francine had told me. The line was silent for a while before he spoke, but his voice was . . . *crushed*. Shocked and hurt. He denied everything Francine had told me, and then he quickly flipped the conversation onto me. He started psychoanalyzing me, telling me that I feared infidelity because my father had cheated on my mother. And the more he talked, the more it made sense. I mean . . . he's the expert, right?"

She paused, kicking a bottle out of her path and feeling some small satisfaction when it rolled against a dumpster and shattered.

"Tell me the rest," said Cort.

"What's the point?" she asked bitterly.

"Why not?" he answered gently. "You've come this far. Get it all out. You'll feel better."

"I doubt it."

"What have you got to lose?"

She looked up at him and shrugged. He was right. She had nothing to lose. She'd already lost her dignity by vomiting in public, so she may as well tell a childhood friend all about her tragic and miserable love life.

"When he got back from LA, our relationship started— I don't know . . . crumbling. We were still together. Still each other's date for every important event. He stayed over at my place. I stayed over at his. We even talked about the future, but . . ."

"But what?"

"Something was lost. I—I didn't trust him anymore." She sobbed softly before taking a ragged breath. "It was dying. Whatever was between us was dying, and I blamed myself. I blamed my suspicions. I blamed my parents for wreaking psychological havoc on my mind." She swallowed over the lump in her throat. "No matter how hard I wanted to go back to where we'd been before Francine's call, I just didn't trust him anymore. No matter how much he explained the suspicious nature of my psyche, I still couldn't get to a place where I *believed* him. And yet I didn't have any *proof* he'd been unfaithful, which meant that I was the one destroying everything between us. And I felt guilty about that, because when he was here, with me, he was such a perfect boyfriend."

"So you stayed with him," said Cort softly, with a tight edge in his voice, like he was trying hard to control it.

"Yeah." Mad gulped. "Which makes me the biggest coward who ever lived. I stayed with someone whom I suspected of cheating . . . who willfully manipulated me . . . just because it was comfortable having someone in my life. Because we'd talked about getting married and having kids, and that felt so safe and—and nice. Because we'd been together for years, and his slippers were next to my easy chair, and my Kindle charger lives at his apartment, and throwing it all away felt even more terrifying than tolerating someone who regularly cheated on me but otherwise treated me like gold!"

She was out of breath when she finished and gasped lightly, the sound of a sob punctuating her words.

By saying the words out loud, it forced Mad to recognize that she was doing exactly what her mother had done—namely, tolerating her father's discreet infidelity quietly, but bitterly, throughout four decades of marriage. Her father, a wealthy Parisian businessman much older than her mother, had plucked country-raised Liliane Roche from the footlights of the Paris Opera Ballet and made her a proper lady with diamonds and furs. He'd given her status in the same way that Thatcher, a world-famous psychotherapist, would have given gravitas to Mad, a children's librarian. But just like her mother, her marriage would have been short in fidelity and long in insecurity. She bowed her head, ashamed that she'd ever considered marrying Thatcher, furious that she'd allowed her life to arrive at this disgraceful place.

"Hey," said Cort gently, poking her in the side with his elbow. "I'll buy you a new Kindle charger."

"I wish that would fix everything."

She wanted to give him a smile, but she didn't have one to give, so she stared miserably at the wet sidewalk instead.

"What happened today?" he asked.

"A few months ago, he told me that his absences from me were an insecurity trigger, so he decided that I shouldn't call him at conferences anymore unless it was an emergency," she said, shaking her head. "And when I called, I should only call his cell phone, not his hotel room, because God forbid a maid answered and I assumed he was cheating on me."

"And then he'd be the victim of your unfounded scorn," said Cort, his voice acidic.

"Playing the victim," muttered Mad. "One of his favorites."

Looking up, she realized that they were approaching Rittenhouse Square now, and the rain was coming down harder, but Cort was slowing down at the corner, probably because he didn't know where she lived. And suddenly, more than anything, she didn't want for him to walk her to her door and leave. She wanted to finish her story, and then she wanted to move past it. Not completely, of course, but symbolically. She wanted to finish telling Cort everything, then move on to a brighter topic—his job, her job, their families, his favorite movies—something, *anything*, so that when she went to bed tonight, her disastrous relationship with Thatcher wasn't the last thing that had claimed her attention tonight, wasn't still lingering front and center in her mind.

"Cort," she said, facing him as she gestured to an elegant arched building over his shoulder. "I live over there. In the Arch. I'd love for you to come up for a bit, but I don't want to give you the wrong idea. I don't want you to think we're going to—"

"I don't." Cort winced, then sighed, dropping her eyes and staring down at the sidewalk for a moment before looking up at her again. "I was an asshole before. I—you're beautiful, Mad. Beautiful and smart and interesting . . . and I'd have to be dead not to be attracted to you. But you're going through something big tonight. I know that. I can see that. And I can just listen . . . I promise."

More hot tears burned Mad's eyes, and she reached up with one hand to brush them away. Cort's unexpected kindness meant more to her than he could possibly know. And calling her beautiful, smart, and interesting when Thatcher had put the final nail in the coffin of their relationship earlier today? It made her want to kiss him.

No kissing anyone but each other tonight.
Kiss him.

God, yes. Kiss him.

Her eyes dropped to his lips, staring at them, wondering what he would do if she suddenly flung her arms around his neck and kissed him. A tiny sound of longing escaped her throat as she sucked her bottom lip between her teeth and leaned closer to him.

Before she could act on her crazy, completely reckless, unacceptable impulse, however, Cort turned sharply away from her and tugged on her hand, pulling her toward the Arch. She would have thought he'd missed her lusty look altogether, except his voice was like crushed gravel when he said, "Come on, *Chevreau*. Let's get you out of the rain."

Chapter 5

His feet pounded on the shiny sidewalk, eating the pavement between the street corner and her building as he tried like hell to get the image of Mad Rousseau about to kiss him out of his head.

For a second—for a split second—he'd almost taken her up on her unspoken offer. God, it would have been so easy to lean forward, wrap his arms around her, and let his lips smash into hers. She was staring at his mouth like a starving person at a buffet, her breath short and shallow, her chest moving visibly under her thin, wet blouse. It had taken a Herculean effort to look away and pull her toward her apartment. Did he want to kiss her? Fuck yes.

But he also wanted her dry and warm. He wanted to hear the rest of her story about her piece-of-shit boyfriend. He wanted to be sure she was going to be okay.

And if he'd kissed her, their night would have been over. He had no doubt. She may or may not have smacked him again, but she definitely would have gone home alone. She would have insisted on it, and he would have been left with no choice but to walk away.

Cort had already decided: he wasn't walking away from Mad Rousseau.

Not yet anyway.

A redheaded doorman in a proper uniform opened the front door for them, greeting Mad. "Evening, Miss Rousseau."

"Hello, Donal," she said. "How are you?"

"Very well, miss."

"Jeanette and the kids?"

"Aw, they're great. Patrick lost his first tooth."

"Well then, you tell him to come and see me on Monday. We have a special book about lost teeth."

"I'll do that, Miss Rousseau."

"This is Cort," she said, holding up their linked hands, then staring at them curiously, like she was only just now realizing that they'd been holding hands since leaving the restaurant forty-five minutes before.

She untangled her fingers from his, and Cort noticed a blush creep into her cheeks.

"How's it going?" he asked, holding out his hand to Donal.

It wasn't typical to shake a doorman's hand when you were a guest of the building where he worked, but Cort didn't care about stupid rules like that. Never had. And listening to Mad greet Donal by name and ask about his wife and children made him wonder if maybe she didn't give a shit about rules like that too.

Donal looked surprised, then took Cort's hand, giving it a firm shake. "Good to know ya."

"Yeah. You too."

"Remember to stop by the library on Monday," said Mad, giving the doorman a smile as she turned toward the elevator.

As he followed her, Cort checked out the posh lobby—way nicer than the buildings near his house on Lombard Street, around the corner from Philadelphia's Magic Gardens. He wondered if Mad had ever seen the gardens but quickly decided that his Bohemian neighborhood probably wasn't a part of her regular stomping grounds. And just as quickly, he decided he'd like to show it to her if she gave him a chance. He'd like it very much.

She leaned forward to press the button for the seventh floor, and they were both quiet, standing side by side against the back wall of the elevator, her bare arm a breath away from his. He was acutely aware of her, of her scent—a mix of baby powder and summer rain—and of her hair, coming loose from its once-tidy chignon. Her shoes looked too high and tight, and her bag looked heavy weighing down her arm, and he just wished she was . . . comfortable. In all ways. In every way that mattered.

When the doors opened, he followed her down the hall to her apartment, stopping behind her in the dimly lit hallway and gently placing his hand over hers as she leaned forward to unlock her door.

"Tell me the rest first," he said, keeping his fingers over hers as she looked over her shoulder and searched his eyes.

"Out here? Let's go in. I'll get us both a towel and—"

"Tell me the rest before we go in," he said softly. "Or else you'll have to bring it home with you."

She slipped her hand out from under his and turned to face him, straightening her arms so her bag dropped to the floor with a thud. Leaning back against the door, she nodded wearily. "Okay."

"What happened today?" he asked softly.

"I got a promotion," she said, a sad smile turning up the corners of her mouth briefly before it faded. "I wanted to tell him."

"Congratulations."

"Thanks," she said sadly.

"So you called him."

"Yes."

"Was he there?"

She nodded, her eyes filling with tears. "She said he was in the shower."

"She?"

"His intern, Chloe. When I called, she thought I was room service. She was trying to order champagne and strawberries. I interrupted and asked to speak with him, which is when she said he couldn't come to the phone because he was in the shower."

He swallowed, wincing at her words.

Throughout her long explanation of what had happened between her and her douchebag, evil, manipulative, chickenshit boyfriend, Cort had somehow managed to hold back his temper. It hadn't been easy, but he'd promised to listen, and he couldn't very well listen and shout "motherfucker" at the top of his lungs every other minute. But now that she was so close to the end, his temper reared its head.

"Fuck."

"Yeah."

"*Fuck*!"

She nodded, her eyes surprised and weary at once, holding his for a long moment before she took a deep breath and whispered "Yeah" again.

"Then what?"

"I told her who I was. I told her to tell him that I called. And I told her to tell him we were through."

"And then you hung up?"

"Yep." She nodded. "And ended up at *Voulez-Vous* an hour later, listening to you play 'Le Cygne'."

"Fuck," he breathed again, reaching up to cup her face in a gesture meant to comfort, not come on. "I'm so fucking sorry."

"I am . . . and I'm not. The reality is that I should have broken up with him a long time ago. Now? Now I will." She reached up and held his hand in place for just a moment before gently pulling it away. "Thank you."

"For what?" he asked, shoving his hands in his back pockets because if he didn't, he'd reach out and touch her again.

"For letting me cry. For walking me home. For listening."

"Well, I promised I would."

"Yes, you did," she said, giving him a small smile.

As he stared back at her sad, tired face, it suddenly occurred to him that by making her finish the story in the hallway, he'd given her the perfect opportunity to say good-night and not invite him in. He'd unwittingly outwitted himself. *Fuck*. And yet, as spent as she seemed, she also seemed more relaxed somehow, and he took some small satisfaction that his presence in her life tonight had afforded her that peace. He wasn't going to ruin that for her by demanding more of her time.

"Well . . ." he said, taking a step away from her. "I guess I should . . ."

"Oh," she said softly, her brow creasing as she stared at him.

"I mean, unless there's more . . ."

"No," she said. "That's the whole story."

He nodded. "Right. You'll be okay? Alone?"

"I . . ." Indecision flitted over her features before she dropped his eyes, looking down at the floor. "Sure."

"Hey," he said, taking another step away, "for whatever it's worth, I think your ex-boyfriend is a total dick . . . and when it stops hurting, you'll see that too. You're well rid of him."

"Yeah," she said, her eyes still wide with—with—what? Longing? Unsaid words? The vulnerability in them was killing him, but without an invitation to stay, it was time to go.

"I'll see you around."

He dropped his glance to her lips one last time before turning back toward the elevator. Halfway down the hall, he heard her turn the key in the lock of her door and forced himself not to turn around. He knew where she lived. He knew where she worked. When a few weeks had passed, he'd throw himself into her path again and see how she was doing. Until then, he'd dream about her some more. He was good at that. He'd been dreaming about her since—

"Cort!"

He spun around at the sound of her voice, hands on his hips, every muscle coiled with hope, waiting to see what she'd say. "Yeah?"

"Do you—I mean, it's so wet out, and I was just thinking— well . . ." She stood in the dim light outside her door, her purse gone, her feet bare, worrying her hands together. "Do you drink tea?"

He couldn't help the sudden and insanely intense smile that took over his face. It came unbidden and stretched his lips, punching up his cheeks and making his heart dance. He started nodding before he could even get the words out.

He fucking hated tea.

"I'd love some."

Mad's stomach flip-flopped like crazy as Cort smiled at her from several feet away, and she giggled softly with something that felt peculiarly like happiness. Peculiar because today was such an awful day, she didn't expect it to bubble up unexpectedly from deep within her, didn't anticipate a sudden shot of that jittery-awesome kind of happiness that she hadn't felt in years and that made her feel a little breathless.

He swaggered back toward her in his sodden, skintight T-shirt, with damp jeans molded to his long legs, and as she admired him, a sudden wave of guilt washed over her. A fleeting thought of Jax tempered her smile, and she promised herself that she would give him a towel, serve him some hot tea, and then say good-night. There was nothing wrong with that, was there? For heaven's sake, it was still raining like crazy. After his kindness tonight, she'd be a shrew to send him right back out into a monsoon, right? Right.

But when he reached her, standing before her, smiling down at her like she'd just hung the moon, her resolve faltered, and her bare feet moved forward, her toes bumping against his sneakers to close the distance between them.

"It's still raining," she said, but her reason for inviting him in sounded as weak out loud as it had in her head.

He shrugged, the small movement making his chest rasp against her distended nipples. His face didn't register that he'd noticed, but his voice dropped in pitch, picking up some gravel on its descent. "I'm already wet."

"Me too," she whispered.

His eyes darkened to black, and when he flinched, she knew exactly what had passed through his mind, because as soon as the words left her mouth, her body, ripe with desire, flooded hot and wet for him. She couldn't remember the last time she'd reacted that way to a man—*any man*—and it startled her. Gasping softly, she spun away from Cort, pushing open the door to her apartment and wincing as it banged loudly against the wall of her foyer.

"Make yourself at, um, at home!" she called over her shoulder, hurrying into her apartment without looking back at him. "Den's to the left. I'm going to change and grab you a towel, okay? Be right back."

"Okay," she heard him mutter as the front door swung shut and she scurried down the hall to her bedroom, closing the door behind her and leaning back against it with her eyes tightly closed.

1. *You need to formally break up with Thatcher.*
2. *You need to recover from your breakup with Thatcher.*

     3. And lest you've already forgotten . . . he's Jax's
     ex-boyfriend.

Sighing deeply, she pushed off from the door and pulled her blouse from the waistband of her skirt, then over her head.

He's Jax's ex-boyfriend.

Huffing with annoyance, she unzipped her skirt and let the damp fabric *whoosh* to the floor. She unclasped her bra and shimmied out of her panties, then padded naked across the plush carpeting to her bureau. Resisting the urge to pluck her sexiest black lace and satin lingerie from the drawer, she grudgingly chose a simple light-blue cotton bra and matching light-blue panties instead.

He's Jax's ex-boyfriend, she reminded herself again, looking up at the picture on top of her bureau of herself with her twin. Jax's smile was bold and brilliant, and her arms were around Mad's neck. She stared at the picture for a long moment, wondering what exactly had happened between Jax and Cort and why Jax had allowed her to believe that Cort only broke up with her because she wouldn't put out. Fingering their smiling faces gently, she felt troubled by the fact that Jax had lied to her outright or by omission. She and Jax were close—as close as sisters could be—and she didn't like the thought that her sister had purposely misled her, no matter how long ago. What could have happened that made Jax feel as though she couldn't be honest with Mad? It was disheartening.

Stepping away from the photo with unresolved feelings, she pulled a pair of dark-gray flannel pants from her pajama drawer and paired them with a soft cotton, scoop-necked, light-blue T-shirt the same color as her bra. Pulling the pins from her hair, she sighed as her chignon unraveled and masses of damp, jet-black, wavy hair tumbled around her shoulders. She stepped into her bathroom to wipe off her smeared mascara, catching a look at herself in the mirror. Jammies, wild hair, and no makeup. This wasn't a look of which Thatcher was particularly fond. He preferred her to wear sexy, silky lingerie when he stayed over, claiming that baggy sweats and loose-fitting T-shirts "didn't do her any favors." Looking at herself in the mirror, she knew he was right: she didn't look very sexy, chic, or sophisticated now, but she was comfortable. And after today, all she wanted was to be comfortable.

Besides, her goal wasn't to seduce Cort in any way, shape, or form. The frumpier she looked, the better. Right? Right. Grabbing a fluffy white towel from the stack under her double sinks, she ignored the throbbing of her heart as she turned away from the mirror to go find Cort.

Thank God she'd given him a few minutes alone, because the boner he'd had at dinner was back with a vengeance after she'd murmured "Me too" at her door. Did she realize that her eyes had widened and darkened after she'd whispered the words? Did she know that she'd released a small "ahhh" noise from the back of her throat? Did she have any idea that her cheeks and chest had flushed pink with awareness and arousal? *Fuck*. She was proper yet provocative. Angelic but arousing. Sophisticated and sexy. And it was going to kill him before tonight was through.

He found her "den" with little problem, skipping the formal living room–dining room combination and opting for a smaller room beside the kitchen that had French doors leading to a cozy hideaway. As he opened the door, overhead recessed lighting turned on, bathing the small space in warm light. On either side, there were waist-to-ceiling bookcases in rich, warm cherry filled with books, and straight ahead, there was a fairly large fireplace of simple black marble. A coffee-colored leather sofa spanned the length of the bookcase to Cort's left, with two easy chairs across the room to his right and a coffee table in the center. The floor was covered with a Persian carpet in deep tones of navy, gold, maroon, and cream, and a cream-colored sheep-skin rug had been tossed casually by the hearth.

It was the sort of room his parents would eschew as "pre-tentious," though Cort felt no pretention in its walls because he sensed that this room was more lived-in than any other in her apartment. The sofa was cracked and worn, and several gray rings, where he suspected a hot cup of tea had been left too long, decorated the coffee table. And there, beside the easy chair closest to the fire, was a pair of men's slippers.

Cort's eyes narrowed as he approached them, staring at them as he would a viper with fangs bared. Without think-ing, he kicked them under the chair, feeling a small measure of satisfaction when they were fully hidden. On the fireplace mantle were several framed pictures—he recognized Jax, J.C., and Ten from the photos, but there were two photos of Mad with a dignified-looking douchebag with salt-and-pepper hair and an overconfident smile. Bingo. The asswipe.

"Hi."

He turned to find Mad standing in the doorway of the small room holding a towel and dragged his eyes hungrily from her bare feet, over the lines of her comfy gray pants, to her soft blue, scoop-necked T-shirt, ending at the shiny onyx waves of hair that framed her lovely face.

His breath caught as he stared into her eyes, recogniz-ing the girl he'd known in the mouthwatering body of the full-grown woman before him and feeling blessed beyond measure to have this glimpse of her that he suspected few were privy to: Mad Rousseau without the heels and chignon—heart-stoppingly beautiful and utterly captivating *au natural.*

He cleared his throat, and she grimaced, dropping her eyes to her toes and the towel to the arm of the sofa.

"I'll get us some tea," she murmured, slipping away in a hurry.

Cort stared at the space she'd vacated so quickly, feeling confused, wondering what the heck had just happened. Why had she grimaced? Why had she looked . . . disappointed? Picking up the towel as he followed her to the kitchen, he pushed open the swing door and stood just inside of it, scrubbing the rainwater from his hair as he watched her work in the small space. She finished filling a kettle with water and placed it on the stove, finally glancing up at him sheepishly.

"Not a good look for me," she said softly, standing up on her tiptoes to open a cabinet over the microwave. "I've already been told. Multiple times."

"I'm sorry . . . you've been told *what* exactly?" he asked. He looped the towel around his neck and stepped toward her, reaching over her head for the mugs she wanted. He held them out to her, and she flicked her glance to them before gesturing to her clothes.

"That I can do better than sweats and a T-shirt." She shrugged. "But I was wet and cold and tired. I didn't feel like putting on another outfit, so I—"

"I'm sorry. Wait a minute," he said, putting the mugs down on the counter and staring at her in disbelief. "Are you *apologizing to me* for the clothes you're wearing?"

She gestured helplessly with one hand. "I saw the way you looked at me."

"Baby," he said, reaching out to touch the soft-blue fabric covering her shoulder and running his fingers over the small sleeve of the T-shirt, then down the length of her arm, "you look good enough to eat. You look beautiful. And anyone who thinks different is a blind fucking lunatic."

"Cort," she gasped, her eyes softening as she stared up at him.

"I'm serious. The pencil skirt and fancy hair? Gorgeous. Sure. But this?" He let his eyes roam slowly, intently over her form, pausing at the luscious mounds of her breasts before stopping at her lips as his fingers threaded through hers. "This is *you*, Mad. And you're . . ." He shook his head looking for the right words, but only one circled around and around in his head. "Baby, you're *music*."

Baby, you're music.

Like rain in the desert.

Like sweet after bitter.

Everything she needed in that moment rolled up into three words she never saw coming. She couldn't help herself. With one step, her chest was flush against his, and with her eyes, which felt wide and hot staring up at him, she gave him unspoken permission.

His lips were soft as they landed on hers—tentative, almost like he couldn't believe what she was offering. Her breasts pushed against his chest, their softness crushed against the solid wall of muscle that she'd felt before when they'd danced on the sidewalk. They stood like that for a moment: their lips and chests touching, barely breathing, almost motionless . . . until their minds and bodies registered what they were doing. And then?

A chemical reaction.

Explosive.

Hungry.

Demanding.

Now.

With a roar of want, Cort jerked her impossibly closer, his hands palming her ass as he lifted her effortlessly onto the countertop. Mad moaned with pleasure as his tongue invaded her mouth to slide against hers. She pushed the towel off his shoulders and wrapped her legs around his waist, locking her ankles behind his back so she was pinned against him. One of his hands wound into her hair, twisting the strands until he held it back tightly, keeping her face upturned as he devoured her mouth with long, insistent strokes of his tongue. Mad arched against him, desperate to feel more of him, and he obliged her, stepping as close to her as he could and gently thrusting his hips so that the hard ridge of his erection massaged the tender, throbbing nub between her legs.

She wiggled closer to him, her fingers dropping from the back of his neck to smooth down his back. Desperate to feel his skin under their tips, she slid them under the hem of his T-shirt to land on the hot, bare muscles of his lower back, her nails curling into his skin to elicit a hiss from his lips, which she greedily swallowed. The hand in her hair slackened in surprise, and she leaned her head forward, kissing her way to the lobe of his ear, which she took between her teeth and bit just hard enough for him to groan and grab her chin roughly, demanding her lips once again. His hand grasped her hair, harder now, his tongue seeking hers with blind determination. She melted against him, into him—breathless, straining, and out of her mind with longing.

In that moment, he owned her.

And until that moment, Mad had never been owned.

She had been kissed, and she had had sex, but never with this sort of rawness, never with this sort of vulnerability. And instinctually she knew why.

Underneath that perfect exterior, I think you're a little dirty too.

From the moment they'd reconnected tonight, he'd seen through her bullshit veneer of perfection, and it had opened a long-sealed floodgate, making her want to bound forth in a wave of reckless abandon. For the first time in years, she had a glimpse of freedom—freedom from her buttoned-up boyfriend and the predictable future she'd convinced herself she wanted. Fuck pearls and heels; she felt like a goddess in flannel and cotton. And she reveled in the guttural, low-toned sounds of their moans and sighs, the smacking of their lips, and the licking of their tongues. It was a filthy melody she wanted to play on repeat forever.

"Cort," she murmured as he bit her bottom lip, then drew away, letting it snap back, swollen and throbbing. For a moment, he stilled, and she opened her heavy eyes, her needy body leaning forward, wanting . . .

"More," he growled, lunging forward to seal his mouth over hers once again.

The hand grasping her hair resumed its iron grip, keeping her head tilted back where he wanted it, but his other hand dropped from her cheek to her neck, the scratch of a calloused palm raising goose bumps all over her body. It caressed the back of her neck, trailing down her T-shirt and slipping into the waistband of her pants. She gasped as his palm slid, warm and rough, under her panties to cup her ass, skin to skin, shoving her flush against his erection until she could feel its pounding throb through flannel and denim.

"I knew it," he groaned, his voice deep and ragged as he dragged his lips to her throat, resting them for a moment against her hammering pulse and murmuring against her hot, sensitive skin. "I knew it would be like this."

And then his lips were upon hers again, gentler now—the hand in her hair easing just a little, his fingers massaging her scalp tenderly as his other hand squeezed her ass, keeping her close, his hips flexing to thrust his erection against her swollen clit.

The numbers on the crease of her thigh throbbed . . . *398.2 . . . 398.2 . . . 398.2 . . .* and she recalled the words she'd spoken to the tattoo artist when he asked why she'd chosen them: *Because I want the fairy tale*, she'd said.

The fairy tale.

Though her eyes were closed tightly, they popped open in an instant, and she felt herself mentally detaching from the intensity of her impromptu make-out session with Cort.

Jax.

Hers was the only face that could have pierced the white heat of the moment—it was the face that had shared the same confined space with Mad for the first nine months of her being, whose heartbeat had pounded in time with hers during that long-ago beginning.

Jax. Jax. Jax.

Jax. Jax. Jax.

He's Jax's ex-boyfriend.

You're kissing Jax's ex-boyfriend.

This isn't *the fairy tale, Mad.*

This is wrong.

"Stop!"

She pushed against his chest, tearing her lips away from his with a gasp of denial just as the kettle started to whistle, as though the chaos in her mind had somehow erupted into the room. Her breasts heaved with the force of her breathing as she stared at him—at his slick red lips and dark eyes that fiercely searched her face. The hand that he'd threaded through her hair loosened, and he dropped it slowly. The fingers clenching her ass gentled, and he removed his hand from her pants but wrapped his arm around her waist to hold her firmly against him.

"What?" he asked, his brows furrowing in confusion and deprivation. "What just happened?"

Her heart pounded with longing, her entire body demanding another touch, another taste. More, more, more . . .

"Cort—"

"Don't throw me out," he whispered, his tone low and challenging.

"I won't," she said, reaching around her back for the hand that clutched her hip and pulling it gently away from her body. "But we *can't* do that again."

Chapter 6

Can't?

Why the fuck not?

He leaned against the kitchen counter and crossed his arms over his chest, gritting his teeth and missing the feeling of her in his arms. She'd been so soft at first—pliant, molded like a kitten against his chest. But only for a moment. And then—bam! The explosive way she'd responded to him was more like a tigress or like a match igniting oil, scorching him until he could barely remember another woman's kiss, though there had been many before. A shiver rippled over his skin as he remembered the way she'd bit his earlobe, her teeth sharp and strong around the tender skin. It still stung a little, and it turned him on so hard, so badly, he pulsated with need behind the zipper of his jeans, his longing so intense, he almost couldn't bear it.

It was heady to finally meet the hot, passionate woman under the cool, polished veneer. And she was so much more intense, more hungry and daring, than he'd guessed. Mad Rousseau was so much more than she seemed, and he wanted to see *all* of it. All of *her.*

. . . which made her declaration bad fucking news for Cort Ambler.

"Why not?" he asked in a harsh tone.

She plopped two tea bags into the waiting mugs and poured hot water from the kettle over them.

"Cream?" she asked, gesturing to the fridge.

Two bright-pink splotches colored her cheeks, and her lips were rosy and swollen. Never, in all his life, had Cort wanted to fuck a woman as much as he wanted to fuck Mad Rousseau. And if that kiss was any indication, they'd be combustible in bed—two lit sticks of dynamite just waiting to detonate. Fuck, it made his toes curl with greed, with raw, raging lust.

She cocked her head to the side. "Or sugar?"

"Fuck the cream and sugar. *Why not*, Mad?"

She rested her hand on the kitchen counter and stared at him, her eyes wary. "I've barely broken up with my—"

"You're going to use your piece-of-shit *ex*-boyfriend as an excuse? Pardon me while I puke," he said darkly, pretending to gag.

"I'm not in the right place for a new relationship, Cort," she added, lifting her chin.

Ah. That patronizing fucking tone he disliked so much was back in full force, and it pissed him off as much now as it had earlier.

"I don't remember offering one," he said snarkily.

She recoiled just slightly, flinching, her eyes registering a hurt that he hadn't expected, and he despised himself for causing it.

"Then what's the problem?" she asked coolly.

He took a ragged breath and sighed. "I didn't mean that."

"So you *do* want a relationship?" she challenged, almost laughing at him.

He shrugged, feeling a little confused and a little miserable and a lot deprived.

"No," he half-lied, because he didn't know what the fuck he wanted from her, but "no more kissing" was definitely not on his wish list. "I don't know what I want."

She picked up the mugs of tea and offered one to him. As she blew the steam over the top of hers, she eyed him. "Maybe you should figure that out before you start making demands, huh?"

Giving him a saucy, annoyed look, not unlike the one she gave him the night he broke up with Jax when she called him a "motherfucker," she slid past him and sailed out the swinging door, leaving him alone with a massive boner and a cup of tea he didn't particularly want.

"Fuck," he growled.

Damn it, but she got under his skin—under his goddamned skin with her wide, injured eyes and her unexpectedly sassy mouth.

Miss Mad, Miss Mad,
You've been so bad,
I'll put you over my knee.
Miss Mad Rousseau,
To stay, to go,
Aw, fuck it. I'll never be free.

What *did* he want from her?

Did he want to fuck her?

Yes. This was a clearly established, incontrovertible fact.

But surprisingly, he realized that he didn't *just* want to fuck her. Though fucking her sounded mighty fine, anything that meant tonight was the beginning and the end of Cort Ambler and Mad Rousseau sounded piss-poor. Not to mention, it made him see red when she'd used her fucking *ex*-boyfriend as an excuse. In fact, the thought of anyone—*anyone*—touching her besides him made him feel murderous.

Grabbing his tea from the counter, he took a sip and counted backward from twenty until his dick had relaxed a little, then left the kitchen, heading for the den where she'd directed him earlier. He paused in the doorway, staring at her.

She sat in the corner of the couch, feet under her butt, tea clasped between both hands on her lap, her beautiful fucking hair like a midnight shawl around her little shoulders. She was hot and beautiful, innocent and sexy. She'd also had a really bad day, and he didn't want to ever see a look of hurt pass over her features again and know that he'd been the cause.

"Sorry," he said.

She shrugged. "Me too."

"I like the way you kiss," he said, taking a seat on the other side of the sofa. "I liked it so much, it might make me go crazy if it never happens again."

Her soft eyes met his. "I'm sorry."

"Because of your boyfriend?" he bit out. "*Really*?"

"No." She shook her head. "Not really. I mean . . . I knew Thatcher was—"

"Wait!" His blood went cold. "Is that his fucking name? *Thatcher*?"

She nodded, searching his face with surprise.

"Thatcher *Worthington*?" asked Cort.

"You *know* him?" she asked, her eyes wide with disbelief.

"Not personally. But I know he went to Princeton."

"Yeah. He did. How . . . ?"

"So did Bree," said Cort, remembering the day his tough-as-nails, all-business older sister came home from college and locked the door of her room for an entire weekend. The only noise he heard coming from under her door for two full days was the sound of sobbing. The only name he heard her say, over and over again—like a prayer, like a curse—was *Thatcher*.

"Oh, my God. Did *Bree* date Thatcher?"

"It didn't last," said Cort, feeling sick to his stomach.

It didn't last because Bree had caught him cheating on her. After that weekend of crying, she'd come out of her room with red-rimmed eyes and a determined grimace. She'd returned to school on Monday morning, and he'd never heard another peep about Thatcher Worthington. But as her thirteen-year-old little brother, how he'd wanted to hurt the mythic giant who had made his sister cry. How small and useless he'd felt, six years younger, unable to do anything but watch her drive away with her broken heart barely mended.

"What happened?" she asked, though he could tell she already knew.

"He cheated on her."

"God," she murmured. She nodded slowly, taking a long sip of tea before saying, "At least I'm in good company now."

"A leopard doesn't change its spots, *Chevreau*."

"Is that right?" she asked, giving him a searing look. "Because you seem to have changed yours."

"We were talking about Thatcher," said Cort, raising his eyebrows.

"I don't . . ." She took another sip of tea, then leaned forward and placed her mug on the coffee table. "I don't want to talk about him anymore. I'm sorry for what he did to your sister, and I'm sorry for what he did to me, and I'm sorry for what he's going to do to every other woman he ever dates from now until eternity. But I don't want to talk about him anymore tonight. Deal?"

She held out her pinkie, giving him a slight smile. Placing his mug beside hers, he hooked his pinkie around hers and shook. "Deal."

What she'd been about to say before Cort had interrupted her was that she'd known for a long while that Thatcher had been cheating on her, and as terrible as today was, now that it was almost over, there was a strange but solid peace descending over her. Maybe she'd wanted to let go of Thatcher for months, but she was scared, or she didn't know how. Now she did. And now she was strong enough to let him go.

The reality was that her "no more kissing Cort" rule wasn't because of Thatcher—not really. Oh, sure, she'd probably be extra vigilant about the next person she dated, making sure they didn't appear to be the cheating kind, but she'd really only used Thatcher as an excuse. The problem with her and Cort hooking up was Jax. And it was the sort of problem that couldn't be overcome. You didn't date your sister's ex-boyfriend, no matter how many years had passed, no matter how sweet he was, or how hot, or how much his kiss made you want to jump his bones until dawn. It was a cement-hard boundary between sisters, and it couldn't be crossed.

But friendship? Friendship was possible, and if she couldn't have Cort the way she wanted him, maybe she could at least have him in her life as a friend. And if not in her life, then she still had tonight, didn't she? Glancing at the clock, she was surprised to see it was after midnight, way past her bedtime. Though her eyes felt heavy, she wanted to stay awake. She wanted a little more time with him.

She pulled a mohair throw from the back of the couch, spread out her legs, and draped it over them.

"We've been talking about me all night," she said. "What about you? Tell me about you."

He kicked off his sneakers and swung his legs up on the couch, side by side with hers, his sock-covered toes resting beside her thigh. Reaching for the blanket, he pulled it over his legs as well.

"What do you want to know?"

"Tell me about your music."

He grinned, and she blushed because she knew they were both remembering his words in the kitchen: *Baby, you're music.*

"I thought we were talking about *me*," he teased.

"Cort . . ." She gave him a look and waited for him to continue.

"Okay, okay. Went to college. Got my degree in music with a concentration in orchestral composition, even though I prefer performing. I play guitar, piano, organ, and harp."

"Harp?" she asked, feeling a smile creep across her face.

"Yeah." He grinned back at her. "You like it? The harp?"

"I love it. But piano's your favorite?"

"My first love," he said, letting his eyes drop to her lips and linger there.

Her skin prickled with awareness, but she couldn't let herself be lured into another bad decision. One kiss would never be enough, but it was all she would allow herself to have.

She cleared her throat. "And since college? What have you been up to?"

He looked up at her, his eyes soft. "I play. Mostly solo piano with an orchestra. You know the pianist that sits in the middle of the stage with the rest of the orchestra fanning behind? That's me—at the Met in New York from time to time, here in Philly, and with the London Philharmonic. With anyone who needs a soloist. I did that for several years, and I liked it, you know? I liked the travel and the rush of applause. But I hooked up with Vic again about a year ago, and I think we've got a good sound as a duo. I played in a trio with her after Curtis, so we picked up where we left off. We just cut our second album, and we're headed to Europe in two weeks."

She blinked as he finished his sentence, a wave of melancholy surprising her as he spoke of his "partnership" and she learned of his impending absence.

"Oh, Europe? For what?"

"Small concert hall tour."

"For how long?"

His eyes held hers from across the couch, searching her face as though looking for something specific. Finally, he shrugged, leaning forward to take a small sip of his tea. "Two months."

"Two months!" She winced. She couldn't help it, and she was grateful he was drinking and didn't notice. Still, she tried to recover as quickly as she could. "Two months. Oh. That's . . . great. Good for you!"

He smiled at her, widening his eyes. "Boy, you're a bad liar. Like, seriously sucky. The worst I've ever seen."

"I *am* happy for you," she said earnestly. And she was. She was happy for his success. She just hated to think of him so far away. Even though she'd resolved they wouldn't see each other after tonight, it still made her sad. Especially since he'd be away for two months with another woman: Vic, the cellist, who was edgy, voluptuous, and beautiful.

"Hey." His toes rubbed against her thigh. "What's going on?"

"You and Vic . . ." she started, then stopped herself, blushing because she had no right to the sudden spike of jealousy she felt and no right to ask him about his love life.

"Are we a thing?" he asked.

She raised her eyes and nodded.

"Would it bother you if we were?"

She *was* a bad liar. He was one-hundred-percent right about that. So what would be the point of lying? She nodded again.

"Why?" he whispered, his voice thick and bitter with longing. "Why would it bother you when I can never kiss you again?"

An unexpected lump rose in her throat as she stared back at him and lowered her glance, staring morosely at his T-shirt.

Why did it have to be you? she longed to shout. Of all the pianists in all the dive bars in all the world, he was the only one off-limits to her. Why did he have to save her from humiliation and hold her as she cried and kiss her like she was beautiful and precious and the sexiest woman on earth? It wasn't fair. It was so goddamned unfair that tonight was "Once upon a time" *and* "The end."

"No," he said gently. "Vic and I aren't together. I wouldn't have kissed you if we were, Mad."

"You're single?" she asked, a shot of relief-fueled adrenaline making her breath catch and her skin tingle.

"Hard to believe, I know."

"So you two are . . . ?"

"Partners. Friends. I screen the chicks she dates. She screens the chicks I date."

"Wait! She's a . . ."

"You need to learn to finish your sentences, Miss Librarian." He grinned, nodding at her. "Yes. Vic's only into women, which means I hold zero allure for her."

"Unless you're playing piano."

"Even then sometimes . . ." He chuckled. "She's a pain in my ass, but I love her like Bree and Sloane." He cocked his head to the side, stifling a yawn. "So, uh, tell me about your promotion."

She yawned back, settling deeper into the couch, her feet sliding along his thigh to rest beside his hip.

"Today I was promoted to the Head of Children's Programming for all the libraries in the city, which means I get to come up with all the classes and courses we offer at all the different branches."

"That's cool. Is that what you wanted?"

She nodded. "Mmm-hmm. I have so many ideas, and . . . now I can make them happen."

"Ideas to help children love books?"

It was harder and harder to keep her eyes open, but she fought exhaustion, smiling at him at he asked her about her favorite subject. "To love books, love the library, love music."

"Music?"

"Sure," she said. "Have you ever seen the music department at the main branch? It's massive. Not to mention, we have a Mommy and Me music class for babies and another for grade school kids. I want to start something for older kids too."

"Well, I happen to know a musician who'd be happy to give you a hand."

"If only he wasn't going to Europe," she shot back, trying to stay cheerful and failing.

He noticed too and reached under the blanket, finding her feet and taking them gently into his hands, kneading her tired muscles with strong fingers.

"Not forever," he said softly, watching her with such intensity she had to close her eyes against the heat in his searing gaze.

"Mmmm," she murmured, concentrating on the soothing pressure of his hands on her feet, the comfort offered in his touch, his skin touching hers so tenderly. "That feels so nice."

"Miss Mad, Miss Mad . . ." he sang softly, the words like a lullaby, the melody the same as before.

Baby, you're music.

She tried to open her eyes one more time to tell him good-night. But they were just too heavy, and she was way too comfortable, and the words stuck to the top of her mouth, refusing to be said. Instead, she nestled against the back of the couch and let the rest of the world slip away, until there was only her and Cort.

Until there was only sleep.

Cort stared at her as she drifted off to sleep, watching as her sweet lips parted in repose and her breathing became deep and even. He sang quietly, a lullaby just for Mad, improvising silly, sappy lyrics as he fell harder and deeper for her with every passing minute.

As he rubbed her feet, it occurred to him that he didn't generally lose himself over a woman with this sort of intensity or speed, but there was something about Mad Rousseau that called out to him and always had. Meeting her again under such emotional circumstances had brought out every caveman-style protective instinct Cort owned, and he couldn't help the immediate rush of infatuation he felt for her. But truth be told, his feelings ran far deeper.

Mad wasn't some random woman in crisis he'd met for the first time today. She'd lived quietly but firmly in his mind, in his dreams, for a decade. And spending the past several hours talking to her and getting to know her again only added to a rooted sense of intimacy. On a primal level, it was just one of those things a man knew deep, deep in his heart, where wild things were free to grow: Mad Rousseau was back in his life now, and he wanted to keep her there. He *needed* to keep her there.

His lips tipped up as he gazed at her sleeping face, remembering the many times she'd been at his childhood home for pool parties or for his mom's weird annual Christmas party that every kid on Blueberry Lane was forced to attend by his or her parents. His mom and dad would dress up like Santa and Mrs. Claus and give out candy canes and musical instruments, then make all the kids sing carols. It was beyond excruciating, not to mention that they didn't fool any of the kids, except maybe Mad Rousseau, who'd stare up at them, wide-eyed and excited . . . at three, at four, at seven, at eleven. Or maybe they hadn't fooled her at all. Maybe she was just the kind of person who wanted his parents to believe they were appreciated. The one kid on Blueberry Lane who went out of her way to make the oddball Amblers feel like they had something to offer.

Mad. It had *always* been Mad. Always.

For many years, when he thought about Jax, a spike of guilt would rush through him as he remembered dating her and the true reason for their breakup. But it was smart of Jax to use the reason she did: it had made Mad hate him in defense of her sister, and Jax knew that Mad's disdain would be the best punishment of all.

He took a deep breath and sighed, shaking his head at the dumbass things that kids do when they're sixteen or seventeen—the choices they make for all the wrong reasons. The lessons that hurt so much while you're learning them, you'd swear you were dying from the inside. Jax had driven a hard bargain that night, but it was hers to make. And his guilt had allowed him to call it fair.

Mad stirred in her sleep, drawing Cort back to the present, and he gently pushed the blanket from his lap and reluctantly let go of her feet. Standing up beside the couch, he looked down at her—at her long black lashes fanned out on the apples of her cheeks and her sweet lips that had tasted better than any fantasy. He wanted so much more from her, but not tonight. Tonight she needed sleep.

Leaning down, he gathered her into his arms, surprised by how little she weighed. The blanket swept the ground as he turned for the door, his heart swelling as she burrowed against him, her soft hair tickling his throat. Careful not to let her dangling feet hit the doorway as he exited the den, he walked in the opposite direction of the kitchen, toward the hallway where Mad had disappeared when they first arrived at her apartment.

Only one room cast light into the dark hallway, and he slipped inside to find her bedroom bathed in soft, warm light. On the floor was the hot-pink skirt she'd been wearing earlier, along with a lacy bra and pale-pink satin thong that made his dick jump as he stepped over it with bare feet. Stealing one last longing glance at her face so close to his, he gently laid her on the bed, then squatted down beside her as she rolled to her side.

"'Night, Mad," he whispered, tenderly brushing her hair from her forehead and wishing he could quell the terrible rush of sorrow he felt in saying good-bye. "See you soon."

Standing up, he pulled the blanket over her, turned off her bedside lamp, then headed for the door.

"Cort?"

Her voice was soft and small, dreamy and deep, but it surprised him enough that he immediately pivoted around to face her. "Mad?"

"Stay."

His breath caught, his feet frozen as he stared at her in the almost-darkness, trying to figure out what to do. *Stay? Like stay overnight? Like stay in her bed with her?* He couldn't have heard her right. Taking two steps closer, he asked, "What?"

"Stay with me," she murmured, her eyes still closed, her head cradled on one bent elbow.

His heart ramped into high gear as he stepped closer to her bed. Was she asleep or talking in her sleep? Was it ethical to slip into bed with a girl who was fast asleep even if she was asking him to?

He squatted by her head again as he had before. "Baby, you're half-asleep—"

Her eyes opened—not much, but enough for him to see them shine through the darkness. "Cort, please. Just hold me for a while? Until I fall asleep?"

"Yeah, okay," he whispered, watching her eyes close slowly as she took a deep breath and sighed, her sweet mint-tea breath warming his cheek.

It had been one of those magical, talk-nonstop nights full of crazy-high emotion and the thrill of reunion. They'd shared way more than strangers could or would, and something about it felt so huge and so real, it was impossible for him to say no. He walked around to the other side of her bed and laid down beside her.

Because fuck it, he couldn't refuse her. Not if she needed him.

Gathering her body against his chest, he breathed in the fresh, clean scent of her hair, groaning softly as she nestled against him, her ass wiggling against his dick as she covered his hands with her own. He pulled the blanket around them both, planting a kiss on her head as he shared her pillow. Her knees were bent, and he folded his into hers so that they were perfectly spooned. Then he took a deep breath and closed his eyes.

As surreal as it was to be lying in Mad Rousseau's bed, holding her tightly against his body, nothing had ever felt so right or so good as being in this bedroom and holding this woman. *And if maintaining my single status is import-ant to me*, he thought, holding her closer as his breath-ing matched itself to hers, *I am utterly and completely fucked.*

Chapter 7

Warm and comfortable.

Mad sighed with pleasure as she nestled closer to the source of warmth, surprised when her lips pressed against skin. Opening her eyes slowly, it took her vision a moment to adjust because she was pressed so tightly against someone else.

Drawing a breath through her nose, she knew right away it wasn't Thatcher. Thatcher always smelled distinctly (and heavily) of V by Clive Christian, and the man-person holding her smelled refreshingly of soap and cedar. Besides, Thatcher hated cuddling, asserting that Mad's body heat made him sweat, so who—?

Suddenly, memories of last night came back to her in a rush of Polaroid-like pictures tossed carelessly on a white comforter: Chloe, "Le Cygne," tequila, Cort . . . Cort . . . Cort.

Cort Ambler, who had saved her from humiliation after being sick to her stomach in public. Who had taken her out to dinner and held her as she sobbed.

. . . who had walked her home and listened carefully as she told the entire sad story of her failed relationship with Thatcher.

. . . who had told her she was interesting and beautiful—who had told her she was music—and kissed her like he meant it.

. . . who had carried her to bed and stayed when she asked, holding her in his arms as she fell asleep.

And yes, Cort Ambler, who is my sister's ex-boyfriend, she thought weakly, at war with herself, burrowing deeper into his neck, unable to form the words that would wake him up and tell him to leave.

Because Cort Ambler was holding her so tightly against his body, chest to chest, his chin resting on top of her head, it felt like heaven. Like plenty after privation. Like a sweet dream from which she wasn't ready to awaken.

The throat her lips were touching belonged to him, and though she knew she should stop, she couldn't. She was grateful to him. No, screw that. She was *attracted* to him—wildly. And she *liked* him—a lot. The feelings she'd had for him so very long ago weren't dead inside of her, as she would have assumed before reconnecting, but were merely long-forgotten seeds coming to life—his kindness showering them, his tenderness warming them. Her tongue darted out, licking his sleep-warmed skin, and he groaned softly.

"Mad," he whispered, a single syllable colored with emotion. *Pain. Pleasure. Longing.*

She drew back to find his eyes open—black in the early-morning light of new dawn. He adjusted his arms around her, pressing his pelvis against hers so she could feel the hard ridge of his erection through his jeans. Instinctively, she arched against him, holding his eyes as the soft, needy space between her thighs cupped his arousal.

"Baby," he murmured, the slow, sweet sound making her whimper softly.

She placed her finger over his lips and murmured, "Shhhh," then drew her finger away and leaned forward to replace it with her lips.

He breathed into her mouth as though he'd been holding his breath, and Mad inhaled him greedily, surprised by the neutral taste of his morning breath and hoping her own was similarly pleasant. Which it must have been . . . because he groaned greedily, sucking her tongue into his mouth and flipping her to her back so that he was lying on top of her, supporting most of his weight on bent forearms and devouring her mouth like he was starving.

As their kiss deepened, he thrust gently against her, his erection working its way into the valley between her legs, and Mad spread her legs, cursing the flannel pants that had been so comfy the night before.

She needed to feel him.

She wanted the heat of his skin pressed against hers.

Skimming her hands down his back, she found the hem of his T-shirt and smoothed it upward, missing his lips for a moment as he reached behind his neck and pulled it over his head before slamming his lips against hers again.

Her hands grappled with her own shirt, trying in vain to push it up and bare her skin to him as he was bare to her. Recognizing her struggle, he rolled to his side beside her and, holding her eyes all the while, pushed her shirt to her throat, letting the heel of his hand skim the warm skin of her stomach and slip over her distended nipples as he worked to bare her to him. Arching up from the bed, Mad reached behind her back and unsnapped her bra, letting the loose ends ride up along her sides until all that was covering her breasts were two scraps of thin, light-blue cotton.

Leaning up on his elbow, Cort stared down at her face, scanning her eyes before bending his head to place a gentle kiss on her lips. He tugged her shirt over her head, and Mad slipped it down her arms and threw it to the floor as he tenderly kissed her chin, her throat, skimming his lips to the high plane of her chest just over her barely covered breasts. Hooking his index finger under the material between her breasts, he pulled the fabric toward him, and Mad raised her arms over her head so that he could pull the bra off and drop it onto the floor beside the bed. She watched as his eyes widened, darkening to onyx as he stared down at her naked breasts.

"Fuuuuuuck," he hissed, reaching for the breast closest to him and cupping it in his hand, the nipple straining against his palm. "You're beautiful."

She closed her eyes as he bent his head and sucked her other nipple between his lips, circling it with his hot, wet tongue before sucking on it, then licking it again. Writhing with the sweet sharpness of his mouth on her sensitive flesh, she arched against him as his lips skimmed her flesh with tiny kisses, taking her other nipple between his teeth and holding it as his tongue flicked over the straining nub.

Her hands shot to his head, burying in his hair, twisting in the silky strands as she bucked off the bed, whimpering with a mixture of pain and pleasure and want. Kissing her breast gently, he swung his leg over her body and thrust his hips against her as his lips reclaimed hers. He groaned into her mouth, his tongue sliding against hers, his hands sliding down the sides of her body to her waist, to her hips. He hooked his fingers in the waistband of her pants and tugged, pulling them down. She felt a rush of cool air kiss her soaked slit and felt the heat of his hand flatten over the mound of her sex.

My . . . sex.

Sex.

The word broke through a haze of white-hot desire like an arctic chill.

Oh, my God. Sex.

No. No, no, no, no. She couldn't have sex with Cort. *No. No!*

She jerked her neck to the side, freeing her lips from his. "No!"

His fingers, one of which was working its way between slickened folds of flesh to caress her clit, froze.

"We have to stop," she whispered, though her body screamed in agony, wanting to feel the velvet steel of his erection inside of her, massaging the walls of her sex, making her scream with pleasure as she collapsed against him and fell back to sleep naked in his arms.

He leaned over her, breathless and panting, the wall of his chest pushing into her bare breasts with every shallow gulp of air.

"What's wrong?" he rasped, looking confused, scanning her face to understand why she'd stopped them when they were a moment away from something both their bodies obviously and desperately craved. "Are you okay?"

"I can't," she sobbed, letting her hands slide from his warm back and flatten on the comforter beneath them. "I can't do this."

"Why not?" he asked, clenching his jaw and staring at her with an expression split between deprivation and fury.

"Please," she whispered.

Tears filled her eyes, and her body—ripe, wet, and throbbing—ached with longing as he rolled off of her onto his back, letting his forearm rest over his eyes.

His dick throbbed for her so hard it ached, his balls tight and high, waiting to explode inside of her. Denied! God, it felt so fucking bad.

He took a deep breath, letting the air out of his mouth in a pissed-off hiss. He had woken up to her kissing his neck, right? Right. She had been the one who kissed him first this time, right? Right. It was her hands that had bared his chest and snapped her own bra open, right? Right.

So why wasn't he buried balls deep inside of her hot, wet body right this minute?

He pursed his lips and squeezed his eyes shut tighter. Part of him was pissed. This was bullshit. She'd initiated this—he had every right to expect more, right? If another woman tried this game with him, he'd already be out the fucking door, and that was the last she'd ever see of him.

But the reality of the situation was that she wasn't "another woman." She was Mad. Which is exactly why it hurt and frustrated him that he'd gotten so close to something he wanted only to have it taken away. He had to find a place, find context for her refusal, or it would eat at him.

"Too fast?"

"What?"

"Were. We. Going. Too. Fast?" he asked again, overarticulating every word. And fuck him, but if she blamed this on Thatcher-fucking-Worthington, he was grabbing his shit and leaving.

"I'm sorry. I just—"

"Say yes, Mad. Say, 'Yes, Cort. We were going too fast.'" He gentled his tone to a ragged whisper. "Say it."

"Yes, Cort," she said, her voice wispy and sad, "we were going too fast."

He lowered his arm, looking at her face, and fuck if his breath didn't catch—she was so fucking beautiful. Leaning up on his elbow, he nodded. "Okay."

Her eyes told him that she had more to say, but he suspected it was more bullshit excuses about her ex, and after making out with her as he just had, he couldn't bear hearing her say that she had any unresolved feelings for such an asshole.

"Are you mad at me?"

"*About* you," he said softly, caressing her cheek.

"Now who's going too fast?" she asked, the hint of a smile playing on her kiss-swollen lips.

"When can I see you again?" he asked.

She stared up at him for a while, and he read longing and regret in her eyes, but before he could search for more clues, she averted her gaze. "I don't know."

"How about later?"

"I don't—"

"Tomorrow?"

"Cort, I . . ."

"Do you *want* to see me again, Mad?" he asked, reaching for her chin and forcing her to look at him.

Tears brimmed in her eyes, and she sobbed softly, the rosy tips of her breasts trembling beside him as she drew a ragged, miserable breath.

"N-No," she whispered as a tear snaked down from the corner of one eye.

His fingers jerked back from her chin as though burned, and he flinched, anger rising up in him like high tide—a wave of sharp denial making him gruffly demand, "Why not?"

She swung her legs over the side of the bed and sat up, presenting him with her back, and he almost barked at her again when she quietly stated, "You dated Jax."

"*What?* A million years ago!"

"Doesn't matter," she said softly, reaching down to the floor and pulling her T-shirt over her head a moment later. She stood up and turned, facing him with her arms crossed over her breasts. "I—I let this go too far. I can't see you again."

He sprang up from the bed on the other side, mirroring her stance—standing in nothing but his tented boxers with his arms crossed over his chest. "This is bullshit."

She shook her head, her eyes grave. "No, it's not."

"It's an excuse."

"A *real* one."

"I dated your sister over ten years ago, for a couple of months, Mad. We were kids. It was *nothing*. It meant nothing."

"It meant something to her," said Mad, wiping another tear from her cheek, then lifting her chin in defiance. But her voice didn't match her stance—it was uncertain, grieved, and sorry.

"Mad! Come on!"

"I shouldn't have asked you to stay last night. I'm sorry. That was my fault."

"I *wanted* to stay!" he exploded, grabbing his jeans from the floor and pulling them on. He reached down for his T-shirt and dragged it over his head. "I haven't felt like this since . . . God! Ever!"

She sucked in a breath and held it, blinking at him, her eyes brimming with more tears. "I'm sorry. You have to go. Whatever this was, it's over."

"No," he said, rounding the bed to stand before her. He scanned her face, reaching up to brush another tear away. "Please, baby."

She stepped away from him, her eyes determined. "It's for the best."

That condescending fucking voice was back, and he could see an imaginary chignon appear on her head and pearls suddenly clasp around her neck like a collar. Pristine, perfect, untouchable Madeleine stood before him where hot-blooded, sensual Mad had stood a moment before.

He covered the distance between them and grabbed her haughty little chin, then dropped his lips to hers in a bruising kiss, forcing his tongue between her pursed lips. Holding her against his aroused body, he kissed her until she surrendered to the chemistry—to the raw, fucking physical fire that burned between them. Only then did he jerk his head away, abruptly releasing her from his arms.

Her eyes changed quickly from lusty to furious, but he spoke quickly, determined to have the last word—"Call it too fast. Blame it on your asswipe ex. Even blame it on your sister if that's what you need to do. But don't you *dare* tell me it's for the best, princess, got it?"

Then he stormed from the room, leaving a gaping Mad in his wake.

Mad stared at the door, willing him to return even though she'd all but forced him to leave. When she heard the front door slam shut, she sat back on her bed, letting her tears flow freely. Yesterday she'd been crying about Thatcher. Today? Cort.

"Can I just get a break?" she wailed, falling back on the bed, which was a big mistake, because it smelled of Cort and made her tears fall faster.

God, he'd been so damn sweet to her, and the way he'd kissed her this morning—the way he'd touched her so hungrily, so tenderly, so reverently—made her want to die. And when he said, *I haven't felt like this since . . . God! Ever!* it had just about decimated her willpower to push him away, because he was verbalizing something that she was feeling too. Her sexual relationship with Thatcher, while satisfying, had never burned this bright, this hot, this intense. What she and Cort shared, in terms of chemistry, was unique in Mad's life.

And if I was free to explore that chemistry? She whimpered softly. *I would. Indefinitely.*

But she wasn't free.

She wasn't lying about Jax standing, figuratively, between them.

It wasn't like Mad could waltz up to Le Chateau, sit Jax down, and ask for permission to date Cort. Jax had recently come home from LA beaten, broken, and tired from being hounded by the Hollywood paparazzi. Then, at their brother's wedding last weekend, she'd been mauled by an old friend who wanted to "make it" with a famous producer. Thank God the Englishes' new gardener had stepped in and saved the day. But the point was, her sister was fragile. The last thing Jax needed was to find out that Mad was involved with the ex-boyfriend who had dumped her in high school and broken her heart. No. It was impossible. For now and probably forever.

It was an idea that made Mad's heart ache with such misery, she pressed her hands against her chest and curled up in a ball on her bed, weeping and eventually falling back to sleep.

Ring, ring, ring. Ring, ring, ring.

The sound of her phone ringing woke Mad from a deep sleep, but the immediate thought that it could be Cort made her grab it from her bedside and press "Talk" without opening her eyes.

"Cort?"

"Madeleine?"

Thatcher. Like a bucket of ice water over her sleepy head.

She sucked in a breath and sat up, leaning back against her headboard, her fingers forming fists against the pillow she'd shared with Cort last night.

"What do you want, Thatcher?"

"You," he said. "I want *you* to be well, darling."

"*Well*?"

"I can't believe we have to walk down this road again, Madeleine. I'm exhausted, aren't you?"

"Yes, Thatcher. Yes, I am. I am tired of—"

"Your suspicious heart? The stories you make up in your head that you somehow convince yourself are true? Darling, I worry for you. So terribly."

"Your slut was ordering champagne and strawberries!" she bellowed.

His silence was disapproving, and his tone was tighter when he finally spoke. "Oh, and no one working late, analyzing data, has ever ordered food and drink."

"She wasn't ordering a peanut butter sandwich and a Coke, Thatcher."

"It's *my* fault she prefers fruit and wine?"

"You were in the fucking shower," she growled.

"Cursing is the linguistic tool of the inarticulate, Madeleine."

"*You're* a linguistic tool," she shot back.

"Very mature." He paused. "Clearly, you're not in the right frame of mind for common sense and adult discourse. We'll talk when I get home."

"No, we won't," said Mad, feeling belligerent.

"Yes, darling, *we will*. There is nothing going on between me and Chloe. You've made it all up in your head . . . yet again. You're projecting. Your poor mother's experience with infidelity, coupled with the latent hostility you feel toward your deceased father, is making you *project*. You know, I'm wondering about regression therapy for you, Madeleine. Perhaps we need to get in touch with your reptilian brain to really discover—"

"My reptilian . . . ?"

"Yes, your most basic self. Because I believe that—"

"The only *reptile* here, *darling*, is you."

"Madel—"

"Let me make this really clear in language you will understand. We are *over*, Thatcher. You and I are *finished*. We've been over for ages, but I haven't had the guts to say it. Well, now I do. We are so, so, *so* over!"

"You're acting rashly—"

"I will have your slippers and toothbrush sent to your apartment via messenger. I'm dumping your wine down the sink as soon as we hang up."

"That's a 1956 Brunel—"

"Too bad. You're fucking your assistant. I know it, and you *certainly* know it. And I'm done being cheated on. Do you understand? Done."

He was silent for a long time on the other end of the line before speaking again. When he did, his voice was eerily composed, as though she hadn't just called him out on cheating and broken up with him.

"I'll see you when I get home, darling."

And the line went dead.

Mad pulled the phone from her ear, staring at its screen with a frown before letting it drop to her lap. *No. You won't.*

But something about the conversation—*aside* from the way he'd patronized and belittled her—bothered Mad. It was like he hadn't heard her at all. Or like he was purposely ignoring her. Was he truly so much of an egotist that he would ignore the fact that she'd just broken up with him? A sudden chill made her shiver, and she jumped when her phone buzzed in her lap.

She hit "Talk" and put the phone to her ear.

"Thatcher, I don't want to—"

"Mad?"

"Jax?"

"The one and only."

"Jax," she sighed, her coiled muscles relaxing as she pulled her comforter over her legs. "God, I thought you were . . ."

"Dr. Wonderful?"

"He isn't . . ." *wonderful.*

But someone else is wonderful, and I just reconnected with him, and it would kill you if you found out, so I sent him away . . . and my heart's dying over it, and my boyfriend is now my ex-boyfriend, but I'm not ready to tell you all this . . . and God, I wish I could, because I don't know how to feel like this and push Cort away, and I just wish we could eat Ben & Jerry's and talk.

"Mad?"

"He isn't always wonderful," she said softly.

"I could have told you that two years ago."

"Leave it, Jax."

"Someone's in a shitty mood, *petite soeur.*"

Mad took a deep breath and sighed. "I'm just . . . tired. What's up?"

"The promotion! You never called me back yesterday after you were called into your boss's office!"

For the first time since Cort left in a huff, Mad smiled. "I got it."

"*Alors!*" screamed Jax. "Of course you did! My beautiful, smart sister. Of course you did. Oh, *ma chérie!* I'm so proud of you!"

Mad's smile faded as fresh tears filled her eyes. Here was Jax in all her thoughtful, loyal, devoted glory. The very best sister she could ever ask for.

Betraying Jax was impossible, unthinkable. She needed to forget about last night and this morning—forget that she'd ever reconnected with Cort. Forget his searing kisses and the way he listened to her. Forget the way he hummed in her ear and held her against him. Forget their chemistry and the way he made her feel. She needed to forget all of it.

"Mad?"

She sniffled, reaching up to wipe her eyes. "I'm so lucky to have you as a sister, Jax."

"We're both lucky, *chérie. Toujours.*" Always.

She wiped away another falling tear, her heart full of love for Jax but aching because that love demanded that she never see Cort again.

"*Toujours,*" she responded.

"Now tell me all about the promotion! And don't leave out a single detail!"

Chapter 8

Walking back to his apartment in the early morning, Cort cursed the moment Mad walked into *Voulez-Vous* last night and promised himself that he was fucking done with her. He didn't need this kind of bullshit in his life. She had barely broken things off with her ex, and once she did, she was going to have a messload of baggage to deal with. Not to mention that using his fleeting—and ancient—relationship with Jax as an excuse not to explore their connection had to be the weakest excuse ever. She clearly wasn't in the zone for someone new, and Cort wasn't in the habit of begging for female attention. *Not to mention* he was leaving for Europe in twelve days. He needed to focus on his career, on his plans, on sets for him and Vic to knock out at every venue. So fine. Fuck it.

It was about a mile from Mad's place on Rittenhouse Square to his house on Lombard Street, across from Seger Park, but Cort's long legs and fierce irritation propelled him forward. In fifteen minutes, he found himself at his door just as the sun was rising, out of breath and a lot less angry.

His dick had finally accepted the harsh reality that relief inside of Mad was not forthcoming, and his head had cooled enough to look at the situation with less emotion and more understanding. He climbed the brick steps, punched in the security code to unlock his front door, and entered the historic row house, built in 1884. The ground floor smelled, as it always did, of over one hundred years of woodburning fires, and he breathed deeply, feeling comforted by the familiar scent of home.

Cort had bought the house with money from his trust when he turned eighteen, happy to get the fuck out of Greens Farms and leave Blueberry Lane behind. And aside from occasional trips to Haverford to visit his Lola or spend Christmas with his parents when they left Sedona once a year, he stayed away.

The Amblers had been the black sheep of his childhood neighborhood, though his inheritance was probably similar to that of the English, Winslow, Story, or Rousseau kids. His mother, Mariah Coopersmith, was the only child and heir to one of the oldest and wealthiest fortunes on the Main Line, though she'd soundly rejected her pedigree and trounced her parents' expectations from the beginning.

Cort's parents had met on a commune outside of Sacramento when his mother was just shy of twenty-five and the youngest anthropology doctoral student to graduate from UC Davis with a completed dissertation on critical thinking. His father, Theodore Dashiel Ambler, was forty-one at the time but had earned his own PhD in classics almost a decade earlier at Yale. Despite a fifteen-year age difference, they'd been a perfect storm of deep conversation, raw sex, and psychotropic drugs until his mother had realized, three months into their acquaintance, that she was several weeks pregnant. Short on real-world common sense, his mother had thankfully had the presence of mind to return to Philly with Theo; however, her extremely traditional Coopersmith parents had insisted on marriage if the couple wanted any measure of financial support. Mariah and Theo married quickly and quietly despite their mutual fundamental disregard for the institution of marriage. Seven months later, Cort's mother gave birth to a daughter, Breezy Day Ambler.

Over the course of the next eight years, his parents added to their brood with sons Dashiel Spaniel and Cortlandt Apple and finally with a second daughter and the youngest child, Sloane Square. With little interest in anything besides academia, rhetoric, and each other, Mariah and Theo kept busy teaching at various colleges and universities in and around Philadelphia, while the Ambler children were raised primarily by seasonal au pairs and the longtime house-keeper of Greens Farms, Lailani Cruz, a Filipino American woman who'd lost her husband in the 1991 Mount Pinatubo eruption and had emigrated to the United States with his parents' help.

For just a moment, Cort thought about calling Lailani, whom he called "Lola," just to hear the soothing cadence of her heavily accented English. She still lived at Greens Farms, puttering around and keeping it tidy. She was the grand-mother the Ambler kids hadn't had in stiff, starched Amelia Coopersmith. Lola was kind and cheerful with big hugs, and she was always available for a long talk about their love lives. But she was almost eighty now, and he'd hate to wake her by calling so early. Maybe he'd head out to Haverford before he left for Europe to check on her, just to get a hug good-bye and hear her say, "*Nandito ka sa puso ko,*" which meant—as every Ambler child knew—that no matter where they were, they were *always* in their Lola's heart.

Just hearing her voice in his head made his lips tremble with a grin as he plopped down on the couch across from the fireplace he used daily in the wintertime. He won-dered what Lola would say about Mad and decided she'd tell him that he hadn't earned the right to pout yet, that he had a long way to go and lots of work to do before he could claim that right. No doubt Lola would add that he was smart enough to win the girl; he just needed to use his head.

. . . which gave him an idea.

He sprang up and walked into the kitchen, opening a door that led to a secret staircase that wound tightly up to the third floor of his house, which he'd renovated to be a studio and study. There he sat down in front of his computer and pulled up the Internet, typing in "Facebook" and searching for J.C. Rousseau.

Since they weren't already friends, Cort sent Mad's brother a friend request, then typed in "Mad Rousseau," waiting for her page to come up. When it did, he couldn't help the smile that spread over his face. Her page was private, but her profile picture—of her and Jax wearing matching gold dresses and smiling into the camera—was full of so much unbridled joy that he chuckled softly, right-clicking on the picture and saving it to his hard drive. Then, with no offense intended to Jax, he opened it and cropped her out so he could stare at Mad alone for a few minutes.

She was wearing her hair up and a double string of pearls around her neck, but her eyes sparkled, and her smile was infectious, like the person taking the picture was someone she loved very much. Cort frowned at the thought, leaning back in his chair with narrowed eyes and wondering if the photographer was her piece-of-shit cheating ex. Clicking back on Facebook, he checked out the caption of the photo and relaxed: "Our brother snapped this one at his wedding! Congrats to Ten and Kate! We love you!"

He sighed, looking at her cheek pressed tightly against Jax's as her words echoed in his head: *You dated Jax . . . it meant something to her.*

Sighing, he rose from the desk chair, walked through the study and past the studio to the main staircase, and headed down to the second floor. He'd have to call Sloane and ask her if Mad's reason for pushing him away was legit.

Passing a guest bedroom on either side of a narrow hall-way, he continued to the large master bedroom at the end of the hall, pushing open the door and throwing off his T-shirt as he headed to the bathroom to take a shower. Stripping naked, he opened the glass door of the shower, climbed inside, and sighed with pleasure as the steamy water sprayed his body from left, right, and above.

Maybe it was true.

Maybe it was some sort of "girl code" or "sister code" that a girl couldn't date her sister's ex, but the thought made him scoff as he squeezed shampoo into his palm. He *barely* qualified as an "ex." He'd only dated Jax for a few months in high school, and they'd never had sex or said "I love you" to each other.

Then again, Mad was clear that dating Cort had "meant something" to Jax. Perhaps she'd been in love with him? His feelings had never even come close to love, so it was hard for him to imagine it, but he supposed it was possible.

He pictured Mad calling him a "motherfucker" by the pool, then fast-forwarded to her smile at her brother's wedding. She was close to her siblings. The Rousseau kids had always been close. Maybe because there'd been a cultural and language bar-rier when they first moved to Philadelphia or maybe because their parents were almost as absent as Cort's, but they'd been closer than most of the other siblings on Blueberry Lane, and Mad and Jax had been practically joined at the hip.

Bracing his hands against the shower wall as the water pelted his back, Cort had his first real moment of despair as he put all these thoughts together.

Because if Mad truly believed that being with Cort would betray Jax, then when she'd said, *Whatever this was, it's over,* she'd meant it.

After talking to Jax, Mad walked around her apartment, collecting Thatcher's things into a box and pouring his 1956 Brunello down the toilet as promised. She also collected all the gifts he'd given her over the years—a juicer, a Fitbit, an antisnore jaw strap, a basil plant (because he liked fresh basil in his pasta sauce), a spätzle maker (because he preferred German-style spätzle to pasta), the trio of bitter marmalades he'd brought her from England, his signed Amazon best-selling book, *Why It Isn't PsychoBabble*, and the pearl-handled letter opener he'd bought her impulsively at a sidewalk fair—and took great pleasure in throwing them one by one into the incinerator and listening to them crash against the metal tubing on the way to the basement furnace.

Thus cleansed, she gathered up all the picture frames holding pictures of them together and took out the photographs, cutting them into little tiny pieces of confetti, and replaced them with pictures of her family.

Once she had finished, she walked up to the library and slipped in through the employee entrance, bypassing the public areas and going straight to her cubicle. Her job as Head Children's Librarian of the main branch would end in exactly two weeks, and her position as Head of Children's Programming for all free libraries would commence one week after that. She didn't know what she planned to do during that week off, though she supposed she would still come into the office and bank the time. She could use the time to ramp up to the new position and maybe even have a couple of new programs to roll out on her first "official" day of work.

For the next two weeks, she'd be in transition, expected to train the Assistant Children's Librarian, Penelope Ford, to take over for her and spend some time reviewing the folders of the person she was succeeding, who was already gone.

She spent a little bit of time at her desk and a little time moving some of her things into her new private office. Checking on Miss Ford, she found that the Saturday-afternoon Eager Readers group was well in hand, so she drifted listlessly back to her cubicle, a feeling of disquiet descending over her.

She knew its root cause, of course, because part of the reason she'd stayed so busy all day was specifically so that she wouldn't have to confront thoughts of Cort. Or worse, *feelings*. They were being kept behind a floodgate that was perilously close to bursting.

She didn't want to remember the different tones of his voice—gentle, tender, amused, sarcastic, yearning, and furious. She didn't want to miss the way it felt to wake up in his arms or remember just how close she'd come to sleeping with him this morning. She didn't want to remember the way it felt when he sucked her nipples into his mouth, laving them with his tongue in gentle circles before suckling at them so strongly, it made her whimper just remembering. She didn't want to picture his eyes as she told him she didn't want to see him again, because it hurt so much, it made her want to cry.

But as she spent the afternoon barely able to form coherent sentences, let alone brainstorm new and creative ways to foster a love of reading in Philadelphia's youth, *not* thinking about Cort became the most exhausting activity of all. Finally, she packed up her things and left the library around five, wandering home to her empty apartment. Tired from a short night's sleep and a day testing her tenuous self-control, she lay down on her bed, burying her face in the pillow they'd shared last night and inhaling Cort's fading scent as she closed her eyes.

Hours later, she woke up in darkness, her body ripe and aching after dreaming of Cort's touch on her skin, his tongue dipping into places he'd only touched with his fingers this morning. Flipping onto her back, she stared at the shadows on the ceiling and desperately wished that things were different.

If wishes were fishes, we'd all cast nets into the sea.

"Well, wishes *aren't* fishes," she said aloud, feeling annoyed. "And he is off-limits."

Frowning, she grabbed her phone from the bedside table and checked it for messages. She found two texts from her friend Jane Story, who invited her to come out for drinks at a swanky local hotel bar with a group of friends. It was only nine thirty, so she could easily catch up with them, but Mad didn't feel like going out for drinks with friends. She didn't feel like much of anything except seeing Cort again, which made a stab of longing knife at her heart. Even if she wanted to, she didn't know how to find him. She had no idea where he lived. They hadn't even exchanged phone numbers.

Noticing a red dot over the phone icon at the bottom of the screen, she swiped at it to find she had a waiting message from a Philadelphia number she didn't recognize. She tapped it and put the phone to her ear.

"Uh, hi. This message is for Madeleine Rousseau. This is Darryl down at *Voulez-Vous*, and, uh, we have your American Express card. Yeah. So maybe come by for it tonight if you get this message, okay? We close at midnight. We'll keep it at the bar for you."

She gasped, and just like that, her listless heart started thumping again. Her eyes opened wide, and she felt more alert, more alive, more excited than she had all day. Clutching her phone in her hand, she lowered it slowly to her lap as a smile broke out across her face.

She couldn't very well leave it there, could she?

No. It would be incredibly irresponsible for her to leave her credit card there and not go back to pick it up.

Tonight. Right away.

The logical thing to do would be to change into jeans—and a cute top—and take a taxi down to *Voulez-Vous* immediately.

"And because I'm a logical girl, that is *exactly* what I'll do," she said aloud, leaping off her bed with a giggle to go get ready.

When Vic started the intro to the Barcarolle from *The Tales of Hoffman*, the sad irony of Offenbach's lyrics was not lost on Cort:

> *Lovely night, oh, night of love,*
> *Smile upon our joys!*

With very little joy and zero will to smile, Cort started the whimsical melody line on cue, staring down at his fingers as they traveled effortlessly across the keys.

He was a professional, of course, so it would take a very sensitive ear to pick up on the fact that his heart wasn't into the performance. Looking over his shoulder and around the bar contemptuously, he highly doubted any of the clientele at *Voulez-Vous* were included in that exclusive group.

The small burst of hopefulness he'd had this morning after messaging J.C. Rousseau had dissipated as the day went on. Mad was like a drug to him, and today had felt like a wicked withdrawal from her awesomeness, leaving him a moody sonovabitch when he arrived at the bar tonight for the second of two booked performances.

"Hey, Cort!" greeted Merit, who was sitting at a two-person table on the sidewalk in the dying sun, sipping a glass of red wine on his own.

"Hey, Merit."

Merit lowered his Oakleys to get a better look at his friend. "You look like shit, man."

"Aw, that's sweet. Thanks," said Cort, sitting down at the empty chair across from Merit and picking up his friend's wineglass. He downed the contents before placing it back on the table.

"Oh," Merit chuckled. "I see."

"I highly doubt it," said Cort, pulling his own sunglasses down and leaning back in his chair.

"Darla, can you bring me another glass?" Merit called downstairs, refilling the glass on the table and pushing it toward Cort. "I think you need this more than me."

"Women suck."

"Yeah," said Merit. "And if you're lucky, they're good at it."

Darla arrived with a second glass, and Cort kept his mouth shut until she turned and walked back down the stairs.

"I didn't mean it like that," he said, lowering his sunglasses to glare at Merit.

"C'mon, man! Lighten up," said Merit. "Or at least tell me her name."

"Fuck you. No chance."

Merit chuckled in that annoying way chicks liked—Cort had seen it work on enough of them to know. "If you won't tell me who she is, that means she's off-limits, and that means you like her."

Cort sat up straighter, bracing his elbows on the table and taking a large gulp of wine. "You have sisters, Merit?"

"Nope. Five brothers."

"You're useless," muttered Cort.

"At having sisters? Yes. But I *know* a lot of girls."

Cort nodded—this was true: Merit was an incorrigible flirt, and women loved him. "Okay . . . So tell me this. Once upon a time, you dated a girl's sister, but you really had a thing for her the whole time. Ten years later, you run into her and—"

"She's off-limits for life," blurted out Merit, all traces of humor gone. "I mean, if you're going where I think you're going with that question, you're shit out of luck, man. You can't dump a girl, then date her sister."

"There must be a statute of limitations," Cort insisted.

Merit took his sunglasses off, and Cort did the same. Merit leaned forward and looked Cort right in the eyes, his expression grave. "*Life*. It's for life, Cort."

"But—"

"Sorry, man. If you like the sister of an ex? You are sadly fucked, my friend."

And that's exactly how he'd felt since that short, unpleasant conversation: fucked by the universe.

As Vic rolled into the Barcarolle's mirror duet, Cort glanced over at her, and she gave him a "fuck you" look. She'd almost been late tonight, and they'd gotten into it outside on the sidewalk before playing, with Vic calling him a "fucking lunatic who needed to get laid" before stomping inside.

She's right, thought Cort, his fingers resuming the main melody for one final lyrical stanza. He hadn't been with anyone for a couple of months now, concentrating hard on getting his and Vic's tour set up after they'd cut their second album. It just didn't make sense to start up something with someone when he was going away, and Cort didn't engage in casual sex the way he had when he'd done the tour circuit. Call him a pussy, but it just wasn't emotionally satisfying anymore. He was ready to experiment with something serious in his life, and he knew exactly with whom he wanted to give it a try.

Too bad—in the eloquent words of Merit Atwell—*I am fucked.*

. . . leaving Cort with option two, which was to take a look around *Voulez-Vous* after their final number and find someone who looked available for a single night of "fun" with zero strings attached. He could only hope that screwing someone else would release the tension in his balls, though he doubted it.

He had it bad for Mad.

Bad.

His melody line finally ended, and he rested his fingers on the keys, waiting for Vic to finish as he mulled over option three, which was to write.

High emotion could lead to good music or bad music, but it would inevitably lead to *something*, and because Cort really wasn't in the mood to fuck just anyone, it looked like he'd be up until dawn penning songs of frustration.

> *Miss Mad, Miss Mad,*
> *I want you bad,*
> *So bad it hurts inside.*
> *Miss Mad Rousseau,*
> *You've brought me low,*
> *My need for you denied.*

The small crowd clapped, and Cort turned to Vic, raising his eyebrows in question. "Now what?"

"You want me to pick the next one?" she asked, narrowing her eyes.

He shrugged. "Why not?"

"Why not? Because *you* fucking choose the sets, Cort."

"Just choose something. Anything. I'll play it."

"Fine," she said, her eyes flicking over his head to the door and pausing for a moment before looking back at him. A shit-eating grin suddenly played on her lips. "I choose . . . 'La Vie en rose.' "

Cort winced. Yes, it was a French-themed café, but another French love song? He just wasn't in the fucking mood tonight.

"How about anything else?"

Vic shook her head back and forth. "Nope. You said I could choose. It's done. Play."

When he stared back at her, she started plucking a gentle intro, leaving him no choice but to come in with the melody, a new set of romantic lyrics taunting him.

Generally, when Cort played, he tuned out the ambient noise around him, focusing solely on the music he was creating. But he had the *ability* to play on autopilot and tune *into* the ambient noise, which is what he did now so that he wouldn't have to concentrate on the sappy lyrics that mocked him as he played.

"What do you have on tap?" (*A nearby customer.*)

"Dogfish IPA, Palm, Amstel Light, Becks, and . . ." (*Darla.*)

He bent his neck the other way.

"I'm the owner. Can I help you?" (*Merit.*)

"Um . . . I left my card here last night?" (*Wait . . .*)

Mad? Cort flinched. *No, it can't be. You're just hearing what you want to hear.*

"Sorry. Your credit card?" (*Merit.*)

"Yes. Someone called to say I'd left it here? They said they'd hold it for me behind the bar." (*Fuck! It is her.*)

Cort slowly pivoted on the piano stool, his fingers moving of their own accord as he looked over his shoulder to find Mad Rousseau at the corner of the bar near the door, talking to Merit. As though she felt his eyes on her, she turned her glance away from his friend, and her eyes slammed into Cort's.

Her lips parted, then turned up into the loveliest grin he'd ever seen. His bitter heart took flight, and he chuckled softly, smiling back at her as he tuned into the music he was playing, pouring his heart into the simple melody as the beautiful words highlighted a perfect moment.

> *I thought that love was just a word they sang about*
> *   in songs I heard*
> *It took your kisses to reveal that I was wrong, and*
> *   love is real*

When the music ended and the applause began, Cort stood up and crossed the room in three strides. He only paused before her for a moment before grabbing her cheeks and pulling her close, his lips crashing into hers before either of them could say a word.

Chapter 9

"What are you doing here?" he asked her, his dark eyes fierce as they stared into hers.

"I forgot my credit card," she said, still breathless from the intense kiss they'd just shared. "I came back to . . ." Her cheeks were still clasped within his palms, the tips of his fingers buried in her hair. She couldn't lie to him. She just couldn't. "I wanted to see you."

"Today was hell," he whispered, touching his lips to hers gently before resting his forehead on hers.

"For me too," she said, closing her eyes and breathing in the now-familiar and infinitely comforting scent of him. "But nothing's changed, Cort. Jax is still my sister."

Cort leaned away from her, and she opened her eyes to find his deeply troubled. "Will you stay until I'm done? So we can talk a little?"

"I shouldn't," she said, though she made no move to leave him.

He leaned forward, his lips so close to her ear that his breath made her tremble. "Please, baby. Let me walk you home."

Talk and walk. That would be okay, wouldn't it? *Oh, God, please let that little bit of time with him be okay.* She wanted it. She *needed* it.

She nodded, relief flooding her body as she made a quick decision to stay. "Okay."

His smile was sudden and blinding, and he kissed her again, just as Vic strummed a few annoyed notes to remind him they were on the clock.

"I'm done in an hour," he said, dropping his hands and taking a step away.

Mad slid onto the stool at the corner of the bar closest to the door, smiling back at him. "I'll be here."

"If you two are done," said Merit, leaning his elbows on the bar, "my customers are waiting for music."

"I'm here at cost," Cort snapped at his friend, "so give me a break. By the way, Merit, this is Mad. Mad, this is Merit. Merit, stay the fuck away from Mad. Mad, ignore whatever he says."

Mad turned to Merit. "Hi, Merit. Sounds like you're trouble."

"Does it?" he asked, turning up the charm with a flirtatious grin.

"I mean it, Merit," said Cort. "She's off-limits."

Merit took a deep breath and lifted his elbows, stepping away from Mad. "Too bad."

But Mad didn't buy his hangdog expression for a second. She was fairly certain that Merit didn't have any trouble finding female company when he wanted some. She grinned at him, shaking her head like he was very naughty.

"Whatever you're drinking is on his tab, so choose something expensive," said Merit.

"Hendrick's and club?" she asked. "With a lime?"

Merit's eyes widened, and he flattened his hand over his chest. "Gorgeous *and* she knows her gin. Why didn't I see her first?" he asked dramatically, sighing as he ambled away to make her drink.

She turned back to Cort. "Good friend?"

"When a woman's not involved," said Cort.

"I think he's just a bad flirt."

"Yeah, well, usually I wouldn't mind that, but tonight . . ." He reached forward to grab a tendril of her hair and tucked it behind her ear. "Tonight I mind."

"I'm here for *you*," she said, surprised to hear the words leave her mouth. She felt her cheeks flush with heat and knew they were turning red, but it was the truth. She refused to be embarrassed and held his eyes to let him know she meant it.

The breath he took was ragged, and his eyes flared with heat as he stared back at her. "Mad—"

A loud, discordant chord ripped from the nearby cello, interrupting him. He looked over his shoulder at his partner, then back at Mad.

"The next one's for you," he said, winking at her before he turned and strolled back over to the piano.

Mad watched him go, her heart throbbing with emotion but also at peace for the first time since he'd left her apartment early this morning in a huff. It was as though her heart was finally at home now that it was in the same room as Cort's heart, a thought that was as inconvenient as it was wondrous.

She watched him whisper something to Vic, who looked at Mad with an expression caught between suspicious and hopeful, then began to play. She recognized the introduction immediately as Elton John's "Your Song," with Cort playing the regular piano line and Vic playing the melody line on cello. And when he got to the point where the lyrics were "how wonderful life is with you in the world," he looked over his shoulder, his eyes so intense and full of unspoken promises, her breath caught.

"Whew. That is some *serious* eye-fucking," said Merit, placing a cocktail napkin beside her elbow, followed by her drink and a small dish with extra limes. "*I* feel violated."

Turning away from Cort, she gave Merit the look she saved for the rowdiest little boys who wiggled their way through Monday-afternoon story time.

"Oh, man," said Merit, shaking his head and chuckling softly. "Now I get it."

"What, exactly, do you get?" asked Mad, sliding her drink closer and plucking one lime from its nest to squeeze it into her lowball glass.

"What are you? A kindergarten teacher? Piano teacher? Hmm. Librarian?"

She gasped softly, giving herself away, but she had to hand it to Merit. He was good at figuring out women from a look.

"Holy shit. He has the whole naughty librarian fantasy going on here, doesn't he?"

"What does that even *mean*?" she asked, taking a sip of the tangy cocktail.

"You know? I never could figure out Cort's type. Always going after the quiet ones when the brassy ones were pushing their tits up against him . . . But he was holding out, wasn't he?"

Mad's eyes widened. *This* was interesting.

"*Was* he?"

Merit propped his elbows on the bar, narrowing his eyes at Mad as if he was trying to figure something out. "Only one question, though I'm almost positive I already know the answer: are you the prototype or a stand-in?"

"The what or a what?"

"How long have you known each other?"

"Forever. We grew up together."

"I had a feeling," said Merit, leaning away as the music started up again. A dramatically *less* romantic song, she noted.

Looking over her shoulder at Cort, she found him staring back at her and Merit's tête-à-tête with a murderous expression. She shook her head and rolled her eyes at him, though his possessiveness secretly pleased her. Thatcher had never been one to mark his territory or treat her like she was "his woman," but from the way Mad's body was responding to the heat of Cort's stare, it was clearly something she'd been missing. She kissed her fingers, then blew on them, watching with fascination as Cort's eyes turned from hot with jealousy to hot with want. Biting her bottom lip, Mad watched as he turned back to the piano, the muscles of his back shrugging under his T-shirt. She remembered the way those muscles felt under her fingers and longed to feel them again.

"You're the prototype," said Merit definitively, "and how."

Mad blinked, cutting her gaze from Cort back to Merit. "I'm the what?"

"The prototype." Merit put his hands on his hips and spoke matter-of-factly as he poured a draft beer into a pint glass. "As long as I've known Cort, he wanted someone just like you. All prim and proper on the surface but burning like a fever under the pastels and pearls."

"You don't even know me," she scoffed, though she reached up to finger the string of pearls she wore over a pale-yellow linen peasant top.

"I don't need to. I know *him*, and I see the way he's looking at you. All the rest were just stand-ins. You're the original. You're the prototype."

He was close, but he was wrong.

"You're a little bit off."

"I'm not," said Merit confidently.

She nodded. "Yes, you are. If anyone was the 'prototype,' it was my sister, Jax. She was his high school girlfriend."

"His high school—you're . . ." His eyes widened. "Oh, God. You're *her*."

"Who?"

His face had taken on a pained expression. "The sister."

"He mentioned me?"

"In a manner of speaking." His eyes narrowed. "Forgive me for asking, but . . . what are you doing here?"

She stared at him, his question searing and uncomfortable because she knew—full and well—that she should have grabbed her credit card and left. She had no business waiting for Cort to finish playing. Letting him walk her home was just going to lead him on, to complicate matters further, especially when he'd already kissed her tonight. She looked up at Merit, the growing lump in her throat making speech difficult, even if she knew what to say.

Merit shrugged, his face segueing from disdainful to concerned. "I only ask because I care about him. And he clearly cares about you. And unless I'm wrong, this can only end badly."

She nodded quickly as her eyes filled with tears. Glancing at Cort's back, she gulped softly before turning back to Merit. As she slipped down from the stool, she said, "Tell him I had to go."

"I will," said Merit, his voice gentle as he held up his hand to wave good-bye.

When he started the song, she was sitting there at the corner of the bar talking to Merit. When he finished playing and turned around, she was gone. Was she in the bathroom, or was she *gone* gone?

"Play a solo," he growled at Vic.

She gave him a hard look, then nodded. And for Vic not to give him shit? He had his answer. Mad was gone, and Vic had watched her go.

"Thanks for letting me know," he snarled.

"We were in the middle of a set," she said softly, her voice guilty.

He turned and headed to the bar, feeling furious, determined to find out what she and Merit had been talking about and why she'd suddenly left.

Merit raised his eyebrows as Cort approached.

"Outside. Now."

"Cort . . ."

"Now!" said Cort, bypassing the bar and walking up the three steps that led to the sidewalk.

When he turned around, Merit was on the second step, and Vic had started playing the old ballad "Stardust."

"Why did she leave? What did you say to her?"

Merit flinched, shaking his head. "Cort, I'm just looking out for you."

"*Don't!*" bellowed Cort. "What the fuck did you say to her?"

"I asked why she was here. I said it can only end badly between you two."

"Fuck!" Cort ran his hands through his hair in frustration. "You don't know that!"

Merit took a step up toward Cort. "Yes, I do. And damn it, Cort, she even knows. She left."

"You know what, Merit? I'm not your little brother," said Cort, his voice lethal. "You can't—"

"Believe me," said Merit, steel entering his voice, "if you were Ever, Ransom, or Reason, you'd be tied up in the back room, and she'd be on a one-way flight to Paris. But we're friends, and I prefer not to see my friends act like stupid jackasses."

"Fuck you, Merit. Mind your own fucking business."

Then he turned and started walking toward Rittenhouse Square. Aside from the fact that he had wanted to spend more time with her tonight, he wasn't particularly happy about the idea of Mad Rousseau walking around Point Breeze alone at ten thirty at night. Lord only knew what sort of trouble—

"No! Help! Please help!"

Cort's eyes flared open at the sound of her voice, and he started running toward her, his heart racing, his hand reaching into the back pocket of his jeans, where he always carried a Swiss Army knife. He opened it as he ran, keeping it down by his side but ready to use it if Mad was in trouble.

"Help!" she yelled again, and Cort turned right, his feet beating the pavement as he grew closer to her panicked voice. God help the person who was hurting her, because he was going to—

He stopped short when he saw her.

She was kneeling down on the street, but to his relief, there was no one with her, no one bothering her. Was she hurt? He didn't want to frighten her, so he walked slowly, with purpose, to where she was kneeling. As he grew closer, he realized that she was leaning *over* something—a furry lump of something.

"Mad?"

She whipped her head up. "Help! I forgot my cell. Call the police. He's been hit!" As she sat back on her haunches, he could clearly see the outline of an animal—a dog, if he wasn't mistaken—whining softly, its back leg covered in slick, black-looking blood.

Snapping his knife closed, he swapped it for his phone and pressed 911.

"This is 911. Your emergency?"

"Yeah, I'm at Twentieth between Reed and Wharton. A dog's been hit."

"A dog?"

"Yeah, can you send Animal Control? We'll stay with it until they can get here."

He pressed "End," then shoved the phone back in his pocket, taking a deep breath. He'd run fast, plus his adrenaline had been pumping at the thought of Mad in danger. He looked down at her now—she was sitting on the street with the mangy dog's head in her lap. Squatting down beside her, he said, "They're coming."

"Thanks," she whispered. She stroked the dog's head gently. "You're okay, sweet baby. You're going to be okay." She sniffled. "The car hit him on purpose. It *swerved* to hit him. Who *does* that?"

"Someone evil," he said.

The dog whined softly with each breath, its dark eyes looking up at Mad in supplication. He saw a tear wind its way down her cheek and reached over to catch it. There had to be a way around this whole "can't date the sister" thing. There had to be.

He sat down on the pavement beside her, surprised and pleased when she put her head on his shoulder. "I'm sorry I left without saying good-bye."

"I understand," said Cort, putting his arm around her.

"I can't hurt Jax. I—she's my sister, my twin. I love her. I'd do anything for her."

"I know."

"You were her boyfriend. Even if you weren't perfect for each other . . . you meant something to her."

Cort didn't say anything, partially because he wasn't sure this was entirely true. After he and Jax broke up by the pool that night, she hadn't reached out to him again, and the next time he'd seen her—over Thanksgiving break—she seemed fine, as though she'd totally moved on from anything they'd once shared. In fact, if memory served, Jax was already dating someone new. So how much could he have really "meant" to her? Still, it wasn't worth a quarrel with Mad.

"It was a long time ago."

"Yeah," she said, sitting up. "But she's going through a rough time right now."

"How so?"

"You know she made that movie? *The Philly Story*?"

He'd heard about it from Lola because it was filmed on Blueberry Lane, and she'd complained about the film crews parking on the street and blocking the driveway.

"Yeah."

"Her life changed a lot after the movie won an Oscar. She was hounded by the press—like, unmercifully. They scared her, and Jax isn't afraid of anything. Anyway, she's just moved home, and I . . ."

"You don't want to rock the boat," he said.

"Exactly." The dog whined, and Mad shushed it, running her fingers over its tangled fur. "I wish they'd get here."

"So . . . just to be clear, if Jax *wasn't* going through a tough time, you'd consider it? Us?"

She shrugged. "I'd probably be more likely to consider it, though I still don't see how it could work."

His heart lifted because the simple reality was that she wasn't saying no. "So, basically, you're not saying 'never.' You're saying 'not right now.'"

She looked up at him. "Cort, I don't know what I'm saying. I'm saying—"

"Wait. How about this . . ." His arm was still around her shoulders, and he squeezed her closer. "How about we give it a try?"

"I can't—"

"Temporarily. Just for tonight and tomorrow, how about we pretend we're together? How about you come back to my place after Animal Control comes, and we spend the night together? How about we forget that I dated Jax and you just broke up with Thatcher? How about we just see what it feels like to be together?"

She laughed humorlessly. "And then we say good-bye tomorrow? Just like that?"

He nodded. "Just like that." It was a big gamble because if they spent the next twenty-four hours together and he had to watch her walk away forever, he'd always have the memories of their time together, which would be torture if he couldn't have her. But he was hoping that those memories would be so potent, so good and perfect and right, that it would force them to figure out a way to be together.

"Twenty-four hours," she said.

"All in," he said. "A real couple for twenty-four hours."

"And then we say good-bye."

He hated her words, but he nodded.

"And you don't call me."

"Not if you ask me not to."

"Why? What's the point?" she asked.

"To know the truth," he answered gravely. "To know if there's really something here."

"What if there is?" she asked, looking down at the injured animal, her voice a whisper.

"Then we fight for it."

She stared at him, her lips parted, her eyes grave. "Fight?"

He nodded, releasing her shoulder as the van from Animal Control turned onto Twentieth Street. "Uh-huh. We fight, baby."

The van's blue lights lit up the block, stopping in front of Mad and Cort. Cort kept his arm around Mad as the driver and a technician lifted the dog into a blanket-filled crate in the back of the van.

"No tags," said the driver, filling out a form. "He'll be over at 111 West Hunting Park until tomorrow. Then we'll move him to a shelter."

"You'll find a home for him?" Mad asked the technician.

"We do our best, ma'am." But the technician looked dubious as he shut the back doors of the van. "He's not that young, though. And that leg's bad."

She could read between the lines, and her heart lurched. Mad followed him to the passenger side door. "You won't put him down, will you?"

The man hopped into the car and closed the door, looking at Mad through the open window. "I can't say."

"I'll pay for his care," said Mad, reaching for her purse.

"No need, ma'am. We'll take him in and get him stitched up."

"I . . . *please* don't put him down."

The driver got into the van and fired up the engine, leaning over his friend. "Ma'am, if you want to help, what he needs is a home. If you can give him one, come and claim him tomorrow, huh? We have to get going now. Thanks for calling it in."

And just like that, they drove away.

Mad watched them go, grateful for Cort's arm around her as the red taillights grew dimmer and dimmer. "My building doesn't allow dogs," she said, feeling helpless. He sighed softly beside her, and she turned to look at him. "Does yours?"

"I'm not looking for a dog, Mad."

She turned to face him, lowering her eyes and flattening her hands on his chest. "Any boyfriend of mine would have to be an animal lover."

"Oh, Thatcher had a ton of pets, did he?"

But he covered her hands with his, squeezing them before pulling them around his waist and gathering her into his arms.

"I thought we weren't talking about Jax or Thatcher for the next twenty-four hours," she said.

"Wait . . ." His face, which had been stormy, softened as though on command. "You agree? To be together?"

Her heart fluttered wildly as she nodded. "For twenty-four hours."

"Why?" he asked, looking bewildered. "I mean . . . Yes! God, yes! But I'm surprised. I didn't think you'd go for it."

"To be honest, I'm surprising myself," she said, locking her fingers together on the small of his back. "I want to figure out what this is, and . . ."

"And?" he prompted, leaning down to press his lips to her neck.

She leaned her head to the side to give him better access. She smiled, feeling happy from the top of her head to the tips of her toes. "I want you to give Chevreau a home."

"Who?" he mumbled against her throat.

"Chevreau," she said. "Your new dog."

"My new"—he lifted his head, giving her an annoyed look that quickly changed into a smile because he couldn't help it—"dog. Right. Fine."

Mad gasped, unlocking her fingers and throwing her arms around his neck. "You mean it?"

Cort stared at her face for just a moment before whispering, "Yes, baby. Anything for you." Then he pulled her close and dropped his lips to hers. "Let's go home."

Mad insisted that she needed to run home and pack a small bag of things before going to his place for the rest of the weekend, so Cort arranged for an Uber car on his phone app, slinging his arm around her shoulders in the back of the car and kissing her senseless until it pulled up in front of her building. As he waited for her to come back downstairs, he had more than a few seconds of anxiety, rapping his fingers on his knees, worried that she'd rethink her decision to spend time with him and send Donal over to the car with a message that she wouldn't be coming down. So when the elevator doors reopened and Mad walked through the lobby with a sweet smile on her face, his heart throbbed with the sort of forever love he'd never experienced before and never intended to experience for another woman ever again. It was wide and deep and as certain as anything he'd ever known in his life. And it didn't matter that he hadn't seen her in years, and it didn't matter that they'd only reconnected last night. All that mattered was that in his whole life, he'd never felt anything close to what he felt watching Madeleine Rousseau walk back through those lobby doors and slide back into the car beside him where she belonged.

As they pulled away from the curb, she stared at him. "What?"

"You came back."

"I said I would."

"You're mine," he said, reaching up urgently to palm her cheeks, to know that she was real and really here.

She covered his hands with hers, the green pools of her eyes soft and tender. "Until tomorrow."

"You're mine," he said again, bending his head to kiss her.

Chapter 10

His tongue tangled with hers, his heart bursting from the knowledge that they wouldn't be parted tonight and reveling in the idea that she would sleep beside him tonight as she had last night, as he hoped she would for many nights to come.

Sliding his hands down her back, he cupped her bottom and shifted her onto his lap. She straddled his thighs, instantly setting off a chain reaction of intense desire within him. His blood rushed to his groin, and his dick sprang to life, pulsing and throbbing, growing larger and harder with every slide of her sweet, silky tongue against his.

God, how he wanted her, but he had no expectations about tonight. They hadn't talked about what would happen over their twenty-four hours together, aside from the fact that they would spend that time as a couple and had tacitly agreed not to talk about Jax or Thatcher. The rest? That was up to Mad, and he wouldn't push or pressure her to give any more than she offered.

She arched her back, pressing her core against him, the pressure of her softly gyrating body against the zipper of his pants making him groan into her mouth. He slid his hands to her waist, slipping them under her shirt until his palms were flat on the warm, soft skin of her lower back.

"Uh, folks? Folks, we're here?"

Cort's eyes popped open. The car had stopped moving, and they were idling in front of his house. But her lips still moved on his greedily, her hands dragging through his hair as she kissed him urgently.

Pulling away from her, he said, "Mad, we're here."

Her lips were parted and slack, and her eyes opened slowly to look at him.

"Cort," she said, her eyes glazed, her voice husky and desperate, "take me to bed."

Heat flared inside of him as she scrambled off his lap and opened the car door. He grabbed her small duffel bag and slid across the seat to follow her out, muttering "Thanks" to the driver as he shut the door.

She stood on the sidewalk facing him, a sweet smile on her lips.

Cort gestured to his front door with a flick of his chin. "Want to come in?"

"Yes. But we have to talk first."

"What happened to 'Take me to bed'?"

She sighed. "Fresh air cleared my head."

He glanced down at his swollen cock, all but bursting against the zipper of his jeans. "I'm dying a little here, baby."

Her eyes followed his, dancing with mirth when she looked back up at him. "So I see."

"I'm not alone either," he said, dropping his eyes to her nipples, which strained against her thin, billowy blouse.

"No," she said, her voice slightly lower, her smile giving way to a hotter, more needy look. "You're not."

"So let's talk inside."

She shook her head no. "Here."

Cort sighed, hitching her flowered bag a little higher on his shoulder, waiting for her to continue.

"No talking about Jax or Thatcher," she said. "If you talk about Jax, I won't be able to stay. I'll feel too guilty. And if you talk about Thatcher, I'll feel too angry. Promise?"

"I promise."

She took a step closer to him. "And this one's big . . . No falling in love with each other. We're just about impossible, you and me, so we can't—you know—bring that sort of emotion into this. We can enjoy each other, but that's all, Cort. Promise."

He flinched as she finished. He could feel the involuntary muscle reaction that narrowed his eyes and told him that it was too late. It was a lifetime too late to tell him not to love her, because he'd loved her for most of his life. Her gentleness, her quiet grace, the peace he'd always found in her presence now combined with the scorching chemistry between them that couldn't be denied. Over and over again throughout his life, he'd looked for her, tried to find someone like her, but his heart had fixed on hers so long ago, it was all but impossible for him not to love her. The only way he could promise her was to promise not to "fall" *this weekend*, only because he'd already fallen years before.

"I promise not to fall."

She smiled at him, though the smile had lost a bit of the lightheartedness it had held minutes earlier. "Do you need any promises from me?"

He nodded, closing the distance between them. "Yeah, I do."

Her eyes widened, flaring with heat, the black of her pupils obliterating the green of her irises as she pressed her breasts against his chest.

"Promise to leave nothing on the table, Mad. Give me everything you've got for twenty-four hours."

"Except . . ." Her voice broke. "Except my love. I promise."

His heart clenched at her omission, and it made him want to push her out of her comfort zone a little. "Promise to touch me everywhere with your hot little mouth."

"I promise," she murmured, her throat moving as she swallowed.

His eyes narrowed. "Promise to open your legs so I can slide inside of you as if I've been doing it all my life."

"Cort," she whimpered, her eyes fluttering closed as she looked down at where her chest heaved into his. "I need you."

"Promise, baby, because I need you too."

"Yes." She lifted her head. "Take me inside. I promise."

His cock jumped in his pants as she said the words, and he took her hand, pulling her up the steps to his house and punching in the security code. The door unlocked, and he twisted the knob, slipping into the darkness of his living room as Mad pushed the door shut behind them.

Leaning back against the door, her eyes tried to adjust to the dim light of the room, but with no lights on anywhere that she could see, she remained blind, only aware of the insistent throbbing of her heart and the warmth of Cort's fingers threaded through hers.

She heard the sound of her duffel hitting the floor, and then his body pivoted, his chest pressing into hers as he lifted both of her hands above her head, pinning her wrists to the door. He held them with one hand while his free palm landed flat on the bare skin just above her breasts.

She lurched forward, and her lips found his in the darkness. They frantically, urgently kissed, their teeth clashing, his hand plunging lower, into her shirt, under her bra, to grasp the tender flesh of her breast. Arching her back against the door, she whimpered, wanting to be naked, wanting to be beneath him, needing to feel like he belonged to her every bit as much as she wanted to belong to him.

Releasing her wrists, his hands dropped to her shirt and bra, bunching the fabric in his hands and dragging both forcibly over her head. Her nipples, stiff and desperate for the heat of his tongue, beaded into hard points as the cool air kissed them. His hands left her body for a split second, but when he grabbed her again, the hard, hot wall of his bare chest crushed her breasts as his hands clutched her ass. With a small hop, she was straddling his body, her ankles locked around his back, and he was backing away from the door, into the room, kissing her madly as he walked blindly through the darkness of his house.

Mad wove her fingers through his hair, razing his scalp with her nails as he started up a flight of stairs, his tongue still dancing with hers as he turned a sharp corner and kept ascending. Her sandals clattered to the floor, and with floor-boards squeaking beneath his booted feet, he walked down a hallway and turned into a room.

"Light on or off?" he asked gruffly, his voice breathless.

"Off," she said as he sat down on a bed with her still strad-dling his hips. She leaned forward to drag her lips along the hot skin of his throat, her fingers sliding between their bodies to tug open the button of his jeans, nimbly unzip-ping the tight denim and reaching for the satin steel of his erection.

He gasped. "Mad, what I said downstairs . . . the promise I made you give me . . . you don't have to . . ."

The long ridge of straining muscle pulsed in her palm, making her mouth water. How she longed to taste him.

"You didn't make me say anything I didn't want to say," she said, pressing the heel of her hand against his balls and making him groan. "I want this. I want you."

His hands were suddenly under her arms, and he lifted her from his lap, transferring her to the bed, where she lay on her back, looking up at him.

"You need to know this," he said, his voice emotional and urgent. "I have to tell you . . ."

Warning bells went off in her head, telling her that she didn't want to know whatever it was he was going to say . . . that whatever he wanted to tell her would end up making things irrevocably messier between them.

"No," she said, her hands trailing down the center of her chest to unbutton her own jeans and open the zipper. Hooking her thumbs into the waistband, she braced her weight on her elbows, and with a shove—*whoosh*—her jeans and panties pooled at her ankles, leaving her completely naked on his bed. "You promised. No declarations. Just be with me."

Staring down at her, he stood up, toeing off his boots and socks, then shoving his pants and boxers to the floor, his eyes never leaving hers as he bared his body to her for the first time.

Her eyes darted to his erection, and she licked her lips before looking back up at him. Lifting one finger, she hooked and flexed it twice, gesturing for him to come closer, and he stepped to the edge of the bed.

She knelt on the side of the bed, placed her hands on his hips, and leaned forward, taking him balls deep into her mouth with one smooth slide forward.

He gasped in surprise—a low, guttural, animalistic sound of pain and pleasure as she laved her tongue around the tip of his hardness, tasting the salty pre-cum as his hands landed gently on her head, neither pushing nor urging, just a point of connection as she slowly backed away, her lips holding tightly as each vein, each ridge, each pulsing muscle slipped between her lips. Reaching for the base of his shaft, she held him tightly as she leaned forward and took him into her mouth again. With a gasp and a hiss, the pressure of his fingers in her hair increased for just a moment—a reflex, not a demand for more. He was taking what she was giving, and she was making good on her promise to taste him, to touch him, to discover him and know him, and to learn what he liked and how she could please him. Because if he only belonged to her for a day, then she would be sure that—as he'd made her promise—*almost* nothing was left on the proverbial table.

Looking up, she found his head thrown back and the muscles of his chest taut in the moonlight—the boy who had so intrigued her as a teenager, unspeakably beautiful as a man fully grown in the throes of pleasure. Sensing her eyes on him, he bent his neck forward and looked down at her, caressing her hair, gathering it into a ponytail that he held gently until she took him as deep as she could.

"Mad," he groaned, his fist in her hair in a trembling grip. "You're going to make me come."

Good, she thought, reaching around to cup the rock-hard muscles of his ass and push him flush against her face, giving him unspoken permission to let go and find his pleasure.

Working him with her lips and tongue, she reveled in the power of her touch, her clit throbbing to the music of his groans and sighs, her fingernails biting into his skin as a growl ripped from *his* throat, his cock pulsing in rhythmic throbs as he came in hers.

Sliding her lips gently from base to tip, she kissed the salty tip of his shaft as she raised her eyes to his face and leaned back on her hands.

"Oh. My. God," he sighed, breathless and bewildered.

He stared down at her, his expression a mix of shock and worship, his lips tilting up into a smile that made him look so happy and so boyish, she could do nothing but return it, lying back on the bed with a satisfied sigh, knowing that she'd given him pleasure.

"Good?"

"Fucking phenomenal."

She chuckled softly, but her giggle stopped abruptly when he knelt on the bed and reached for her legs, rearranging them so that he could kneel between them.

"Do you know what's coming next, baby?"

Thatcher wasn't into oral sex, claiming that Mad "smelled ripe," so she nervously looked up at him. "Oh, you don't have to . . ."

"Yes, baby. I do."

She licked her lips, feeling an awkward blush creep into her cheeks. "I don't think you should."

He caressed her thighs tenderly. "You don't like it?"

"I do . . . I just . . . Oh, God."

"What?" he asked. "What's wrong?"

"I just think that maybe I don't . . . um . . . smell right," she finished, dropping his eyes as her whole body flushed with embarrassment.

"Mad," he said softly. "Can I touch you there?"

"Um . . . if you want to, but remember, I warned you . . ."

She gasped as his index finger slid into the thatch of neatly trimmed curls, slipping effortlessly into the soaked folds of her clit, and she whimpered as he rubbed it gently. Then, holding her eyes all the while, he withdrew his finger and lifted it to his mouth, sucking on it. His eyes closed, a look of pure bliss taking over his features.

"You taste like heaven, Mad Rousseau. Any other warnings you want to give me?"

"N-no," she murmured, closing her eyes and leaning back on the pillow as her tense muscles unbunched and she exhaled with relief.

Lifting her legs over his shoulders, he leaned his head down, parted the lips of her sex with two fingers, then licked, in one long, smooth stroke, from the base of her clit to the hood. She was already sensitive from making out against the door and taking him in her mouth to climax, but nothing prepared her for the shock of desire she felt as his tongue made a second pass. Her hips bucked off the bed, shoving her slit into his face, then she whimpered with a mix of embarrassment and pleasure.

With one hand holding her left thigh tightly, he chuckled as he licked her again, slower this time, as though he wanted to test and taste every ridge, every indent, every slick, sweet, soaked morsel of skin between her legs.

"Coooooort," she moaned.

"Too much?" he whispered, his breath kissing the throbbing nub of her clit.

The way he touched her—so carefully, so tenderly— brought tears to her eyes, but she let them slide away unnoticed, reaching for the soft hair of his head and plunging her fingers into it. "More. Oh, please, more."

"Whatever you want, baby."

He circled her clit with his tongue, the point tracing lazy rings around her pulsing, throbbing skin, and Mad writhed beneath him, moaning shamefully, straining to get closer to his mouth as the pressure between her legs focused to a diamond point, building into an almost unbearable crest of impending pleasure.

"Cort. Oh, God . . ."

"Let go, baby," he whispered, pursing his lips around the swollen nub of hidden flesh and sucking. "Come for me."

Like an electrical charge to her clit, the strong sucking of his mouth made her explode beneath him, coming apart in deep, throbbing waves of pleasure. Her eyes rolled back in her head, and her body hummed like an instrument expertly played by the ministrations of a master.

As the waves of pleasure ebbed and slowed, she sighed, opening her eyes to find Cort leaning over her, watching her with an expression filled with such profound love, she knew that he'd already broken his promise to her.

"You weren't supposed to," she murmured, a tear slipping down the side of her face as she reached up to cup his cheek.

"I can't help it," he answered, dipping his head to lick the tear away before kissing her lips.

She nodded because she couldn't help it either—this freight train of intense emotion that propelled her forward, into his arms, into his heart, into his life. They were like supermagnets, destined for each other since the moment they'd reconnected, and she felt utterly helpless to stop the forward motion that would lead to love.

"Are you angry?" he asked.

"No. I can't help it either."

His eyes narrowed, but he didn't push her to explain. Instead, he asked, "What do you want?"

"You."

"Now?"

She nodded, opening her legs wider as he settled between them.

"Are you on the pill, baby?"

She nodded again, smoothing her hands down his back as he reached between them to grab the base of his cock and position it at the entry of her sex.

"Mad," he said reverently, holding her eyes as he slid inside her body, "it was *always* you."

She cried out as he drove into her to the hilt, his balls slapping against her skin as he touched his forehead to hers, peppering soft kisses on her face as he held himself still from the waist down, waiting for her to adjust to his girth and length.

"Are you okay?" he asked.

She nodded, and he lifted his head to look down at her. "I mean it. I know you don't want me to say it, but you have to know. It was *always* you, Mad."

His words, meant to reassure her, split her heart in half, because if they were true, it meant that all the time he'd been with Jax, he'd wanted to be with her. And that made her sad for Jax, and for him, and for her. Because all the while he'd wanted her, she'd wanted him too.

"Kiss me," she said, sliding her hands up his back and winding her arms around his neck as he began to move slowly inside of her.

He bent to taste her lips, his tongue finding hers as tears slipped from the corners of her eyes. Moving with deep, rhythmic strokes, he massaged the walls of her sex with the ridges of his cock, claiming her, owning her, mimicking his movements with the slide of his tongue against hers. Reaching between their bodies, he found the swollen nub of her clit and rubbed it, sending shockwaves of pleasure radiating throughout her body like electricity. She hooked her ankles around his back as he pumped harder and faster, his finger moving in circles on her clit and the whole world swirling with love and betrayal, pain and pleasure, until Mad couldn't keep up anymore. And her body tightened to the point of breaking.

"Come with me, baby. Tell me you're mine," panted Cort, withdrawing almost totally from her body as his finger stilled on her clit.

It was true. She was his. He owned her, and she owned him.

"I'm yours," she whispered.

His throbbing cock surged forward, filling her again as his fingers pinched her clit. They exploded together in the most intense, all-consuming orgasm Mad had ever experienced.

They rode the crest together, muscles contracting in symphony, kissing madly, a lifetime's worth of want, of need, of destiny slamming into them and forcing them to recognize what the universe had always known: they were meant to be together.

She lay back against the pillow, exhausted but replete as Cort emptied himself, in pulsing spurts, deep within her body. And Mad felt the blistering awareness of something her heart had always known: Cort had never belonged to Jax because he had always belonged to her, and here, now, their hearts were finally home.

With Cort still imbedded deeply within her, she stroked his hair as her tired eyes closed and her heart sought his rhythm, and their hearts beat in tandem as they fell asleep.

I'm yours.
You're mine.
We fight.

When Cort woke up two hours later, it was after midnight, and Mad's smooth legs were tangled around his, her breath sweet and warm in the crook of his neck as she slept peacefully in his arms.

Miss Mad, Miss Mad,
In nothing clad,
Your body bared to mine.
Miss Mad Rousseau,
I love you so,
From now to the end of time.

He nuzzled her forehead, and she sighed in her sleep, burrowing closer, her nipples rubbing against his chest, her arms tightening around his torso. His heart swelled. Despite the other women who had shared his bed over the course of his lifetime, he couldn't remember a single one, because none of them mattered except this one.

I'm yours, she'd said as they climaxed together in the single most earth-shattering moment of his life. *And I'm yours*, he thought. *I always have been.*

"I'm going to marry you," he whispered, pressing his lips to her hair. "Marry me, Mad."

"Mmm," she murmured. "Yes."

He froze, holding his breath as his eyes widened. *My God, did she hear me?*

"Mad?" he whispered, but she didn't answer. "Baby, are you awake?"

She didn't stir, didn't murmur, and there was no hitch in her breathing or tightening of her muscles. Had she said "yes" in her sleep? Had her subconscious heard him and asked her lips to answer? He smiled, relaxing as he pulled her closer.

He'd take a dreamy yes.

For now.

When Mad's eyes fluttered opened, it was dark, and she was alone. Leaning up on her elbows, she looked at the clock on Cort's beside table: 3:21 a.m. Feeling the pillow beside her, she found it was still warm but cooling. He hadn't been gone long.

From somewhere in the house, she heard the sound of a harp playing, and for just a moment, she wondered if she was dreaming or awake—it sounded so beautiful, so ethereal. Remembering that Cort played the harp, she grinned, and somewhere inside, she knew he was playing for her. She knew because he was playing "Le Cygne."

Wrapping herself in the bed sheet, she stood up and walked toward the flowing ripples and waves of music. She peeked up a steep spiral staircase and realized that the music was coming from upstairs. Unable to see her destination from the landing where she stood, she took the steps carefully, winding around and around the narrow staircase until she found herself in the doorway to a large, open space. Cream-colored walls with exposed ceiling beams and hardwood floors made the attic studio feel cozy even though the loft was vast by Center City Philadelphia standards.

To her left was a glassed-in room with padded walls and a microphone hanging from the ceiling, and inside, with his back to her, Cort sat on a low stool in nothing but jeans, a harp between his legs and leaning against his shoulder. Mad stepped closer to the glass, listening as Cort played, her heart swelling with affection for him. Her fingers rested on the glass, and for just a moment, she allowed herself to imagine that this was truly her life—or rather, that this was her life beyond tomorrow—sleeping in Cort Ambler's bed, wrapping herself in a sheet that smelled of him, and finding him here, in an attic studio, playing music that was too beautiful to be real.

It was always *you.*

Deep in her heart, she knew his words were true. He had dated her sister, but he'd wanted her, just as she'd always wanted him. She didn't know—yet—how that had happened, but when their twenty-four hours were over, she would seek out Jax and find out the truth.

Tears of longing pricked her eyes just as Cort finished, resting his hands on the strings until they were silent. As though he felt her watching, he turned slowly, his eyes scanning her face, his hand lifting to beckon her in.

Swiping at her weepy eyes, she gave him a smile and pushed open the door, stepping inside the small, transparent, strangely intimate room.

"That was beautiful," she said.

"Sit with me," he said.

He scooted the chair back a touch, and she slipped between Cort and the harp, perching on his lap.

"What were you working on?"

"Something new," he said, "for you. Want to hear it?"

She gasped. "Yes, I'd love to."

Reaching forward, he pulled the harp closer, between Mad's legs. To reach the strings, he circled his arms around her, and the sheet around her loosened to expose the peak of one full breast. Mad reached for the sheet, but Cort placed his hand over hers.

"Leave it, baby," he whispered into her ear, his voice husky. "Please." He leaned the harp against her shoulder, then took her hands and placed them on the soundboard. "You'll feel it here," he said, caressing the backs of her hands before sliding his palms to the part of the sheet still covering her thighs. Smoothing it up until it bunched around her waist, he slid the harp all the way back, until it was cradled in the apex of her naked inner thighs. "And here."

Mad's breath hitched, her eyes fluttering closed with anticipation as she realized exactly where she would *feel* his music.

"Ready, baby?"

"Mmm-hm," she murmured, leaning her head back on his shoulder.

His hands, which rested on the strings, started moving, and the seductive waves of melody issuing from the instrument vibrated against her thighs, massaging the tender flesh between her legs. As his arms reached for the strings, plucking and sweeping, his elbow rubbed and nudged the bare skin of her exposed breast until her nipple strained for his touch, stiff with arousal.

It was the most erotic experience of her life, being practically naked in Cort's arms as he played the harp for her. Exposed and vulnerable, she had also never felt so alive, as though she was placed on earth for the sole purpose of finding herself here, now, with him.

The music poured from the harp in glorious waves, and she realized she'd heard the song before. It was the same one he'd been humming last night as they danced in the rain. It was the song he was writing about her.

And suddenly it was too much—the wetness between her thighs where she ached to be filled by him again, the erect peaks of her breasts that longed for the slick warmth of his tongue, the song he was writing for her on the instrument she loved the most.

All the air in the small room seemed to be disappearing, and she could barely breathe from the assault of sensation. Trembling in his arms, she reached for his hands, stilling them, keeping her eyes closed as she tried to fill her lungs.

It had always been her for Cort.

It had always been Cort for her.

She was falling in love with him.

She was falling madly in love with him, and there wasn't a single thing she could do about it.

She was already in the middle of it—a forgotten song from long ago now present with new verses being written—before she'd even realized it had begun.

"Did you like it?" he whispered.

"I loved it," she answered, desperately trying not to sob.

"What now?" he asked.

Her body cried out for his, throbbing with longing.

"Make love to me," she murmured on a sigh. "Right here. Right now."

Tilting the harp back up, he pushed it away several inches, then reached for the sheet around Mad, gently pulling it from her body. He stood up to shake it out, then placed it on the padded floor. She heard the zipper of his jeans being pulled down and the shimmy of fabric as he slid them down his legs. Circling the stool, he stood in front of her a moment later, naked and erect, his thick shaft straining toward her.

He surprised her by dropping to his knees and putting a hand on each thigh.

"The numbers," he said, looking into her eyes with fathomless tenderness. "Can I see them?"

She nodded, and he pushed her legs apart until she was fully exposed to him, the most private, secret parts of herself on full display. And while he'd had his lips on those parts not three hours ago, it was different now, here, in the bright light of his recording studio, perched on a stool and completely naked. She waited for her cheeks to flush with heat as he drew closer, but they didn't. And then it occurred to her: they didn't because she didn't feel embarrassed; she didn't feel less than perfect in Cort's eyes. In fact, she felt like every moment of her life kept leading here. To Cort. To now.

His palms smoothed up her inner thighs, and he leaned forward until he found them, the size of a penny, on the crease of her thigh: 398.2 in an elegant script.

He looked up at her. "Three ninety-eight point two?"

She nodded, and his thumb rubbed absentmindedly against her skin.

"What does it mean?"

She licked her lips. Would he laugh at her? Would be understand?

"In the Dewey Decimal System, fairy tales are shelved at three ninety-eight point two."

"Fairy tales?" he breathed.

She nodded, feeling even more naked than she had before. "I want the fairy tale, Cort."

"Oh, baby," he sighed, leaning forward to press his lips to the black numbers as he held tightly to her hips. "I want that too."

His lips lingered on the tattoo, and Mad felt a surge of profound tenderness. She placed her hands on his head, stroking his hair, glorying in the feel of it between her fingers.

She wanted him.

She *needed* him buried deep inside her body.

"Make love to me, Cort."

Pulling her into his arms, he lay down on the sheet and positioned Mad over his hips, gasping as she grasped the root of his sex and lowered herself onto him. He flexed his hips, invading her tight, wet sheath and claiming it for his own.

"We fight, Mad," he whispered, staring up at her, his eyes holding the promise of forever. "Tell me we fight, baby."

"We fight," she whispered back, lacing her fingers through his as she moved rhythmically over his cock, faster and faster, taking him deep, surrendering to the power of their forever connection, and yielding to the strength of a bond that should have weakened over time but hadn't.

And now, reborn, she prayed it would never, ever forsake them again.

Chapter 11

Cort sat at the bistro table in his kitchen wearing jeans, with Mad perched on his lap, dressed in nothing but a pair of panties and one of his old T-shirts. It swam on her much smaller frame, but he loved it because it was his, and she was wearing it like it belonged to her, as if fishing a shirt from his dresser drawer on a Sunday morning was something she did all the time. She picked up a piece of the buttered toast he'd made for them and took a bite before nudging it to his lips too.

After they'd made love on the studio floor, he'd carried her back downstairs, and they'd fallen into bed—a tangle of naked limbs and sated bodies. And waking up midmorning, hours later, he'd reached for her again, sliding into her waiting warmth with sleepy gratitude. Moving smoothly and slowly within her to savor every blessed skin-to-skin stroke, he brought her to orgasm before claiming his own.

Afterward, she'd turned to him with a shy grin and asked, "What do you have for breakfast?"

And now here he sat, with Mad on his lap and buttered toast on a plate, his heart so full of wonder, it bordered on disbelief.

"Can I ask you something?" she asked, reaching for the mug of black coffee they were sharing.

"Sure."

She took a sip, then placed the mug back on the table, turning around and swinging her leg over his lap to straddle him. He slid his hands under the T-shirt, resting them on the soft, bare skin of her hips and searching her eyes, which looked unsettled.

"Hey . . . what's up?"

She rolled her lips together and took a deep breath. "If you were into me, how come you dated Jax?"

"I thought we weren't talking about Jax and Thatcher today," he said.

She shrugged. "That was before we decided to give this a real try. I think we need to talk about Jax a little, don't you?"

No. Talking about Jax sounded complicated, not to mention that Cort's memories of his two months with Jax weren't the proudest of his life. He'd just as soon not talk about it, but Mad waited for an answer.

"Because I was young and stupid," he said.

She nodded. "I'm sure that's part of the story, but I feel like you're leaving a lot out."

Was there any way out of this? His lips twitched as he dropped her eyes. Yes, it was ten years ago, and yes, he'd grown into a man since then, and yes, teenage boys were notoriously stupid . . . but he hated to say anything that might jeopardize his chances with Mad.

He looked up at her luminous green eyes that waited patiently for him to figure out how to answer her, and finally he decided that the truth would be best, no matter how much it sucked.

"Okay . . . the truth?"

"It's my favorite."

"That spring of senior year? Bree was already out of college living in London, and Dashie was at UC Santa Barbara. My parents were barely around. They were in Sedona almost every weekend, and little by little, they'd added Fridays and Mondays to their weekends until they'd just come home for a day or two every other week. Lola was pretty much raising Sloane, and I was . . . well . . ."

"You were what?"

"I had just gotten into Curtis. No one was keeping an eye on me. I mean, Lola did, as much as an elderly housekeeper can look after a teenage boy, but otherwise, I was pretty much left to my own devices."

Mad nodded, and he knew that she understood what he was saying on a personal level because her parents had been jet-setters, always headed to a different city, leaving the Rousseau kids alone with house staff and each other.

He held onto her tighter. "You and Jax have the same hair color, and you were the same height. You looked about as alike as fraternal twins could look, always borrowing each other's clothes . . . I mean, if I was talking to one of you when I was sober, I knew exactly who was who because your personalities are so different, but . . ."

"But you weren't very sober that spring," she said softly.

"I was an *alcoholic* that spring," said Cort. "I was only *occasionally* sober."

"Tell me the rest," said Mad, sadness filling her voice like she knew exactly what he was going to say, and man, but he hated to have to say it.

"It was spring break. I barely remember that week. The *only* thing I remember is making out with *you* one awesome night but somehow having Jax for a girlfriend on Monday morning."

She sprang off his lap, hitting her hip on the table as she turned in the tight space to face him. Her eyes searched his face, blinking rapidly like she was trying desperately to hold back a deluge of tears. Standing between his open knees, her hands formed into fists over her heart as she stared at him.

Finally, she whispered, "You thought Jax was me?"

He flinched but held her eyes for a long moment before nodding slowly. "I thought Jax was you."

She sucked her top lip between her teeth and dropped his eyes, looking down miserably. "You made out with Jax thinking she was me? God, that sucks on so many levels."

"I know," he said softly.

"You were *that* drunk?"

"I was a mess, Mad. The Friday I got my acceptance letter to Curtis, it was the day before spring break. Bree and Dash weren't around, and Sloane was staying after school for cheerleading practice. Lola had left a note that she was organizing bingo at her church that evening and wouldn't be back until late. I called my parents, but their housekeeper said they were leading a retreat in a desert, which essentially meant they were taking peyote and dancing naked all weekend around a campfire or some such shit. I sat down with my acceptance letter and poured myself a glass of my grandfather's best scotch to toast myself alone. I drank a glass, then two, then four, then eight. When I woke up a few hours later still drunk, Lola was yelling at me, and Sloane looked frightened. Probably because I'd smashed every crystal tumbler in the dining room except the one I was using. My little sister had called Lola home from her church game night because she couldn't wake me up and thought I might be dead. I smashed the glass in front of me, told them both to go to hell, moved into the pool house, and went on a bender for the whole week."

"Everyone partied at your house that week. I remember hearing about it," she said, her eyes still heavy with betrayal, but her posture had relaxed a little, and Cort used it to his advantage, reaching for her hands and feeling an intense rush of relief when he laced his hands through hers and she didn't pull away.

"I honestly don't know how I survived it, but Sloane got me sobered up in time for school on Monday and informed me that Jax was waiting by the front gate for a ride."

Mad was nodding her head like she remembered what he was talking about. "She was excited. When I came home that afternoon, she said she had a boyfriend for the end of senior year."

"She kissed my mouth when I backed out of the driveway and rolled down the window, and I was like 'What the fuck? Why is Jax Rousseau kissing me?' Then she jumped into the passenger seat beside me, talking about 'last night' and how much fun we were going to have until graduation. I was so confused. I asked her where you were, and Jax said that . . ."

"I was coming home from Paris later that day?"

Cort nodded. "And then I knew. I'd made out with Jax the night before. And I would have to be a monumental asshole to make out with her, then dump her because she wasn't you, so . . ."

"So you decided to be her boyfriend."

"Yeah. I mean, sort of. I meant to break it off quickly, but she was talking about prom and senior skip day, and she'd already told all her friends that we were a thing. It was already a mess."

"That's Jax," said Mad, nodding affectionately. "Off to the races before the gunshot."

"But Mad . . . I was always watching you, hanging out at Chateau Nouvelle with Jax, hoping you'd show up too. And those conversations we'd have while she was busy talking to everyone else?"

A slight smile tilted her lips. "I loved talking to you. But I felt guilty . . ."

". . . because you felt something for me too?"

"Because I felt something for my sister's boyfriend."

"Just so you know . . . Me and Jax? We kept it light. We *never* slept together."

She lifted her chin. "If you had, I wouldn't be here now. It would have been impossible, Cort. Being together would have been impossible."

"I know that," he said, thanking God things had never progressed that far for him and Jax.

Mad unlaced her fingers from his to cup his cheeks and give him a tired look. "You've gotten us into a fine mess, you know?"

"Young and stupid," he said. "I told you."

He searched her eyes, wondering what she would say next. Finally, she cocked her head to the side, her expression just shy of jealous. "You two dated for almost two months. You must have liked her."

"Aw, baby. Of course I liked her. Jax was my friend. I cared about her enough not to fool around with her and then act like it was a mistake or let her tell all her friends we were an item, then dump her. And yes, part of me probably hung out with her because I had better access to seeing you. Plus, I didn't want you to think I was a dick."

"I ended up thinking you were a dick anyway."

He shrugged, twisting his head to kiss her palm.

"But I'm glad you didn't hurt her," she said softly, stepping closer to him. She took his chin in her fingers, making him look up at her. "You really thought she was me?"

He nodded. "But I'll never make that mistake again. Jax is awesome, baby, but she's not you."

Mad took a deep breath and sighed, and Cort, sensing her anger subsiding, reached for her hips and pulled her back onto his lap. She straddled his hips in the straight-backed kitchen chair, and his cock hardened, pressing against his jeans, ready for her again and needing the reassurance that making love would bring—that despite these hurtful confessions, she still wanted him.

"When will you tell her?" he asked, his voice husky as he kneaded her lower back with his fingers, nudging her T-shirt aside with his nose and nuzzling her shoulder.

"I don't know. I told you . . . she's going through something right now."

"But soon?"

"As soon as I can." Her lips twitched. "I'm seeing her for dinner at Jean-Christian's on Thursday. Maybe then if the time feels right."

"Do you still—I mean, does what I told you change things? Between us?" he asked, staring up into her eyes and cursing the love he felt for her, which made him feel so small, so uncertain, so desperate for her to love him back just as deeply, just as strongly.

Her smile was small at first, but it grew into something so beautiful, Cort felt the music of Mad again—of this stunning woman who was grace and warmth, first love and second chances, forgiveness and hope.

"Does it change how I feel about you?" She pressed a kiss to his forehead. "Because you were sad and alone?" Another kiss to his right temple. "Because you were seventeen and drunk and made a stupid mistake, confusing one girl for another?" Another to his left. "Because instead of humiliating my sister, you dated her for a while so she could save face?" She shook her head, widening her thighs and pressing her soaked core against his jeans. "It makes me wish I'd been there when you got the letter from Curtis. It makes me wish I hadn't been in Paris that week. It makes me wonder where we'd be right now if I'd been around."

"Nowhere," he whispered, running his hands up her ribs to cup her breasts, "because I was too young and stupid to love you right."

She lifted the T-shirt over her head, covering his hands as she dipped her head to kiss him.

"Then thank God," she whispered against his lips, "it happened now."

After sex at the kitchen table, they'd showered together and dressed. Cort called Animal Control and found out that Chevreau's leg had been set and bandaged, and they were free to pick him up for adoption at four o'clock, which had won Cort a passionate kiss from Mad, who called him her hero.

With most of the afternoon open, Cort had taken Mad on a tour of the Magic Gardens, a three-thousand-square-foot mosaiced space spanning three city lots and including indoor galleries and an outdoor labyrinth. Because Mad spent most of her time in the posher areas of Philadelphia, it was eye-opening to experience such a spectacle of urban regeneration. She couldn't wait to share this hidden gem with her brother, Jean-Christian, and friend Jessica English. She could just imagine the exposure that two of the city's most wealthy and fervent supporters of fine arts could bring to such an amazing grassroots project.

At one bend in the labyrinth, they found a dreadlocked musician softly playing the bongos beside an unusual-looking stringed instrument.

"Hey Cort-man," he said, grinning up at Cort. "Play wit' me a while, yeah?"

"Got a girl with me today, Aza," said Cort, squeezing Mad's hand.

"Look to me like you got a *woman* wit' you, Cort."

Cort chuckled. "And what a woman."

"So play 'er a love song, man," said Aza, his body moving gently to the beat his fingers played on the bongos.

"A love song, huh?" Cort looked at Mad, his eyes so happy, it made her heart clench with joy. "You want a love song, Miss Mad Rousseau?"

She smiled at him and nodded, stepping back so he could pick up the instrument and sit on the wooden crate beside his friend. He looked up at Mad. "It's a lyre."

"You know how to play it?" she asked.

"It a *kissar*," said Aza, stressing the "kiss" and winking at Mad. "From de Sudan. You been to de Sudan?"

"No," said Mad. "I've never been to Africa."

"Well, you should go," said Aza, "and take dis one wit' you. We got rhythm you ain't never dreamed of, *Haba Haba*." He turned to Cort. "You want to jump in on this, man?"

Cort nodded. "I can work with it."

Mad leaned back against the wall across from them to allow passersby to move between them and watched as Cort placed his fingers on the lyre and started playing a melody that almost perfectly complimented the soft bossa nova beat of Aza's drums.

Though she couldn't place the tune, she hummed along with the deeply romantic song, staring at Cort as he grinned at his friend and occasionally looked up at Mad with a joy-filled smile that spoke volumes about a man who could hold his own with the Philadelphia Orchestra or play with a street performer on a lazy Saturday afternoon. And she loved both.

Her heart stuttered, and her breath caught as she realized the thought that had materialized so effortlessly in her head. She loved both. *Loved.* Both.

Loved *him.*

At that moment, he looked up at her, finishing the closing bars of the song and cocking his head to the side as he scanned her face.

You okay? he mouthed.

She nodded, offering him a smile that was filled with emotion. "That was beautiful."

"It's from *My Fair Lady*. It's called 'The Street Where You Live,'" he said, placing the lyre back down and shaking Aza's hand before they waved good-bye and ambled down to the end of the labyrinth. "And that's where I'm happiest, Mad. Wherever you are."

Leaning down, he kissed her leisurely, only breaking away when a small group of waiting art lovers had piled up behind them, one of them clearing her throat loudly with disapproval.

"We have an hour before we can go check on Chevreau. Want to get some coffee?" he asked, chuckling as the older woman stomped by in a huff.

"I'd love it," she said as he put his arm around her waist and tucked her into his side.

"I want to ask you something, but I don't want to freak you out," he said after they'd walked a short way down the block and found seats outside of a neighborhood café.

Mad's heart fluttered a little at the mixture of excitement and hope in his voice, but she gulped and grinned. "I won't freak out."

"I was wondering . . . You know how you said you're supposed to take a week off between your old job ending and your new job starting? That would be the week after next, right? The same week I leave for Europe."

She nodded, her heart speeding up, longing for him to invite her, but scared too. It was the same feeling she used to get on the high dive of the Winslow's swimming pool—excited but terrified in that moment before she jumped.

"What would you think?" he asked. "About coming with me?"

"Um . . . I don't . . ."

"I know it's sudden, but I'm going to be away for two months, and I was thinking that if you'd come with me, then two weeks later, I'd come back to Philly, or we could meet in New York for the Fourth of July. And then you could come back for a long weekend at the beginning of August when I'm in France. And then I'll be back at the end of . . ." His voice drifted off as the waitress reappeared with their iced coffees and a fruit and cheese plate. He scanned her face, no doubt noting she'd gone mute. "Too much?"

Listening to him plan for their future did serious things to Mad's heart—a heart that had already recognized during the romantic strains of "The Street Where You Live" that she was falling in love with him. Thatcher hadn't believed in "planning" a future with actions, only in "visualizing" it with promises that had never been kept. They'd never moved in together, he'd never given her a ring, and they'd certainly never made any solid plans to marry. But Cort? Cort wanted to nail down a two-month plan with her right out of the gate, and it made her feel so reassured and so grateful, so treasured and precious to him, she could cry.

But the same problem that had been an obstacle in their relationship since they first reconnected still stood between them: Jax—Jax and so many unanswered questions Mad needed her to answer. Why had Jax lied about her breakup with Cort? What had happened between them, and why had Jax allowed Mad to think the very worst of him? Would Jax give Mad permission to be with Cort after she'd dated him first?

And yet, for the first time, Mad felt a sharp wave of protectiveness, not just over her sister, but over Cort too. She wanted what he was offering. She felt this visceral pull to explore the possibility of something real, something beautiful, with him. It's just that she needed to reconcile matters with her sister first in order to give her heart to him unreservedly.

"*Not* too much," she said gently, taking a sip of her icy-cold coffee, "but slightly premature. I have to talk to Jax. I have to tell her about us. And I have to make sure she's okay with it."

Cort's eyes narrowed. "What if she's not?"

"I don't want to hurt her," said Mad, her heart clutching. "You think it will?"

"You were hers first."

"I was *never* hers," he said darkly, "no matter how it looked."

Mad reached for his hand and squeezed it. "She doesn't have to love it, Cort. At least not at first. I can live with her not loving it. Let's just hope she's able to see that something that didn't work out for you two in high school is totally different than the connection we have as adults." Mad sighed. "When are you leaving for Europe?"

"Two weeks from yesterday," he said, staring at his coffee, his lips turned down. "Thirteen days."

"Then I'll try to talk to her before then, and as long as she's able to handle it . . . yes," said Mad. "I'll go with you."

His head snapped up, a smile taking over his face. "You will?"

She shrugged, unable to contain a giggle. "I haven't taken a vacation in ages. I deserve one."

Cort reached for her other hand, lacing his fingers through hers and squeezing. "I'll make sure it's a trip you never forget, baby."

Mad leaned over the table to kiss him sweetly. "I'll hold you to it."

Chapter 12

Two hours later, after they'd picked up Chevreau and Cort had filled out the adoption papers, they took a cab back to his apartment, and Mad placed a brand-new dog bed on the floor at the foot of Cort's bed.

"Chevy," as Cort started calling him, could get around okay on his three uninjured legs and had the sweetest disposition ever, his big brown eyes sad but grateful as he checked out his new room. Mad made sure to praise him enthusiastically when he did his "business" in Cort's small outdoor courtyard, after which Cort carried him back upstairs to his waiting bed, where poor Chevy promptly fell asleep.

Mad knelt by his side, stroking his clean, wiry, gray, short-cropped fur as huge tears pricked her eyes. The sun was waning, casting shadows in Cort's bedroom. It was just about time to go—time to go back to her quiet apartment, do some laundry, and get ready for work in the morning. Time for real life to start again. The most magical weekend of her life was almost over.

Turning to look at Cort, she saw that his face mirrored the misery she felt.

"Don't go," he whispered, his eyes beseeching hers, his voice gravelly with emotion.

She launched herself into his arms, resting her cheek on his shoulder as his strong arms came around her, pulling her into his lap and against his body.

"I don't want to," she sobbed, tears wetting his T-shirt.

"Then don't," he said, gently stroking her back. "Stay here tonight with me and Chevy. I'll make us dinner and draw you a bath. I won't even touch you if you're tired. You can just go to sleep. And I'll take you home in the morning to get ready for work. Stay, baby. Don't go."

She sniffled, leaning away from his shoulder to look up at him. "There's no such thing as me not wanting you to touch me. I want you all the time."

His lips crashed down on hers, his tongue slipping between her lips to tangle with hers, and the bulge in his jeans became hard and long under her bottom. She straddled his lap, placing her feet flat on the floor behind his back and arching her breasts into his chest. His hands slipped into her jeans, under her panties, to squeeze her bare ass as he groaned "Stay" into her mouth.

"I can't," she said, nipping at his lips gently as she pulled away. "I have to go home."

"Why?"

She sighed. "Because I want the fairy tale. And I can't have it if I'm deceiving my sister."

He growled with frustration but hugged her close. "When will I see you again?"

"After I've talked to Jax."

His lips were close to her ear. "I'll miss you until then."

A wave of pure misery washed over her as she clung to him. What if Thursday at dinner wasn't the right time to talk to Jax? Could she go a whole week without seeing Cort or talking to him? She didn't want the magic to fade. She didn't want to go back to her cold life when she'd already discovered how warm life could be with Cort by her side.

"Maybe we could . . . text?" she asked meekly.

He leaned back, raising an eyebrow. "Text?" He kissed her, lingering over her lips with a needy sigh. "It's better than nothing, I guess."

And somehow, it was. It meant that tonight wasn't an ending. They would still be communicating, and she could tell he was as comforted by the notion as she was . . . or he had been, until his face clouded over. "And meanwhile, my bed will be empty, and I've got Gimpy here as a new roommate."

Mad looked at Chevy over her shoulder. "He's darling. You're going to love him."

"I love . . ."

Her neck whipped around so that she faced him, her lips slack, her eyes wide. "What were you about to say?"

She felt him holding his breath, his eyes boring into hers as he stared back at her in the dying light of early evening.

"Yeah," he finally said softly. "I'm sure I'll grow to love him."

Mad stared at him, wondering if he'd been about to tell her that he loved her, and part of her wished he had. Part of her wished she'd heard the words leave his mouth, even if they were impetuous and impulsive. But a larger part of her knew it would be premature. There was work to be done before they could love each other freely, and she needed to begin that work by leaving him now.

Bracing her hands on his shoulders, she stood up, and his palms trailed lightly down her legs before dropping back into his lap. She reached over his head for the packed duffel bag on his bed.

"See you soon?"

Cort nodded. "Soon, baby."

Before she could change her mind, she turned and left the room.

CORTAMBLER: Ur on ur way downstairs, and I can hear ur footsteps, and I swear, baby, it's taking every ounce of willpower not to run after u. I know u have to go. I know we need to do this right. But u blew my mind this weekend. I would spend every second of every day with u if u'd let me. I miss u. God, I miss u already. *6:42 p.m.*

MADELEINEROUSSEAU: In a cab and hating myself. I should have stayed. *6:47 p.m.*

CORTAMBLER: Come back, baby. *6:47 p.m.*

MADELEINEROUSSEAU: Just got off the phone w Jax. She's officially dating someone, and he's staying w her at Le Chateau for a while. *7:04 p.m.*

CORTAMBLER: Good for Jax. Did u tell her about us?

MADELEINEROUSSEAU: Not yet. Seeing her on Thur in person. Better.

MADELEINEROUSSEAU: Oh God . . . *7:08 p.m.*

CORTAMBLER: What?

MADELEINEROUSSEAU: My apartment is covered in flowers. Covered.

CORTAMBLER: It wasn't me. I was too distracted to come up with that.

MADELEINEROUSSEAU: Ugh. From Thatcher. He wants another chance.

CORTAMBLER: And?

MADELEINEROUSSEAU: Like u even have to ask? HELL NO!

CORTAMBLER: I fucking love it when u swear.

MADELEINEROUSSEAU: U make me smile like no one else.

CORTAMBLER: U do the same for me.

MADELEINEROUSSEAU: I need to throw them all away. I'll text u before bed, k?

CORTAMBLER: I'll b here.

MADELEINEROUSSEAU: Cort? *9:03 p.m.*

CORTAMBLER: I'm here, baby. Bedtime? *9:08 p.m.*

MADELEINEROUSSEAU: ☺ Thatcher called. Said I misunderstood everything. Said we need to talk and that he has a "very important" question to ask me when he gets home next wk.

CORTAMBLER: What did u say?

MADELEINEROUSSEAU: That he should go fuck himself. And then I hung up.

CORTAMBLER: MAD!

MADELEINEROUSSEAU: Ur a bad influence. LOL.

CORTAMBLER: And ur fucking perfect.

MADELEINEROUSSEAU: ☺ How's Chevreau?

CORTAMBLER: Snoring. Smelly. No substitute for u.

MADELEINEROUSSEAU: Thank u for adopting him. Meant a lot to me.

CORTAMBLER: WE adopted him. As far as I'm concerned, he's half yours, and he wants u to come the fuck home.

MADELEINEROUSSEAU: Tell him I'll see him soon.

CORTAMBLER: Oh, I almost forgot. JC asked me to play at his gallery opening on Fri.

MADELEINEROUSSEAU: What??

CORTAMBLER: Yeah. I FB'd him for tix, and he asked if I still played music. I said I did, and he told me his cellist crapped out. I said I'd fill in.

MADELEINEROUSSEAU: Did u tell him about us?

CORTAMBLER: No.

CORTAMBLER: But I thought about it.

MADELEINEROUSSEAU: Please don't. U have to let me do this my own way.

CORTAMBLER: I know. But it kinda sux, baby. I want you here.

MADELEINEROUSSEAU: Be patient. BTW . . . U don't play cello. How can you fill in?

CORTAMBLER: I offered to play harp instead. This chick I know digs it.

MADELEINEROUSSEAU: She does. She loves it.

MADELEINEROUSSEAU: So you'll be there on Friday?

CORTAMBLER: I'll be there. Talk to Jax before?

MADELEINEROUSSEAU: I'll try.

CORTAMBLER: This weekend was the best, Mad. The best ever. I can't stop thinking about u. I don't want to stop thinking about u. Not ever. Tell me u'll come on tour with me for a week.

MADELEINEROUSSEAU: I want to. So badly.

CORTAMBLER: Okay. I won't pressure you right now. But at least stay at my place after the gallery opening on Fri. If not for me, take pity on Chevy. He's barely wagged his tail once since u left.

MADELEINEROUSSEAU: We'll see.

MADELEINEROUSSEAU: And Cort . . . It was the best weekend ever for me too. I know I said we weren't allowed to fall . . . but I am falling. So hard.

CORTAMBLER: Chevy just opened his lazy eyes because I whooped so loud. Go ahead and fall, cuz I'll catch u, baby. I'll fucking catch u every time.

MADELEINEROUSSEAU: ♥ See u Fri?
CORTAMBLER: See u Fri.
CORTAMBLER: Sweet dreams, Miss Mad Rousseau. ♥

After four days of texting with Cort about all the little things in their lives, Mad had learned a surprising amount of everyday information about Cort, each morsel of which was precious to her.

He was composing a lot, and at least twice a day, he'd send her one- or two-minute recordings of music. A lot of it sounded familiar—like the piece he'd played for her on harp the night she'd stayed over at his place. Lying in bed, she'd play the sound bites over and over again, staring up the ceiling and wishing he was lying beside her.

He drank coffee almost constantly—he was always at some coffee shop or other, and sometimes he'd send her pictures of especially delicious-looking cappuccinos and lattes. And they made her smile because he'd add some sweet little comment like "Look at this lonely mug that wishes ur mug was beside it," or "The barista made me a heart, but I had to tell her mine was already taken."

On Wednesday night, he and Vic played a Mozart concert to a packed house at Christ Church of Philadelphia, and though Mad dared not enter the church (she didn't trust herself not to run to him on sight), she purposely walked two miles out of her way to stand outside, against the ancient brick building, under an open window, and listen. The strains of cello and harp combined to make the sweetest music Mad had ever heard, and all the while she fell harder, remembering the feel of the harp between her legs, his warm breath against her neck, his elbows gently bracketing her breasts as his fingers moved over the strings. After the last piece, she walked quickly back to Rittenhouse Square, swiping at her eyes and missing Cort more than she'd ever imagined was possible.

"Only forty-eight more hours until the gallery opening," she whispered to herself as her heels clacked on the pavement, putting distance between her and her love. "I can make it."

On Thursday morning, Mad woke up with the jitters, anticipating her conversation with Jax that evening at Jean-Christian's place. She'd thought it over and decided that because her brother lived in an apartment overlooking the water, she would ask Jax to take a walk with her after dinner. She'd start the conversation by asking about Jax's new boyfriend, and when the timing was right, she'd casually mention that she and Cort Ambler had reconnected and pay close attention to Jax's reaction before steering the conversation into a place where she could share that she was developing strong feelings for him.

Usually, the twins spoke once or twice a day at least, but over the past week while Mad had avoided calling Jax due to an uncomfortable sense of latent guilt, Jax hadn't picked up the slack. Mad knew instinctively what this meant: things were going so well with Jax's new boyfriend, she was throwing herself completely into her new relationship with him, which was awesome on many levels. First of all, it was a long time since Jax had been swept off her feet by a man, and no one deserved happiness more than her sister. Not to mention, the happier Jax was with someone new, the better chance their conversation would end with Jax giving Mad her blessing to date Cort.

On Thursday evening, as Mad walked to Jean-Christian's after work, her phone buzzed.

CORTAMBLER: How was work, baby? *7:12 p.m.*

Mad's heart filled with longing, and an instant smile exploded across her face as she felt a tightening on the string that tethered her heart to Cort's. Instead of trying to walk and text, she sat down on a park bench across from the Arch Street Meeting House and typed a message back.

MADELEINEROUSSEAU: Really good. Week one of training Miss Ford is almost done.
CORTAMBLER: Getting excited about the new job?
MADELEINEROUSSEAU: Yes! I have so many ideas!
CORTAMBLER: Can't wait to hear about them. #LuckyKidsOfPhilly. And let me know how/if I can help. Promise?
MADELEINEROUSSEAU: I promise. How about u? What have u been up to today?
CORTAMBLER: More writing. I have a new muse.
MADELEINEROUSSEAU: Anyone I know?
CORTAMBLER: Maybe. ♥
MADELEINEROUSSEAU: How's Chevy?
CORTAMBLER: Chevy's doing good. Sometimes he howls to the music I'm writing. I wonder if that's bad or good? LOL.
MADELEINEROUSSEAU: Let's assume it's good. He looks like a man of good taste. Like his owner.
CORTAMBLER: Buttering me up thru my dog?
MADELEINEROUSSEAU: It's been known to happen.
CORTAMBLER: LOL. Are u nervous about tonight? About talking to Jax?

Mad stared at the screen, biting her lower lip.

She was.

She was nervous that Jax would be hurt, that Jax wouldn't understand, that Jax might make her choose between an obligation to her family and an obligation to her heart, or that she would just make her feel like a rotten sister for letting something happen with someone Jax used to love.

But on the other hand, Jax loved Mad more than anyone else in the world. She wanted Mad to be happy, right? It wasn't like Jax and Cort had been engaged, or had dated for years, or had sex, for heaven's sake. Jax had a temper, yes. But Mad hoped that reason would prevail and that even if it was a little awkward for Jax at first, she would see how happy

Mad and Cort could be together. And hopefully that would make it worth it.

> MADELEINEROUSSEAU: A little. But I'm sure it'll be okay. I'll ask her to take a walk after dinner so we can talk. Speaking of which . . . I have to go or I'll be late, and JC gets pissed about us being late. #PrimaDonna
> CORTAMBLER: Write back and tell me how it goes.
> MADELEINEROUSSEAU: Okay. See u tomorrow?
> CORTAMBLER: Hell yes, baby. Living for it.

She had butterflies in her belly anticipating her talk with Jax, of course, but her smile never wavered as she started walking to her brother's apartment because of the tingles in her tummy as she kept replaying his text—*Living for it*—over and over again in her head. With her dreamy grin still in place, she knocked on Jean-Christian's door.

"*Bonsoir, petite soeur*," said Jean-Christian in a sour voice, opening the door for Mad and giving her a kiss on each cheek. "Glad *you're* here at least."

"At least?" she asked, following him into the kitchen, where containers of Chinese food and a fantastic Sauvignon Blanc waited. She hefted herself up on the counter, taking the glass her brother offered and waiting for him to tell her what was going on. When he didn't, she said, "Kate and Ten are still on their honeymoon . . ." Mad's heart clutched as she cut her eyes to Jean-Christian. "Wait. Where's Jax? Did something happen to her?"

"Happen? Huh. Well, something happened if you think her going away for the whole fucking weekend with the guy she told us about last week is a 'happening.'"

"Wait. Going away? With the gardener?"

Jean-Christian nodded. "Yep. Aaaand I only found out because I just texted her asking if she'd bring chopsticks, and she said sorry, she couldn't make dinner because she was on the train halfway to New York. Apparently, she meant to let me know, but she forgot and then—"

"New York?"

"She said something about talking to a contact at a TV studio about a new project. But does it fucking matter?" He stared at Mad, his face fixed in pissiness. "She's missing my gallery opening, Mad! She was supposed to tweet about it and splash it all over Instagram. Instead, she's missing it to hang out in Manhattan with some *putain de merde jardinier*. What a supportive fucking sister, huh?"

"Ohhh," Mad murmured, nodding dumbly as a feeling of intense relief made her whole body slump. To hide her reaction, she took another sip of her brother's delicious wine.

I don't have to tell Jax yet. I don't have to tell Jax yet.

Thank you. Thank you. Thank you.

"Well?" asked Jean-Christian, obviously waiting for her to validate his feelings.

"Yeah, that sucks. But you know Jax. She never does anything halfway. And between the new guy and the new show, I'm sure she's not thinking straight."

"Exactly. She's thinking with her cunt." Her brother shook his head with disgust. "And you know what else she said? She said she's not introducing the fucking gardener to me and Ten yet because she said we're pigs when we're being protective, and she knows we'll do something to try to drive him away." He scowled. "As if I give enough of a shit to do something like that."

Except you do, thought Mad, thinking that Jax was right, and it was probably best if Jean-Christian and Étienne were the last to know about Cort too.

"I'm sorry about that," said Mad, trying very hard not to smile, "but *I'll* be there tomorrow, and if you want me to, I'll tweet about it and splash it all over Instagram."

"No offense, sis, but *you're* not a Hollywood producer."

"And no offense, but *mange de la merde*."

"Eat shit?" Her brother chortled. "*Zut alors! Petite Madeleine* pulling out the big guns."

Mad shook her head and laughed at her asshole brother, because she loved him just the way he was—hot-tempered, charming, and dirty-mouthed as hell. "Back to Jax. Just wondering . . . did she say how long she'd be gone?"

"All fucking weekend," he growled, his mood darkening again. "What have I been saying?" With a sour look, he took the Chinese containers off the counter beside Mad and plopped the boxes on a pile of plates. "Want dinner?"

She nodded as he walked away, calling, "I'll bring the wine."

Whipping her phone out of her back pocket, she typed a quick message to Cort.

MADELEINEROUSSEAU: Jax couldn't make it tonight. Away until Sun. I'll stay over 2morrow and talk to her next week. xoxoxo *7:40 p.m.*

Then she shoved her phone back in her pocket, picked up the wine bottle, and ignored the happy hop in her step as she followed her brother into the dining room.

The following evening, she walked into her brother's gallery an hour after its opening, her heart bursting to be around Cort again, her body parched for his touch, her eyes desperate for a glimpse of him.

As a nod to his less conservative style, Mad had chosen to wear something outside of her usual comfort zone. But while part of her liked the way she looked in superskinny jeans paired with a nude, off-the-shoulder asymmetric draped top with matching four-inch nude-and-gold Louboutin sandals, another part of her missed the cream suit with matching pumps and pearls she'd originally planned to wear. With a long chain-link necklace in fourteen-carat gold around her neck and several clinking bangles on her wrist, she felt conspicuous (and noisy!). And with her hair down around her shoulders in loose waves, she felt much younger than usual.

Nervous, she grabbed a flute of champagne from the waiter who greeted her at the entrance and looked around for her brother, her breath catching as the soft strains of harp music floated over the din of conversation from a hidden nook in the intimate gallery.

"Madeleine!" exclaimed Jean-Christian, appearing from nowhere and welcoming her with a kiss on each cheek. He took her hands and leaned away, checking out her new style with appreciation. "When the hell did you get so chic, *petite soeur*?"

"Maybe when my brother implied I was a slouch on social media," she said, winking at him. "This place is amazing!"

"You like?" he asked, putting his arm around her waist and leading her toward a cubist-style painting of a nude woman looking over her shoulder. "Jess English has a great eye. Fuck Alex English for getting there first."

Mad slapped her brother's arm gently. "You're, like, ten years older than she is! Pick on someone your own age."

"I have no intention of *picking* anyone. Keeping it casual is more my style, *n'est-ce pas*?" He chuckled softly, lifting his chin toward the painting. "What do you think of it?"

"I think she looks chilly."

"Ha!" Jean-Christian leaned closer. "It's an Alfred Rech. I'll get a hundred thousand for it tonight."

Mad clinked her glass against her brother's. "You deserve it. I know this has been your dream for ages, *mon grand frère*."

"Well, I'm glad at least one of my siblings is here to see it come true." Nodding to someone across the room, he turned back to Mad. "Grab some food. The caviar is ridiculous. I'll find you later?"

"Mmmm," she said, smiling at him. "Congratulations, Jean-Christian."

"*Merci, mon doudou.* Have fun."

Stepping to the left of the painting, she waved good-bye to her brother, then turned her head to look straight ahead, directly into the eyes of Cort Ambler.

He saw her before she saw him, and for a second, *just a split second,* the whole world paused as he waited for her to turn, to find him, to nail and level him with those bright-green eyes. When she did—even prepared as he was—his breath caught, his heart stuttered, his very soul swept unrestrained from his person, seeking only to be bound to hers.

And if there had been any ambiguity about his feelings, about the profundity of his regard for her, or his desperate longing for her steady and unending residence in his life, all doubts were assuaged in that single second that tethered them back together.

His feelings for her were forever.

Forever.

He was done.

Finished.

Finished with dating. Finished with looking at other women. Finished with a life that didn't include Mad Rousseau. Like a snake that had been in the process of shedding its skin to make way for the new, Cort's old life slipped from his being with a soft *whoosh,* and the only life left for him to live was one that he spent with Mad.

It wasn't just that he was fiercely attracted to her or that he'd secretly loved her since childhood. It was that the universe felt wrong unless she was standing on this spinning planet beside him, within reach, her eyes seeking his, the fluttering heartbeat in her throat never more than a touch away.

She plucked a flute of champagne from a passing waiter, keeping her eyes locked with Cort's. Drawing the glass to her lips, she sipped, watching him over the narrow rim, and Cort turned his thoughts to the texts they'd exchanged late last night.

Anticipating having her back in his bed tonight, he'd texted her boldly, in filthy detail, describing everything he planned to do to her body once she was naked with him again. And she'd responded with the kind of heat he'd come to expect from this dazzling woman. She'd put the phone on the pillow beside her head as he texted what he wanted her to do, how he wanted her to touch herself, ready herself, prepare her body for his impatient invasion tonight. After she'd said good-night, he'd touched himself as well, groaning with frustration, crying out with shallow pleasure, their conversation too hot and too intimate to bear the mile-long distance between her bed and his with any patience.

Now, from across a short space, he undressed her with his eyes, which telegraphed his hunger as his fingers plucked the final stanza of "Greensleeves," his body tightening with desire as a hundred milling art lovers surrounded them, oblivious to the electricity of the abstraction in their very midst.

Her wide eyes darkened as she slowly made her way from a portrait to a sculpture, from a sculpture to stand beneath a blown-glass mobile the same color as her eyes. Her tongue slid between her lips to wet them, and whether she realized it or not, as she tucked her one hand in the back pocket of her ridiculously sexy jeans, she thrust her breasts toward him. Her nipples beaded under her skin-colored top and the bra that covered the perfect mounds of warm flesh that he longed to touch.

A lust, raw and real, gripped him so tightly, he didn't realize that he'd ceased playing "Greensleeves" and had segued without preamble into "Mad's Song" until a new verse quickly materialized in his head:

Miss Mad, Miss Mad,
By you I'm had,
By you my heart is owned.
Miss Mad Rousseau,
First fast, then slow,
Tonight won't be postponed.

Ending the song, he rested his hands on the strings, staring up at her standing before him. The light applause of nearby guests tapered away as they turned back to their portraits and conversations, ignoring the tattooed musician and his beautiful girl.

Tipping the harp until it was upright, Cort stepped around it carefully until they were no more than a breath apart. He searched her eyes, drinking from them, drowning in them, happy to die if this was the way he'd go.

"I love you," he whispered, the words unbidden yet unflinching.

She gasped, her eyes glistening but tender as she closed the distance between them.

"Let's get out of here," he said.

He grabbed her hand, leading her behind a panel and through the dark hallway he'd used to bring in his harp when he arrived two hours ago. Slipping out the back door and into the alley behind the gallery, he pinned her body against a brick wall, grasped her beloved face between his hands, and kissed her.

Chapter 13

Pulling her down the alleyway, he hailed the first available cab that passed them and dragged her onto his lap, muttering, "Lombard and Eleventh," before blindly locking his lips with hers again. With her cradled on his lap, he finally felt the restlessness of the past few days without her slip away, and he buried his face in her hair, holding her close.

"I fucking missed you," he said.

Her fingers played with the hair on the back of his neck as her lips slid, hot and soft, along his throat, pressing kisses to his skin, her tongue darting out at his pulse to circle the frantic beat.

"I missed you too," she sighed, the sound making blood funnel to his cock.

"We have to figure this out, baby."

"We will," she said, her lips still dragging against his skin, making him so fucking hard, he didn't know how there was room in his lap for her to sit.

"I meant what I said in there," he said, his teeth grabbing the tender skin on the lobe of her ear and biting gently. "I love you, Mad."

She leaned away, scanning his face, her eyes drugged and dark but worried beneath a fog of lust. "You're going too fast. We *just* reconnected, Cort."

"Yeah." He shrugged. "But I've loved you since we were thirteen."

"Thirteen!" she blurted out, jerking back. "What are you *talking* about?"

He smiled at her shock, tenderly smoothing her hair behind her ears and cradling her cheeks. "Two thousand and two. Jane Story's birthday party."

She nodded, though he could tell she wasn't sure where he was going.

"There was a rivalry between my sisters and the Story girls. Remember?"

"Well," she said, offering him an adorable cringe, "Jean-Christian *did* date both Bree and Alice."

He dropped a kiss to the tip of her nose. "Right. And since he broke up with Alice to date Bree, Bree's little sister, Sloane, was excluded from Alice's little sister's birthday party . . . even though all the other girls on Blueberry Lane were invited."

"Now I remember," said Mad softly, a smile blossoming on her face as she nodded for him to continue.

"But J.C.'s little sister, Mad, didn't think that was fair. She walked over to our house and helped Sloane pick out a party dress. She let Sloane sign her name to the gift she was giving Jane because our parents were MIA, and there was no time to buy a last-minute present. And then Mad Rousseau put her arm around my little sister's shoulders and walked her over to the Storys' house, acting like she was invited all along."

"I remember," said Mad, shaking her head, "but I'm shocked you do."

"I followed you," he confessed. "I didn't trust you at first. To my eternal shame, I wasn't sure you meant well, so I hid behind the stable to be sure you weren't going to do something mean to my sister."

Her fingers locked at the back of his skull, and she cocked her head to the side. "It wasn't Sloane's fault that my brother had gotten between two old friends. It wasn't okay to blame her for something that was between Bree and Alice."

"It was the kindest thing I had ever seen. Kind. Gentle. Generous. Brave. That was the day I fell in love with you. That's when you became *my* Mad."

Because he couldn't stop himself after such an emotional declaration, he raised his lips to hers and kissed her softly, slipping his tongue into her mouth to find hers. She moaned softly, leaning into him, her fingers spreading and then forming fists in his hair as the kiss deepened. His hands slipped under the hem of her top, and he flattened them on her back, letting the warmth of her skin permeate his own and become a part of him physically, just as she'd become a part of his heart so long ago.

"*Eh-hem,*" muttered the driver, clearing his throat.

Mad drew away, her lips shiny in the dim light as she grinned at him. "This keeps happening to us."

Climbing from his lap, she opened the door and hopped out onto the sidewalk. Cort fished his wallet from his back pocket and paid the driver before following her. He grabbed the shiny black-painted wrought-iron railings at the bottom of his three-step stoop and looked up at her on the top step. Her black hair was glossy under his front door lights. Her body, in the jeans and clingy top, sexier than ever. She was a fucking goddess come to life, and after loving her for most of his, it was a relief that she finally knew.

"You're at my house again," he said, grinning up at her.

She smiled back. "I was invited."

"Move in with me," he whispered passionately.

She gasped before giggling. "You're crazy, Cort Ambler!"

He shrugged, chuckling with her at his boldness and because, fuck it . . . he was happy. She made him deliriously fucking happy.

"I left my harp at the gallery," he said.

"I doubt my brother will throw it out."

"I bet he's pissed I left early."

"Unlikely. He was in his glory, surrounded by art lovers, set to make a hundred thousand a piece."

"I'm in the wrong business."

"Like you need the money," Mad deadpanned, knowing full and well that his share of the Coopersmith trust rivaled whatever was in hers and her brother's.

He sassed her back. "And J.C. does?"

"Of course not." She took a breath, her forehead creasing as though she was putting a thought together in her mind. "It's nice to have a trust, you know? It's nice to be a librarian or a musician and not have to worry about how we pay the rent or buy our groceries. But I've never lived like my siblings. The money I inherited makes my life comfortable, but sometimes I feel like I could figure out a way to live without it too."

He nodded, using his arms to swing his body up the two steps that led to the landing, his feet falling directly in front of hers. "We're on the same page, baby."

"I know," she said, closing the distance between them, her sweet face peering up into his, a feeling of fellowship enveloping them. "And isn't that weird?"

He searched her eyes, loving this conversation and knowing exactly what she meant but wanting her to articulate her thoughts anyway. "How so?"

"The rest of the—I mean, most of the other kids we grew up with—they're all trying to make more, aren't they? The Englishes and their finance company. Étienne and J.C. selling our shipping shares to the Englishes for a profit. Jax producing her movie. Bree on Wall Street and Sloane sell-ing antiques."

"The Winslows?" asked Cort.

Mad grinned. "They had about ten times more than the rest of us. They don't need to make any more."

"True." His eyes narrowed in thought. "Priscilla Story?"

Mad burst out laughing, nodding in agreement at their flighty, sweethearted, Bohemian neighbor. "Okay. Maybe not Pris. But the rest?"

"Maybe we're all just trying to find our way," said Cort, reveling in this moment beside her when they were talking about life philosophy veiled in reminiscence and thinking that he loved the way she thought, the way she lived her life, the way she . . . looked.

"Did I mention how fucking hot you look tonight?"

She shook her head. "Nope."

He placed his finger in the small alcove at the base of her throat and let it trail slowly down to the valley between her breasts. "If I tell you now, it'll sound like a line."

"Tell me anyway," she whispered, her voice husky and low.

He reached over her shoulder, popped the keypad cover, and entered the security code for his front door. "How about I show you instead?"

The door unlocked with a soft click, and his arm brushed her waist as he reached for the doorknob and twisted. Back-ing her into the dark living room, he let the door close behind him with a quiet thud, leaving them alone in near-darkness.

"I need you, Mad," he rasped, reaching for her hips.

"Your bed," she murmured.

"Chevy's there. I get you first."

"Then here," she said, winding her arms around his neck. "I need you too."

In the blinding blackness of the unwindowed room, he jerked her against his body, his lips descending upon hers with precision, his fingers moving to the waistband of her pants to hook his fingers inside. With a yank, her ass and cunt were bare, and he slipped his hands under her blouse to unhook her bra as she toed off her spiky heels and used her feet to push her pants down to her ankles. Her bracelets clinked together as he raised her arms over her head to dispatch her top, the only noise in the darkness other than her frustrated moan to be free of her pants. Cort leaned down to pull them from her ankles and smelled the musky sweetness of her ready sex, which made him swell and throb in his jeans, painfully hard for her. Kneeling on the floor, he reached for her hips and pulled her body closer, burying his face—his nose and lips—between the tightly trimmed strip of hair between her thighs.

Her fingers tangled in his hair as he spread her lips and licked her slick, soaked slit, inhaling her deeply as his fingers trailed lower, two of them sliding inside of her honeyed warmth, and listening with satisfaction when she moaned his name.

"Cort," she panted, "I don't want to come without you."

"It's okay, baby," he groaned against her pulsing clit. "I'll make you come again."

Her legs wobbled, and he tightened his one-handed grip around her, sucking her tight nub of flesh between his lips and finger fucking her until she screamed, coming on his face with pulsing waves.

He doubted she realized that he'd gathered her into his arms until he laid her out on the couch behind them, and though part of him wished he'd been able to see her face when she climaxed, the darkness made every touch more potent, made him aware of every sigh, every breath, every almost-silent whimper for mercy.

Standing beside her, he stripped quickly, then lowered himself over her, covering her naked body with his and positioning the throbbing tip of his sex at her still-quivering entrance.

"We were meant for this, Mad. To find each other again. To be together. We were meant to be. Tell me you know that."

"I . . ." she moaned, arching her back, trying to take him inside. "Please . . ."

"Tell me you know."

"I know," she whispered. "I've always known."

Her words were all the permission he needed to drive purposefully into her body, sliding effortlessly into her liquid heat until he was balls deep inside of her, one with the woman he loved.

She cried out at his sudden possession, and he felt the walls of her sex tremble and stretch to accommodate his girth and length. He remained as still as possible, letting her accustom herself to his size, her nails curling into his ass—his cue that she was ready for him to move once again.

Cradling her skull, he slid back almost completely, then thrust forward again, his tongue plunging into her mouth when she opened it to sigh. She whimpered with need, her tongue tangling with his, her lips sucking on his as her fingernails broke the skin on his back.

Staying lodged deeply within her body, he moved his hips in short, quick thrusts as she arched her back, her beaded nipples razing his chest as he felt the inviolable fucking perfection of her cunt squeezing his cock while she cried out his name in the throes of orgasm number two.

And only then did he give over to the building throb of his own release, pumping into her over and over again until he exploded into a million pieces, bathing her womb with his seed and wishing that tonight could last forever.

Mad wasn't sure how she got upstairs, but when she woke up, she was in Cort's bed, her back against his chest and a beam of bright moonlight shining down on them through the open French doors that led to a small terrace. A light June breeze cooled her exposed breast, tightening the nipple and making her sigh. She snuggled back against Cort, and his arm tightened reflexively as he snored softly into her hair.

He snored.

That made her smile.

Cort snored.

. . . and drank coffee and wrote music. He played the harp and adopted stray dogs and rescued vomiting girls from disgrace. His best friend was a cello-playing lesbian, and he loved his little sister so much that a single act of kindness from a decade before became the basis for everlasting love.

She pulled his hand from under her breast, gently examining it, marveling at the tattoos layered over his fingers and thinking that he was just as much of a contradiction as she was. He looked so edgy and tough but played Mozart like a virtuoso. He'd saved Jax from humiliation in high school, just as he'd saved Mad from humiliation the night they'd found each other again. And yet he'd always seemed like he didn't give much of a shit about the other kids on Blueberry Lane.

She pressed her lips to his fingers, loving the way he saw her more clearly than anyone else ever had. He saw the woman under the tailored suits and strings of pearls. He praised her dirty mouth but fell in love with her for her kindness. It was perfect. *Almost perfect.*

They had happened quickly, Cort and Mad, and when he told her he loved her or moved within her, hot and deep, she felt the rightness of being with him. More and more, losing him wasn't an option she'd be able to bear, yet she didn't have permission to be with him . . . and the same kindness that he first fell in love with wouldn't allow her to continue their affair much longer without talking to Jax.

A sharp wave of melancholy overwhelmed her, and her eyes filled with tears.

Tonight was supposed to be a reprieve, she thought sadly, placing his hand back on her chest. But suddenly it didn't feel like a reprieve, because the only thing she had been temporarily pardoned from was telling the truth.

Earlier tonight, Cort had praised her for being kind, gentle, generous, and brave, but now, lying naked in bed beside her sister's high school boyfriend, her body still aching from his use, she didn't feel like any of those things. While Jax slept miles and miles away in New York, Mad lay beside Cort, feeling unkind, duplicitous, selfish, and cowardly.

A tear rolled from the corner of her eye, over the bridge of her nose, and plopped on Cort's arm, the salty water mixing into the tattooed swirls of color and vanishing into his ink as if she'd never felt regret at all but only indulged her own hedonistic lust.

"Hey," he whispered near her ear. "I felt that."

"You're asleep," she said softly, sniffling pathetically.

"Why are you crying?"

"Because we're good for each other," she said, "but my happiness comes at the cost of betraying my sister."

His arm around her tightened, and the hand she'd placed on her chest smoothed to rest on the soft, warm flesh of her breast.

"You need to talk to her, baby."

"I don't understand."

"What?"

Mad rolled toward him, onto her back, and he released her breast. "I get it that you hooked up one night, and she jumped to assumptions about your status, so you started dating her so that you wouldn't hurt her. I get it. I approve. I even admire you for it because I love her, and I wouldn't have wanted you to hurt her. But . . . what happened between you two, Cort? Why did she lie about you that night at the pool?"

Cort braced himself on his elbow, staring down at her, his voice sober. "We were already over. How we broke up publicly was up to her."

She flinched, narrowing her eyes at him. "Wait. You mean . . . it was staged?"

This just didn't feel right. Jax had always been dramatic, yes. For heaven's sake, she was a Hollywood producer—she had a streak of drama a mile long—but a staged breakup? Why?

"No," he said, then bit his bottom lip, taking a deep breath. "Sort of. It had ended the weekend before."

"At prom."

He nodded, but his eyes slid away from her in the moonlight. "We were over after prom, but appearances were important to Jax. She was the social director of Blueberry Lane. She didn't want it to look like . . ."

"Like what?"

He sighed. "Like she'd been dumped."

Mad pulled the sheet over her breasts, still staring up at him, a shot of defensiveness for Jax making her feel cool. "Was she? Dumped?"

"Not exactly."

Huffing with frustration, Mad fixed him with an irritated look. "Can you please just tell me what happened?"

The back of Cort's fingers trailed over the skin of her neck. "No."

She reached up for his hand and pulled it away. "Why not?"

"Because I promised I'd never speak about it."

"You promised Jax?"

He nodded, locking his eyes with hers. "Yeah."

Mad exhaled the breath she'd been holding. She wouldn't ask him to break a promise, but it took all her willpower to respect his confidence. "So something happened at prom, and Jax didn't want to look like she was dumped, so . . ."

"I told her she could handle the breakup however she wanted."

"Why would you do that?" she asked. "Why would you let her handle it 'however she wanted?' Why would you let her ruin your reputation? Why . . . why would you be okay with that? What did *you do* that made *her choices* okay?"

His tongue slipped between his teeth, and she watched him bite down on it for a moment before dropping his eyes.

"I'm sorry," he said, his voice thick and gruff. "But it's her story to tell."

Taking a ragged breath that filled her lungs, Mad flipped over to her side, presenting him with her back and listening as he let out a long, tired breath.

"Can we not let this ruin our time together, Mad?"

Honestly, she didn't have an answer for him. As much as their love felt preordained in some ways, if something truly egregious had happened between Cort and her sister, it would further complicate matters between them. And worst of all, the fierce, terrible love she bore for him would have nowhere to go, nowhere to grow—a thought that made her imagine her heart was made of red glass and a hammer-smash was imminent.

"How bad was it?" she whispered, drawing her knees up and curling around them. "The thing that happened between you and Jax?"

"At the time? Unforgivable."

Unforgivable.

Such a damning word.

Her breath caught on a sound of pain that escaped from her lips before she could keep it tucked safely behind the lump in her throat.

"And now?"

"Mad," he said, putting his arms around her and trying to pull her rigid body against the warmth of his, "I can't betray her. I promised. And yes, it was a long time ago, but I can't just take a shit on my word no matter how many years have passed. If I do that, I'm not the kind of man you deserve, baby. I promise you, I will never keep anything from you from this day forward . . . but what happened between me and Jax belongs to Jax. And it's her story to tell." He nuzzled her neck, but Mad used all her energy reserves to remain stiff in his arms, and he gave up, letting his arms slip away from her, leaving her alone. "I can say this, though . . . Think about Jax. Think about you. Think about me. Think about who we were. Think about how I felt, because I wasn't honest about my feelings then, but I've been honest with you now about how I felt then—about which sister I actually loved."

"You're speaking in riddles," she sobbed, frustrated and angry. "I *knew* this was a mistake." She swung her legs over the edge of the bed and sat up. "I—I knew this was wrong. I knew it last weekend and all this week, and tonight I knew it. I just . . ."

"You want it as much as I do."

"Yes!" she cried, springing up and turning to face him, her body blocking the light and thrusting him into darkness. "I do. But *not* at the expense of my sister!"

He sat up, crossing his arms over his chest. "I see."

She licked her lips, surprised to find them salty from tears.

"This was a mistake," she whispered again.

"Stop saying that. Don't fucking say that."

"Then tell me what happened!" she yelled, making Chevy whine in his bed.

"You're scaring the dog," Cort said quietly. Then he continued firmly, "No. I can't."

"You *won't*," she said, walking around the bed to his dresser and pulling open the drawer where he kept his T-shirts. She took one out and yanked it over her head.

"Fine, I won't."

"A promise you made to Jax over ten years ago is more important than telling me the truth about something *unforgivable*? How do I know I should even *be* with you?"

"After your experiences with Thatcher-fucking-Worthington, I'd think you'd want to be with someone who had a fucking sense of honor!" Cort's lips thinned. "And if you question whether or not we belong together after what we've shared—"

"Just sex!" she shot back, hating herself the second the words left her mouth, because the moments she'd spent with Cort were the most precious of her life. But she was on a rampage and couldn't seem to stop herself. "And I value honesty, not secrets!"

"Don't kid yourself. It was a *lot* more than sex, baby," he growled, a mean edge creeping into his voice. "As for secrets and lies, *I'm* not the one who deserves your anger. Why don't you go talk to your precious sister?"

Mad's eyes widened to uncomfortable burning saucers in her head. "Did you just call my sister a liar?"

"In your heart," he spat, thumping his palm over his chest, "you *know* she lied that night!"

"No, Cort," she said primly, "I don't. I don't know that because you won't tell me the truth."

They stared at each other across the beam of moonlight that separated them after the full-blown standoff that neither had ever seen coming and neither knew how to handle.

"Fine. Here's some truth for you, princess," he said, swinging his body out of the bed and standing naked before her. "Your sister lied about me . . . and you know it. I love you . . . and you know it. We didn't just 'have sex' . . . and you know it. And last but not least? Here's some more goddamned truth: I'd love to see a fucking *glimpse* of the bravery you showed that day you came to get Sloane for Jane Story's birthday party. Because, for the life of me, I cannot understand why you're so chickenshit to stand up to your sister and tell her about us."

Mad's heart clenched as she turned and walked to the bedroom door.

"It wasn't bravery that day," she whispered over her shoulder. "It was easy because it was right."

"This is easy too," he said firmly. "So do what's right, and talk to your sister so we can get on with our lives together."

"Or what?" she asked, lifting her chin with a bravado she didn't feel.

Cort clenched his jaw, letting out a frustrated puff of breath from his nose.

"Or this is done," he said, his eyes holding hers until she nodded sadly and slipped from his bedroom, holding her tears back until she quickly dressed and closed his front door behind her.

Chapter 14

It was three o'clock in the morning when Mad left, and after cursing so loudly he made Chevy whimper again, Cort pulled on jeans and stalked upstairs to the sound-proof studio, where he plugged in his guitar to an amp and played angry riffs in minor keys over and over again until he was sweating. And he didn't feel a bit better when he was done.

Heading back downstairs a little after five, he picked up his phone to text Mad and make sure she got home safely.

CORTAMBLER: Be as mad as you fucking want, but let me know you got home okay.

He threw his phone back down on the bedside table and stripped down, then turned on the shower and stepped inside. Ruthlessly, he scrubbed his body, but he was still agitated when he got out of the shower and toweled off.

Because it was still dark outside and he was exhausted, he crawled into bed, hating his weakness when he buried his nose in the pillow they'd shared, in search of her scent. And upon finding it, his stupid cock stirred to life, wanting more from someone who'd left hours ago. Rolling onto his back, he stared up at the ceiling, his body rigid with anger.

Who the fuck did she think she was, anyway? Calling him a liar? Implying that he was somehow betraying her by keeping a promise to her sister? Fuck, but this was way more complicated than he'd ever imagined. Never having dated sisters, he didn't realize the landmine he'd been walking into the day Mad Rousseau suddenly reappeared in his life.

Grabbing his phone from the bedside table, he checked it for messages, hating it that she hadn't written back. Pulling up his sister Sloane's number, he sent her a quick text.

CORTAMBLER: I need to talk. When?

Then he closed his eyes, rolled to his side, and tried to get another hour or two of sleep.

When he woke up a few hours later, there was still no message from Mad, but Sloane had texted that he was welcome to come by the shop before ten, providing that he brought two mochaccinos with him.

Pulling on a fresh pair of jeans and a "BeethOVEN's HOT Revival" T-shirt, he stopped by Starbucks and still made it to Sloane's place with an hour to spare. The bell over the door jingled cheerfully as he stepped into the Painted Pony, a tony antique shop specializing in estate treasures that his sister had opened several years ago.

Sloane's platinum-blonde head popped up from behind the cash register, and she lowered her black-rimmed glasses, arching one kohl-black eyebrow. "Coffee?"

He held up the two cups.

"Proceed," she said.

Cort shook his head. "Psycho."

"Weirdo."

He maneuvered around several tables of silverware and crystal, almost tripping over a needlepoint footrest and side-stepping a grandfather clock on his way to her.

"Cortie," she said, locking her eyes with his over the rim of her coffee cup and not bothering to test the heat of her beverage before taking a gulp that must have scalded her throat. Damn, but Sloane was made of tough stuff.

"Sloanie," he answered, putting his untouched cup on the glass counter beside the cash register and placing his palms flat on either side of it.

"So?" she asked.

He sighed, shaking his head, uncertain of where to begin. "A woman."

"Hmm." Sloane cocked her head to the side, her ice-blue eyes all-seeing. "Who?"

"Mad Rousseau."

She pushed her glasses back up to the bridge of her nose and winced. "That sucks."

The thing about being the two youngest, mostly abandoned Ambler kids, was that Cort and Sloane had only had each other to turn to for most of their adolescence, and Sloane had even lived at Cort's house for long periods of time while she was in high school and college. Only two years apart, it didn't matter that they were completely different people with totally different interests who were incredibly undemonstrative with one another—they would die for each other, and they both knew it.

Sloane had known, all those years ago, that Cort was only dating Jax so that he didn't hurt her feelings. She watched as her brother escorted Jax to all the senior festivities, keeping his arm around her but never sneaking over to her place in the dead of night because he couldn't bear to be away from her. She also watched the way he looked at his girlfriend's twin sister. The remarkable thing, Sloane had always said, was that Mad and Jax had never seemed to notice, because Sloane thought it was so obvious.

She knew him well.

She shook her head back and forth gravely. "It can't work."

"It has to."

Sloane didn't smile much. Her face was always set in the offensive, which, more often than not, resembled a resting-ultrabitch face. But now her eyes softened, and Cort hated to see it, because it meant that his sister, his most trusted confidante, was telling him to give up.

"It's beyond girl code. It's *sister* code. And that shit is Kevlar."

Cort took a sip of his coffee, grimacing at the heat as it gave him a fuzzy tongue. He plunked it down on the counter and narrowed his eyes, feeling angry.

"So you're saying that if the world gave you a second chance with Co—"

Sloane's eyes shot to his, icy and unforgiving, and he stopped speaking midname, feeling instantly chagrined by the sudden pain in her eyes. "Sorry."

"No," she whispered, rolling her blood-red lips together once before tightening them. "It *still* wouldn't matter."

"Sloane—"

"Shut up and listen," she said, fluffing the huge ruffles on the sleeves of a snow-white gauzy blouse. "Bree shouldn't have dated J.C. Rousseau after he broke up with Alice. But she did because she's Bree, and she does whatever the fuck she wants. But mark my words: Even if I fell head over heels for J.C., I could *never* date him. Never. And if I fucked him, I'd be dead to Bree."

"I get it."

"Do you?"

"Yes. But I love her."

"That's a pity."

"You're a bitch."

She nodded slowly. "Established fact."

"I *love* her," he said again.

"Irrelevant. Go to Europe. Get over it."

"And if I can't?"

"Life is long."

"And not worth living without her."

"Bold words."

"Truth."

Sloane bowed her head, the bright off-white of her hair catching an iridescent light overhead. "Then *she* has to do it."

"*Do it?*"

"Get permission."

"From Jax?"

Sloane looked up and nodded solemnly. "And God only knows what that would cost if this was me and Bree."

They're not like you and Bree, he almost blurted out, wanting to remind her that some sisters loved each other deeply—would even sacrifice their own happiness for their sibling. His mind played a million slides of Jax and Mad throughout their shared childhood, ending with Mad by the pool, fists curled, love for her sister blazing in her eyes. If Jax loved Mad as much as Mad loved Jax, wouldn't she want her sister to be happy? Wouldn't she give her blessing to Mad and Cort if it meant Mad's happiness?

Sloane leaned forward, a crystal pendant around her neck grazing the shiny glass counter between them. "Let her go."

"No."

"Your funeral."

She straightened, chugged the rest of her coffee, then crushed the cup in her hand, fire-engine-red fingernails almost garish against her white skin.

He could tell from her eyes: Sloane was finished discussing this.

"You going to the Winslows on Friday night?" he asked.

"Is Mad?" she countered.

"Probably."

Sloane took a measured breath, then slowly released it. "I received an invitation from a Skye Something-or-Other."

"So?"

Sloane shrugged like she didn't give a shit. "I owe a visit to Lola anyway. You?"

He shook his head. "No. There's nothing for me there."

"Wise," said Sloane, taking a step away from the counter but holding her brother's eyes. "Words are cheap, Cortie, but I know you wanted this. I'm sorry."

And after that very brief, rare display of compassion, she turned on her five-inch black patent leather Mary Janes and walked behind a curtain and into the back of the store.

Sloane had never learned the fine art of bullshit, and it was what he loved most about her. Cort sighed as he watched her go, wishing that her insight had been different, though he'd already known what she'd say.

Let her go.

As he turned and walked away from the counter, the finality of Sloane's words started to sink in. A cold chill rushed through his body, strangely electric but uncomfortable, like iced lightning in his blood, as a terrible thought occurred to him.

Their fight this morning wasn't the end, was it? It was just a fight. When she left, she wasn't *leaving*; she was just angry, right? What they had wasn't actually over. It couldn't be.

He walked out of the store in a daze, pausing on the sidewalk as he remembered the final words he said to Mad:

Or this is done.

"I didn't mean it," he whispered under his breath, crossing the street to a park bench in Rittenhouse Square and staring at Mad's building across the park. He was on the street where she lived, but the ice in his veins made him feel a kind of fear he'd never known before. His fingers were cold as he fished his phone out of his back pocket, and his heart plummeted when he saw he had no waiting messages.

He typed quickly.

CORTAMBLER: I didn't mean it. We're not done, Mad. We'll never be done.

Staring at her building, his knee bounced to a frantic rhythm as he prayed for her to write back.

"Please, baby," he murmured.

He checked the clock on his phone. Nine fifty-five. Mad didn't sleep in late. She went to sleep early and woke up early. He'd bet anything she was awake.

CORTAMBLER: I'm downstairs in the square. Come and talk to me, baby. I'll wait here for you. I love you.

But after sitting on that bench for a full two hours, staring desperately at her building, there was still no answer, and she never showed.

With Sloane's heartbreaking advice ringing in his ears, he stood up, turned around, and walked home.

By Thursday, Cort's texts had piled up, but Mad was determined not to respond to him. His parting words—*Or this is done*—had gouged her heart like a lead drill over the past five days, hollowing out a deep hole that made her ache with sadness. At times, she'd wished she'd never gone to *Voulez-Vous* that fateful night, only to hate herself for such a wish, since the moments she'd spent with Cort had been among the happiest of her life. But to know the ecstasy that could be found in his arms only made her present state unbearable.

Part of her felt bad that she'd pressured him to betray Jax's trust. No matter how long ago he'd made her a promise, Mad had no right to ask him to break it. After a day or two, she had cleanly identified jealousy as the motivator for the tantrum she'd pitched in his bedroom. While she respected him for keeping Jax's confidence, she hated it that he and Jax had a secret of any kind.

. . . which is why you're not supposed to date your sister's ex-boyfriend, snarked her conscience dryly. *Because of course they shared secrets, dumb-dumb. And spit too.*

Jealousy had been an emotion that Mad *thought* she'd felt about Thatcher's many liaisons, but in truth, she hadn't. She'd felt disappointment and hurt feelings, but never the kind of white-hot jealousy that had made her jump from Cort's bed and stomp out of his room. And frankly, she didn't like it much.

Something else she didn't like? That he'd used the word "unforgivable" about whatever had happened between him and Jax. At first, she'd reacted to that word as though he'd earned it as a result of something terrible—like battery or assault—but the more she thought about it, the more she knew that assumption couldn't be true, which just served to confuse her more.

She *knew* Cort. She *knew* him. He had dated Jax to preserve her feelings, the same way he'd rescued Mad from *Voulez-Vous* to preserve hers. He wouldn't have purposely hurt her . . . which meant that in order to allow Jax to slander him so viciously, he must have hurt her inadvertently but badly. The question was . . . how badly? Badly enough that Jax would never give her blessing to Mad and Cort? With the wisdom of an adult, Mad knew that whatever had been "unforgivable" to her dramatic sister at seventeen was likely forgivable through the lens of a mature adult. But still, she didn't like it. And even more, she didn't know how to handle it with Jax.

Her curiosity gnawed at her like a feral rat, making her antsy and angry and giving way to a narrow-eyed indignation at his use of the word "chickenshit" to describe her behavior in not talking to Jax. But what exactly did he have in mind? Was she supposed to knock on her sister's door and blurt out, "Remember your high school boyfriend who you loved? Who made you cry? Who did something unforgivable? Yeah, him. I'm in love with him. Okay with you?" Sure. That'd be just ducky.

Not to mention that Jax's life looked like it was spiraling downward again. Their mother refused to let Jax live at Le Chateau any longer, which meant Jax was moving in with Mad even though she hated the idea of moving into the city. And Jax's new boyfriend, about whom Jax was head over heels, had suddenly disappeared. He said he needed to go to New Orleans to deal with some family business, but he'd been gone for four days, and Jax was starting to worry that he wasn't planning to return at all.

By Thursday evening's dinner at Mad's place—the first dinner with all Mad's siblings and Kate, her new sister-in-law, together again after Étienne and Kate's honeymoon—Mad was a mess of jealousy, confusion, and heartsickness, all of which Jax had overlooked this week because she was dealing with a heartbreak of her own.

Jean-Christian arrived, complaining that "Bree's weirdo brother" had left his "fucking harp" at the gallery last Friday and asking Mad why she left without saying good-bye. Before he had a chance to connect the two things, she made a quick excuse about getting a headache that night, then shoved a glass of wine into his hands, relieved when the doorbell rang immediately to announce Étienne and Kate's arrival. On their heels was Jax, who arrived with about six suitcases, which Donal dumped in Mad's vestibule with an annoyed grimace.

"Where's Gard?" asked Mad hopefully, looking over her sister's shoulder. "Wasn't he coming with you?"

"*Still* in New Orleans," she said, unable to keep the worry out of her voice.

Mad led her twin to the couch, grateful when Kate handed Jax a full glass of wine.

"I thought he was supposed to be home by today," said Mad gently, knowing how hard her sister had fallen for the Englishes' new gardener.

"Me too," said Jax quietly, her lips tilting down in a frown. She took a gulp of her wine and looked up at Mad. "What about Thatcher? Another conference?"

Mad's face froze for a moment before recovering. "That's right. Back on Sunday."

She knew this was the truth because Thatcher had been calling and texting her at least once a day, insisting they needed to talk on Sunday when he returned to Philadelphia.

"Mad?" prompted Jax. "Is everythin—"

"I have to check on dinner," she said, standing up quickly and forcing a smile.

It was unbearable to talk about Thatcher like he was still her boyfriend when she was estranged from the man she ached for. She wanted Cort. In her dreams—her fantasies— she told Jax about Cort, and her sister hugged her with a huge smile, telling her to chase down her own happiness. And Mad would race to Cort, throw herself into his arms, and never let go.

But "unforgivable"?

That made it difficult to dream. Difficult to hope.

She stirred the coq au vin, her ears perking up as she heard Kate ask who was going to the Winslows' movie- themed summer party tomorrow night. Mad flinched. She'd forgotten about the party, which was Skye Winslow's way of having a Blueberry Lane "block party reunion."

Surely Cort wouldn't be there, would he? Her heart raced with joy at the thought of seeing him, but her mind forced her racing emotions to see reason: she and Cort were deadlocked. She couldn't talk to Jax, and if she wouldn't, he said they were over. What good would it do to see him?

She stepped away from the kitchen, carrying a plate of cheese and grapes back into the living room.

"What about the Amblers?" asked Mad, shocked that the words had left her mouth, though thankfully, they were appropriate to the conversation.

Jax looked up and nodded. "Bree, yes. Sloane, yes."

"What's Sloane up to these days?" asked J.C.

"She owns an antique store," said Mad without thinking.

Jax's eyes widened in surprise. "You keep in touch with her?"

"N-not really," said Mad, standing up quickly and snatching Jean-Christian's glass from his hand. "Someone needs a refill."

Turning her back to her siblings and Kate, she crossed over to the wet bar and refreshed her brother's glass.

"What about Cort, Jax? He coming?" she heard Étienne ask Jax, and her breath caught.

Jax's tone behind her was offhanded. "As far as I know."

"New boyfriend and old boyfriend all in one place, huh?" said Étienne.

Mad turned around, nailing Étienne with furious eyes. "Shut up, Ten."

Mistaking her jealous outburst for loyalty, Jax winked at Mad with a little grin.

"Oh, my God!" exclaimed Kate, turning to Jax. "That's right! I almost forgot you two used to date. You hooked up during spring break, right?"

"Ancient history," blurted out Mad, heat creeping into her cheeks at the words "hooked up."

"Dark-ages ancient," said Jax softly, giving Mad a curious look as she scanned her sister's face.

"And Dash?" asked J.C.

Mad could just about have kissed him for his timely interruption.

Jax slowly turned away from her twin, facing her oldest brother as she shrugged. "No idea. He never got back to Skye."

"That's because he's in Calcutta," said Mad matter-of-factly.

Shit. Shit. Shit. Shut up, Mad! You're saying too much!

Every set of eyes in the room—Jax's, Kate's, Étienne's, and Jean-Christian's—turned to look at Mad in unison in various stages of surprise, baffled that she would know something so random about Dash Ambler.

"Umm . . . I think I heard that he's in, uh, India . . . or something." She fixed a nonchalant expression on her face and smiled awkwardly before backing out of the room. "I need to check on dinner."

Back in the safety of her kitchen, she braced her hands on the counter where she and Cort had had their first kiss and tried to catch her breath. Was it true? Was Cort going to be at the Winslows' tomorrow night? Jax's noncommittal "As far as I know" didn't mean very much, but her heart soared at the thought of seeing him one last time.

He'd said if she couldn't talk to Jax about them, they were over. And she couldn't talk to Jax because the timing was shit, and she refused to hurt her sister when she was already hurting.

But if he was there, at least she could say good-bye.

And maybe . . . someday . . . when the timing was better . . . she and Cort might find each other again.

Red and green martinis, thought Mad, checking out the colorful cocktails that greeted the guests who arrived at the Winslows' sailing-themed summer party. *Port and starboard. Clever.*

Picking up a green martini, she took a sip as she stepped onto the slate patio. Technically, her weeklong vacation started tonight. She may as well start it by getting drunk. That had worked out so well for her last time.

Out on the lawn, there was a full-size movie screen, and the Winslows had rented comfortable theater-style seats that were set up in five or six rows of four chairs each. A popcorn machine made the air smell like a cinema, and Mad checked out a cheerful concession stand Skye had set up at the back of the "theater." A movie night under the stars— what a charming idea.

She wished she could enjoy it.

But it had been an awful week, and she was mentally and emotionally drained. And frankly, if Jax hadn't coplanned the party with Skye, Mad would have stayed home in her apartment, eaten a pint of Häagen-Dazs, and cried herself to sleep.

She missed Cort.

She was still angry at Cort.

She was very much in love with Cort.

Which made the sight of Cort hurrying up the marble steps toward her both welcome and disastrous.

His unruly dirty-blond hair brushed his shoulders, and his blue-gray eyes were trained, like lasers, on hers. The sleeves of his white button-down dress shirt were rolled up to reveal the intricate tattoos that covered his forearms. Other guests at the party would have to guess if the tattoos rose higher than his elbows, but Mad knew the swirled designs by heart. She knew that they rose to his shoulders, some trailing down his back and others connected to more ink on his chest. Her fingers twitched with a sensory memory of his skin, of hours spent mapping the contours of his beautiful body.

Her lips parted to speak, but a lump in her throat trapped all the words she longed to say.

"Hi," he breathed, his eyes trailing tenderly over her face.

"You said we were done," she whispered, shocked to see him, her voice perilously close to a sob.

"I know. But I needed to see you." He paused to wet his lips. "This week was hell."

She nodded. "For me too."

"I'm sorry we fought. I'm sorry I tried to force you to do something you're not ready to do."

I am ready, she thought, the words streaking through her mind like phosphorescent white on a jet-black background. *But Jax is not.*

"How are you?" he asked, and the familiarity of his soft, gritty voice made her heart throb, made her eyes burn.

"Not good," she whispered. "I miss you. So much."

"You don't have to miss me," he said evenly. "I want to be with you, but the ball's in your court."

She gulped over the massive, growing lump in her throat. If Gard's absence was his way of dumping Jax, losing him would be a tremendous blow for her sister.

"The timing's not good," she said.

He nodded, the light in his eyes dulling. "The timing's never going to be good, Mad."

"Please be patient," she begged him.

He leaned closer to her, his breath kissing her ear. "Every second without you is a fucking eternity."

His desperate voice twisted her heart, but Jax would be here any minute, and with the uncanny insight of a twin, she would know way too much if she caught Mad talking to Cort. She had to get away from him. Now. The sooner the better.

Her heart cracked open as she whispered, "I have to go."

As she turned to leave, he grabbed her wrist, his fingers gentle but still somehow searing, and suddenly every nerve ending in her body was concentrated in her right forearm. His long fingers, tattooed at the knuckles, wrapped around her slim wrist with ease, and Mad had to bite her bottom lip to keep from whimpering. She'd missed his touch so desperately.

"Mad, *please*," he beseeched her, his voice low but firm. "Come with me tomorrow."

She turned to look up at him, her eyes caressing his face without her permission—memorizing the omnipresent dark-blond scruff on his jaw, the high, regal cut of his cheekbones, the long, dark lashes that shielded his stormy eyes. She didn't know when she would be this close to him again, if ever. She couldn't seem to turn her eyes away or loosen her wrist from his grasp. She stood, trapped and silent, wishing that things were different.

Reaching into his back pocket with his free hand, he pulled out a ticket jacket that read "British Airways." Scanning her eyes, he folded it and quickly shoved it into the purse hanging from her elbow.

"I leave tomorrow at nine."

"I can't," she whispered, her voice breaking as her eyes filled with more useless tears.

He moved closer to her, and she could feel the heat of his body through the thin fabric of her sundress as his hot breath kissed her neck. "Please come with me, baby. I miss you so much, it hurts."

"Skye!" exclaimed Jax's voice, entering the terrace several yards behind them. "You've got the perfect weather for tonight!"

Mad glanced over her shoulder at her sister, then back at Cort. "I have to go."

Cort dipped his lips to the shell of her ear and whispered, "I love you, Mad. It was *always* you. It will *always* be you."

Her eyes fluttered closed, burning with tears as she felt his fingers slip from her arm. When she opened her eyes, he was gone.

"Mad? Mad! Oh, my God! Look who's home! You have to meet Gard . . . and I have *so much* to tell you!"

Though her heart ached with so much pain, it should have been impossible to bear, Mad took a deep breath, fixed a bright smile on her face, and turned around to greet her sister.

Chapter 15

8:52 a.m.

She stared at the digital clock on her bedside table with no will to move, barely able to read the bright-red numbers because of the tears in her eyes. Closing them briefly, she imagined Cort sitting in first class, in seat 1A by the window, with seat 1B empty beside him. Was he still waiting for her? With the arrival of every new passenger that wasn't her, did his heart sink lower?

When she opened her eyes, the clock read 8:54 a.m., and she rolled onto her back, streams of tears leaking from her eyes and onto the pillow.

"This is hell," she muttered, wiping them away.

Last night, after Cort had left, Jax had joyfully introduced her to Gard, who, as it turned out, had bought Le Chateau for her sister. That's what he'd been doing in New Orleans: buying Jax her dream house with his inheritance. And though Mad's own heart was breaking, she loved Jax and found it easy to be happy for her sister. *Genuinely* happy, even in the face of her own sorrow.

She'd stayed with them to chat a little before begging off with a headache and slipping away before the movie started. It had occurred to her, as Jax was gushing about Gard's thoughtfulness, that she could interrupt her sister and pull her aside. She could explain to her about reconnecting with Cort, she could tell Jax how much she loved him, and then she could pack a bag and run to his house. In a fantasy world where Mad had zero sense of decorum, maybe she could do that: make a scene at a party and live impetuously for once.

But the sad reality that faced her now was that she was still the same Mad who'd known about Thatcher's cheating and tolerated it. She was still the same Mad who'd desired so much more but contented herself with complacency. She *was* a chickenshit who'd rather endure an unfulfilled life than rock the status quo.

It made her tired and ashamed to realize that she hadn't changed, hadn't grown, after all. It made her hate herself.

Glancing at the clock, she winced to see it read 8:58 a.m.

Two more minutes, and Cort would be gone.

And then what?

No sense in telling Jax what had happened with him.

By the time he returned, he might already be over her or have a new girlfriend.

She winced at the thought, whimpering like a hurt animal as she wrapped her arms around herself and held her breath, willing a wave of nausea to pass. The idea of Cort— *her* Cort—connecting intimately with some random European girl made her sick, made her want to die.

8:59 a.m.

Sixty more seconds until his plane left.

She grabbed her phone off the nightstand, frantically unlocking the screen and checking to see if he'd written her one last time.

There was no red notification badge waiting.

No final words of love.

No last farewell.

He'd left it all on the table last night, and what had she done in return? She'd told him to go.

9:00 a.m.

He was gone.

She buried her face in her pillow and cried herself back to sleep.

She woke up at noon feeling awful.

Her head was ringing . . . and something else was ringing too.

Sitting up in bed, she realized her phone was buzzing, and she picked it up and answered. "Hello?"

"Madeleine, it's Thatcher. I'm home."

The bitter realization that it wasn't Cort on the other side of the line made her lie back in bed, all her flexed, hopeful muscles relaxing.

"Uh-huh."

"Darling, I hope you've had a chance to cool off."

Not by half. "Thatcher, there's no use. You need to—"

"*You* need to listen, Madeleine!" he yelled. Clearing his throat, he assumed a gentler tone when he continued. "I haven't stuck by you for three years just to let you go now over some trite misunderstanding. Think of our plans, darling. Don't be so hasty. You've made assumptions that simply aren't true."

"I'm not a moron."

"No one is name-calling, but you must let me have a chance to exonerate myself. One final conversation after three years together—don't you owe me that much?"

Yes, she thought, feeling sad and tired and not in the mood to fight. *After three years, you deserve one last conversation.*

"I'm barely up," she said. "You can come by in an hour or two. I'll be waiting in the lobby."

"Tsk. I'll be there at six and pick you up at your door. Dress up, darling. I'm taking you out. We're celebrating tonight."

"No, Thatcher. I didn't agree to that. I only said we could ta—"

"Six o'clock, Madeleine. Good-bye."

The line went dead, and Mad groaned, swinging her legs over the bed and shuffling to the bathroom. After fifteen hours horizontal, she was achy. Getting a glimpse of herself in the mirror—wild, snarled hair; smeared makeup from last night; and red, bloodshot eyes—she grimaced. This wouldn't do for Thatcher at all.

But then, just before she allowed herself to feel bad about the way she looked, another stronger voice echoed in her head:

Baby, you look good enough to eat. You look beautiful. And anyone who thinks different is a blind fucking lunatic . . . The pencil skirt and fancy hair? Gorgeous. Sure. But this? This is you, Mad. And you're . . . Baby, you're music.

Sobbing, she turned from the mirror and ran back into her room, getting into bed and throwing the covers over her head as she curled into fetal position and let her tears flow.

When Mad's doorbell rang a little after five-thirty, she was sitting on the couch in the same flannel pants and old T-shirt she'd been wearing since last night, with a half-eaten pint of melted Häagen-Dazs on her lap and a marathon of *Married at First Sight* on the television.

The only people approved to come straight upstairs without being announced were her mother, her siblings, her friends Jane and Elizabeth Story, and Thatcher.

Thatcher.

Fuck.

For the first time since talking with him, she remembered that he insisted on taking her to dinner tonight. Was he a half hour early to pick her up? The nerve. Her temper flared as she plunked her ice cream on the coffee table and marched over to the door, swinging it open.

"I never said I'd go out to dinner with you!"

Jax stood on the threshold, looking surprised. "Good thing I didn't suggest it then."

Mad sighed, turning back into her apartment. "I thought you were Thatcher."

"I see," said Jax, closing the door behind her and following Mad into the den.

Mad curled up on the couch, muting her program and pulling her blanket around her. It was the blanket that she and Cort had been wrapped in the night he'd slept over, and the memory made her ache with longing. But it was way too late for that now. He'd been in London for hours. She'd made her choice, and she'd chosen Jax. Lifting her eyes to her sister, it stunned her how empty the thought made her feel. Jax had a new man, a new house, a new project she was working on, a new . . . life. And Mad? Mad had loyalty, yes, and gentleness and kindness. But her arms were empty. Her heart was empty. Her life felt . . . empty.

"What do you want?" she asked, feeling angry.

"Drop the attitude and I'll tell you," said Jax.

Mad swallowed. "I'm not in the mood for company. Can't you see that?"

"*Oui*." Jax sat down on the other side of the couch and raised an eyebrow. "You look like shit, *petite soeur*."

"I don't care," said Mad, looking down at the blanket, plucking at the threads with her fingernails.

"After that greeting, I assume Thatcher's finally home and coming over tonight?"

Mad shrugged. "Yes."

"When did you two break up?"

Mad raised her head, looking into Jax's emerald-green eyes. "I never told you we broke up. How did you know?"

"I got a little distracted for obvious reasons, but I started putting the pieces together last night," she said, fishing in her purse for a moment before pulling out two Tootsie Roll pops and offering the cherry-flavored one to Mad. "I think we need to talk."

All the sadness and nerves and worries and longings of the past several weeks came to a head as Mad peeled off the red wrapper and stuck the lollipop miserably into her mouth.

"I don't know where to begin," she sobbed, her speech garbled.

"At the beginning," said Jax, slipping a chocolate pop into her own mouth. "When did you and Thatcher break up?"

"A few weeks ago."

Jax nodded. "When *exactly*?"

"The Friday of my promotion."

Jax's lips twitched, and Mad knew it was because her feelings were hurt that Mad hadn't shared this information.

"You've been a little MIA," said Mad.

"I'm sorry," said Jax.

Mad shrugged. "I'm happy for you. About Gard."

"But I've been checked out?"

"A little."

"Well, I'm here now . . . and aside from obvious reasons," said Jax, who'd never liked Thatcher, "why did you two finally call it quits?"

Mad winced, hating to tell the truth but knowing that it was time to say the words aloud to her sister. "He cheated on me."

Jax's eyes narrowed. "Cheated?"

Mad nodded, sucking on her lollipop.

"Was it the first time?"

"No. The third or fourth that I know of. But there could have been hundreds of times I never found out about."

"Bastard," growled Jax.

"Yes." Mad nodded. "But I knew, Jax. I knew what he was doing, and I stayed with him."

Jax took a deep breath and sighed heavily. "How does Cort Ambler fit into this?"

Mad gasped softly, her breath hitching at Jax's unexpected question. Searching her sister's eyes desperately, Mad felt her own fill with too many tears to hold back. She let them fall, the rivulets streaming down her cheeks as a sob broke from her throat. Jax's arm looped around Mad's shoulders, and she scooted closer to hold Mad, comforting her as she cried.

Mad rested her head on Jax's shoulder, wetting her elegant silk top with tears until she had none left to cry. She sniffled, moving the lollipop from one cheek to the other before looking up at Jax with blurry eyes. "When did you know?"

"Last night," said Jax gently. "I saw you together when I arrived."

"I'm sorry," wailed Mad. "I'm so fucking sorry."

"For what?"

"He w-was y-your b-boyfriend."

"In high school, Mad. A long time ago."

"B-but you l-loved him."

"Oh, Mad. No. No, *chérie*. I never loved him. Not like . . . not like you do."

Mad's head jerked up to look into Jax's eyes. "W-What? You did! It b-broke your heart when he . . . when you . . . I mean—"

Jax clenched her jaw for a moment before exhaling a long, labored breath. "I owe you an explanation."

"Me?"

"*You.*" Jax nodded, her eyes heavy and full of portent as she popped her lollipop out from between her lips and gestured with it. "We need to unravel this, Mad. Tell me what's been going on, and I'll—"

Her doorbell rang again, and Mad sucked in a breath, meeting Jax's eyes and saying, "Thatcher."

"The cheater," said Jax, her green eyes narrowing with fury. Mad nodded.

"You want to talk to him?" asked Jax.

"No," said Mad, shaking her head, "but he wouldn't take no for an answer on the phone."

"Uh-huh," said Jax, hopping up from the couch like a woman on a mission. "Stay here. I got this."

Following her sister to the front vestibule, she stood back as Jax swung open the door.

"J-Jax," sputtered Thatcher.

"Motherfucker," answered Jax pleasantly, grabbing the bouquet of flowers out of his hands and throwing them over his head into the hallway. "Let me make this very simple: you're not welcome here."

"Last I checked, this wasn't your home," he answered, composing himself. "And it's certainly none of your business."

At Thatcher's imperious tone, something snapped inside of Mad. Maybe it was her relief that Jax finally knew about her and Cort. Or that she and Cort were, for all intents and purposes, over. Or that she had grown up over the last few weeks, after all, and was no longer willing to accept a half-full life when the promise of a full-to-bursting life awaited. Her own words circled in her head:

It wasn't bravery that day. It was easy because it was right. This is easy too.

Mad lifted her chin and crossed the vestibule to stand beside her sister, Cort's encouragement strengthening her steps and her purpose. Remembering his words made her feel his presence beside her—and with his presence, the way he believed in her, the way he saw her, the strong words he'd used to describe her: brave, generous, gentle, and kind. And suddenly, that was the person she wanted to be.

This is the person I am, she thought, placing a hand on Jax's shoulder.

"This is my fight," she said evenly, giving Jax a look that told her to back away.

"Thank heavens," said Thatcher, reaching for Mad as Jax backed up into the center of the vestibule a few feet behind them.

Mad blocked his hand with hers, pushing it away.

"Don't touch me," she said firmly. "You are not ever allowed to touch me again."

"Madeleine—"

"You're a cheater and a liar and a manipulator, and you are not welcome in my home, or in my life, from this day forward."

"Now darling—"

"We are done."

"You don't get to decide that!" he bellowed.

"Tell me you hear me, Thatcher," she said, her eyes capturing and holding his. "Acknowledge what I am saying to you. We are finished."

"But our plans . . ."

"We have no plans."

"Three years together."

"Wasted," she said softly. "To my undying regret."

He narrowed his eyes. "You're making a mistake."

"Maybe so. But my decision is final."

"You little French bitch," he snarled, his face red with fury. "I'm a *doctor*. My family fortune is older than this town. My name is one of the best in Philadelphia," he said, his dark eyes flinty with rage. "Who are *you* to break up with *me*?"

"*Je suis Madeleine Rousseau*," she said, placing her hand on the center of his chest and pushing hard enough to make him stumble backward into the hallway. "*Et tu, fils de pute—tu me gonfles! Va te faire foutre* . . . and *never* call me again!"

She slammed the door in his face, out of breath as she turned around and leaned against it, facing her sister.

Jax's mouth was scraping the floor as she clapped slowly, one hand still holding her lollipop, her green eyes wide with surprise and appreciation. "'Son of a bitch,' 'You're pissing me off,' *and* 'Go fuck yourself.' Nicely done, Mad!"

"Yeah?" Mad took a deep breath, blowing a rogue lock of tangled hair out of her face and popping her lollipop back into her cheek.

"Fuck, yeah! I wasn't aware you *knew* some of those words, but you swear like a champ!"

"Étienne and Jean-Christian are my brothers too."

"True, true," said Jax, throwing her arms around Mad. "*Merde*, I'm proud of you."

Her sister's praise sat like a stone in her stomach as she pulled away. She needed to explain to Jax what had happened with Cort, and she prayed her sister would understand and not interpret Mad's feelings and actions as a betrayal.

"We need to talk, Jax."

"I agree."

"Regular place?"

"*Oui.*"

Mad led the way to her room, where Jax kicked off her heels, and they sat down on her bed, cross-legged, across from each other.

Mad started. "I've known for a while that Thatcher was cheating on me, but I overlooked it. I've always wanted to be married, to have kids and a nice home. I thought that's all I wanted, and I thought Thatcher was going to offer it to me, and I think I even convinced myself that a little cheating wasn't such a big deal for a beautiful life. *Maman* tolerated it, didn't she?"

"She did." Jax nodded. "Keep going."

"I'm ashamed—so ashamed," she said, "that I ever felt like that. I think . . . after three years together, our lives were intertwined, and I just . . . I don't know. Maybe I feared finding someone else. Better to be with someone for the wrong reasons than be alone."

"It doesn't matter now," said Jax, reaching forward to take Mad's hands. "You came to your senses, and I just watched you kick him to the curb. That's over now. Tell me about Cort."

"The night Thatcher broke up with me, I decided to get drunk. I ended up at a dive bar downtown and got sick all over a cocktail table after chugging tequila. Cort was playing the piano there that night. He—I don't know why . . . or I didn't then . . . but he took care of me." She watched Jax's face for hurt or jealousy but saw none and was encouraged to continue. "He . . . he made me feel like I could be myself. Like I was enough. Just me. And after being with Thatcher, it felt so good. We talked and laughed. He stayed the night— not sex or anything. He just held me, and it was—" She looked up at Jax, a sudden pang of guilt making her talk faster. "But I broke it off, Jax. I promise I did. I told him I couldn't be with him because he'd been *your* boyfriend. It felt disloyal to be falling for him when he used to belong to you, and I told him we couldn't see each other again."

"Go on."

"But I couldn't stay away either," admitted Mad in a small, broken voice laced with tears. "I went to see him again. We slept together. We adopted a dog," she said, chuckling through tears. "He made me feel . . . more precious, more loved, more beautiful, more wanted than anyone has ever made me feel in my entire life."

"That's because he's been in love with you since we were kids," said Jax gently, reaching forward to wipe away Mad's tears with the back of her hand. "Was I right before? Do you love him?"

Mad nodded. "Totally."

"Am I all that's standing in your way?"

"You . . . and the Atlantic," she said before her voice gave way to sobs.

"Wait! He's in Europe?" exclaimed Jax.

"He l-left t-today."

"Oh, Mad," Jax sighed, shaking her head and sighing. "I *wish* you'd talked to me."

"I didn't w-want to h-hurt you! We haven't t-talked about C-Cort in years, but you l-loved him! I thought you l-loved him!"

"I didn't," said Jax, scooting forward. "I wanted a boyfriend for senior year, and he was . . . convenient."

"What do you mean?"

"You were in Paris for a month, and I was hanging out with Jane and Pris, who both had boyfriends. I wanted one too. I saw them sneaking out at night, going on dates to the movies, having fun . . . I wanted that too."

"But why Cort? I mean, if you didn't like him like that?"

"I did *like* him," said Jax. "I mean, I wasn't crazy about him, but I liked him. He was always nice. We were already friends. I thought he was cute in that broody musician sort of way. And both Pris and Jane said he was always looking at me." She sighed. "The last night of spring break, we were both hammered, but he'd been smiling at me more and more as the night went on. So . . . I followed him to the pool house and made a pass at him, and we kissed for a while. The next morning, I thought to myself, 'Here's your chance,

Jax. Best take it.' So I showed up at his house, treating it like more than it was and acting like we were boyfriend and girl-friend. I knew he wasn't with anyone else. And I was pretty sure if I made it sound like he'd promised me something, he wouldn't be an asshole about it. So I'd have a date for prom and the graduation party and everything else. No big deal, right? Except . . ."

"What?"

"I quickly realized that just because he wasn't with any-one didn't mean he was available." She dropped Mad's eyes for a moment before looking back up. "The reason he was always smiling at me was because I looked like you. The longer I observed, the more I realized he was totally in love with you." Jax took a deep breath and held it before letting it go. "The thing is? Once we were together? I started liking him a little, or at least I convinced myself I did. It was fun going out with Jane and Pris and their guys. I liked dating. I loved dating. And he was *my* boyfriend, even if he wished I was you. He was *mine*, not yours, and it hurt me—made me jealous—that he wanted to be with you instead of me."

"I understand," said Mad in a tight voice, trying to process all this new information and contextualize it into the past.

"We didn't make out a lot, Mad, almost like we both knew the relationship was a sham. If we drank too much, we'd kiss, but I think—no, I *know*—he was always pretending I was you. I know that because on prom night . . ."

Mad bit her lip because it hurt to hear about her sister touching Cort at all, even if it was a million years ago, but she needed to know what had happened between Cort and Jax.

"Tell me what happened."

"He—" Jax shook her head the way she did when she was having trouble saying something. She took another deep breath, then looked up at Mad. "He said your name while we were making out. He said, 'Mad, I love you so much. It's always been you, Mad.'"

Unforgivable.

Something unforgivable.

"And I realized," continued Jax, "that anytime we'd made out over the two months we were together, he was drunk. Because when he was drinking, it was easier to trick himself into believing that I was you."

"Jax," said Mad, imagining how it must have felt to realize that the boy whom you thought you were falling for was totally in love with someone else. "I'm so sorry."

But at the same time, her heart swelled with love for Cort, who'd only really ever loved Mad, just as he'd said. A stupid kid. A stupid kid who'd chosen the wrong sister. A stupid kid who'd tried to do the right thing. A stupid kid who'd blurted out the wrong sister's name in a moment of passion. Her heart clutched for Cort. And Jax. And herself, standing beside the pool, calling him a "motherfucker" when he loved her so terribly.

Jax sighed. "I started crying. He started apologizing. I said we were over, and he looked relieved, which made me furious. He said that I could tell our friends anything I wanted. That the 'breakup story' was completely up to me. I made him promise never to breathe a word about that night, and he promised me he wouldn't. And Mad," she said, tears filling her eyes as she looked at her sister, "I didn't blame you, but I wanted you to hate him as much as I did in that moment. I didn't want him to have a chance with you. So I told you he'd broken up with me because I wouldn't put out. He went along with it. And you hated him because you loved me and thought that he'd hurt me."

Mad pursed her lips, looking down at her lap and feeling bleak. "Yes, I did."

"A few months later, I felt bad about it when I saw him again over Christmas break when we were all home from freshman year. I pulled him aside and apologized at that weird party his parents always hosted. He accepted my apology and made one of his own, but the damage was done, and we both knew it. You hated him. And that was the worst punishment of all."

"I understand why you did what you did." Mad gulped over the sorrow lodged in her throat. "But it makes me really sad, Jax. You didn't have to tear him down like that."

Jax nodded, her eyes sorry. "At the time, I was angry and hurt. I may have even convinced myself I was heartbroken, and my ego had taken a blow for sure. I was selfish. I wanted to hurt him."

A tear snaked its way down Mad's cheek as she stared back at Jax. "You succeeded."

"Forgive me?" whispered Jax.

"I do," said Mad.

"We need tissues," said Jax, sniffling and swiping at her eyes.

"In my purse," said Mad, gesturing to the bureau, where she'd dropped her purse last night when she got home from the Winslows'.

Jax hopped off the bed and grabbed the purse, putting it between them on the bed. As she opened it, Mad suddenly remembered the airline tickets sitting on top and reached for them just as Jax pulled them out of the bag. Jax opened the British Airways envelope and nailed Mad with surprised eyes.

"These are for today."

Mad nodded, more tears falling. "He asked me to g-go on t-tour with him for a week."

"Well, what did you say?" asked Jax, leaning forward, her eyes hopeful.

"Obviously, I said no," sobbed Mad. "He was your b-boyfriend. I have no right to—"

"Wait!" said Jax, breathing faster as she waved the tickets at Mad. "You didn't go because of me?"

"Sister code! He was yours first. You loved him . . . or you didn't, but I thought you did! Not to mention, you were depressed after coming home from LA . . . then Gard was away, and I didn't know when he'd be back—*if* he'd be back. You seemed so fragile. I mean, I couldn't do that to you—suddenly go off on a vacation with your ex!"

"My *ex*? Oh, Mad!" cried Jax, throwing her arms around her sister. "I'm so sorry! I *never* loved him like that . . . of *course* you should be with him if he makes you happy, *petite soeur*! All I want is for you to be as happy as I am!"

"Do you mean it?" asked Mad, pulling away from her sister to look into her eyes but still holding on to her tightly. "You really . . . you really don't mind if Cort and I . . ."

"If you get together?" said Jax. "Of course I don't mind! He always wanted you, Mad, and I ruined that for both of you. That you could find your way back to each other means I didn't destroy something that was meant to be." She grinned at Mad. "Not to mention, I have a hot Cajun I'm going to spend my life with. If Cort is the man for you, *please* don't let me stand in the way! Oh, my God! It kills me that you'd do that for me!"

"I love you," sighed Mad, squeezing her sister closer as the burden she'd been carrying around for weeks took flight and disappeared. She was free to be with the man she loved.

And yes, Cort was far, far away, but maybe there was hope for them. She could fly over to London and still try to meet up with him. Or stop by Sloane's shop and find out where he was staying so she could call him. She'd figure out a way to—

"Mad," said Jax, "I don't get something. What did you mean when you said, 'Obviously, I said no,' when he asked you to go to London?"

Mad sniffled. "I mean . . . his plane left this morning, and I wasn't on it. But you know? I was just thinking . . . maybe I can track down his tour schedule and see if I can fly out tomorrow or—"

Jax jerked away from her sister, opening the ticket jacket she still held in her hands. "Mad!"

"Jax?"

"Did you *read* these tickets carefully?"

Mad nodded, scanning Jax's face. "Yes. Philadelphia to London on British Airways at nine."

"Exactly. At nine *p.m.*," said Jax, a massive smile blooming across her face. "He hasn't left yet!"

"What?" screeched Mad, ripping the tickets from Jax's fingers, her heart soaring, more tears pouring from her eyes as her lips tilted up into a smile she never felt coming. "Oh, my God! Oh, my God! Oh, my God! *Jax*!" She stared at the tickets and felt her heart race with anticipation as she looked up at her sister. "It's not too late!"

"It's not too late!" Jax giggled, nodding at her twin with joy-filled eyes. "But we have to get a move on. You go get ready and leave the packing to me!"

Cort sighed heavily, looking to his right, out the first-class window.

Rain trailed down the double panes, blurring the ground crew loading the bags into the hold and mirroring the bleakness of his mood. The seat beside him was empty, and across the aisle, Vic was already asleep.

He hadn't really thought Mad would come. Not really. But he'd stupidly hoped she would, and seeing her at the Winslows' last night was just an added bit of torture. Knowing that she missed him and was suffering as he was didn't relieve his pain; it only added to it. He didn't want her to be sad, and he was sorry that he had anything to do with bringing sorrow into her life. All he'd ever really wanted to bring into her life was love.

Love.

It occurred to him last night as he packed his bags after returning home from Haverford that despite the number of times he'd told her that he loved her, she'd never responded in kind. He believed that she cared for him, but maybe she didn't *love* him. Maybe she hadn't returned the words because she simply didn't feel them.

Maybe he'd been a distraction for her. Or a rebound from Thatcher.

Maybe he'd been the flattery she needed to lift her confidence after a bad breakup.

Maybe she enjoyed their chemistry, but her heart wasn't really invested.

Or maybe, as she'd insisted last night, the timing was truly bad for her to talk to her sister, and maybe one day—someday, *please, God*—the stars would align, and they'd have a second chance at forever.

But for now? With an empty seat beside him and a heart that felt full of lead knowing that he wouldn't see her for the next two months? He hurt. He hurt and he ached, and part of him hated Mad and hated love. At least for today.

"Sir?"

Cort turned to the flight attendant. "Yes?"

"We should be taking off in about ten minutes. Can I get you anything else before we close the galley prior to taxiing?"

He shook his head. "No thanks. I'm good."

"Will you be having dinner with us tonight?"

He pulled his earbuds from his lap. "I think I'll try to sleep."

"Then we won't disturb you, sir."

"Great," he said, offering her a polite smile. "Thanks."

Popping the buds in his ears, he decided to torture himself just a little more and scrolled through his song list until he found the one he was looking for and tapped on the title: *Mad's Song*. A smooth guitar riff—a little folk, a little Irish, and a lot fluid—strummed a full chorus before the gentle plucking of the harp joined it for a completely unique sound. And over these unusual instruments blending carefully together came Cort's voice, ripe with sorrow, recorded just today.

Miss Mad, Miss Mad,
A heart so sad,
And shattered glass for eyes.
I'll stay, you know,
Miss Mad Rousseau,
'Til you say otherwise.

He thought of her at *Voulez-Vous* that first night in her chignon, Chanel, and pearls. The way she'd let him take her out to dinner and walk her home, and all the while, he'd hoped for a few more minutes with her. Just a few more precious seconds.

Miss Mad, Miss Mad,
Mi caridad,
My arms were made for you.
You stay, you go,
Miss Mad Rousseau,
To you I will be true.

He remembered dancing with her in the rain, humming the first incarnation of this song while she wept against his chest after slapping his face so hard it had left a mark. He hadn't minded the slap because she'd let him hold her, and that had meant everything to him.

Miss Mad, Miss Mad,
You've been so bad,
I'll put you over my knee.
Miss Mad Rousseau,
Aw, fuck this! I'll go.
No, fuck me. I'll never be free.

And when he kissed her for the first time in her kitchen, the fucking heat between them was so combustible, they both should have gone up in flames. That's when he'd known that whatever had started between them that night wasn't going to be easy to let go.

Miss Mad, Miss Mad,
I want you bad,
So bad it hurts inside.
Miss Mad Rousseau,
You've brought me low,
My need for you denied.

She'd turned him away the next morning, telling him to go. And though he was determined to see her again at some point, it had looked like—for all intents and purposes—their short affair was over . . . until she'd come walking back into *Voulez-Vous* that second night like an angel, and he'd kissed her at the bar like she was water and his thirst was unquenchable.

Miss Mad, Miss Mad,
In nothing clad,
Your body bared to mine.
Miss Mad Rousseau,
I love you so,
From now to the end of time.

His heart throbbed as he remembered making love to her in his bed, in the studio, in the shower . . . her body perfectly matched with his, the beautiful fucking memory of being one with the woman he'd loved since childhood.

Miss Mad, Miss Mad,
By you I'm had,
By you my heart is owned.
Miss Mad Rousseau,
First fast, then slow,
Tonight won't be postponed.

And when she'd arrived at her brother's gallery after a week apart, how he needed her, how fucking badly he needed to know that there was a chance for them. And they'd run away, into the alley, back to his house, falling into each other as they both admitted that they were meant to be.

He gulped with misery as his voice tapered off and a final guitar riff tied up the love song in a beautiful fucking bow.

No such beautiful ending awaits me tonight, he thought, wondering how long it would take for him to stop aching every time she passed through his mind. Days. Weeks. Fuck it, he knew better . . . a lifetime.

He felt the plane start moving back from the gate and took a deep breath, opening his eyes as he took out the earbuds and leaned away from the window. Sighing with melancholy, he turned his head to check on Vic only to find the seat beside him occupied . . .

. . . by Mad Rousseau.

"Wh—Are you really here?" he gasped, holding his breath, his entire body rigid as he stared at her lovely face only inches from his.

"Yes," she said, her eyes glistening with fat tears. "Hi."

"Mad," he managed, blinking at her in shock. "When . . . and how did you—"

"I told Jax," she said, biting her lower lip as her eyes searched his. "I told her about us."

"What did you tell her?"

"That . . ." She whimpered softly, looking down at her lap before cutting her eyes back up to his with such stark vulnerability, it took every ounce of his strength not to unbuckle her fucking belt and drag her into his lap. "That I love you. That I want to be with you. That you're the best thing that's ever happened to me. That you and I were meant to be."

His eyes searched hers. Did she know what he'd done to hurt her sister?

"Did she tell you what happened? After prom?"

"That you said my name?" She nodded. "She told me. And she told me that she wanted me to hate you."

"It worked," he said.

"Only for a while," she said, gazing at him with green eyes full of tenderness.

He needed to be sure. "She's okay with this? With us?"

"Completely," said Mad, placing her hand palm up on the bolster between them. "She drove me to the airport. She wants me to be happy."

"And I make you happy?" he murmured, sliding his fingers through hers.

"You make me the luckiest," she said, leaning closer to him.

"Hey, wait a second," he said, nuzzling her nose with his, happiness warming his voice. "Did I just hear you say you love me, Mad Rousseau?"

She smiled, happy tears falling at will. "I love you, Cort Ambler."

"I love you too," he said, reaching up to cradle her cheeks in his hands as he captured her lips with his. He kissed her tenderly, lovingly, pouring his relief and joy into the gentle movement of his lips, into the fingers that kneaded her soft skin, offering her his sighs of utter contentment and swallowing her low moan of pleasure.

When he pulled away from her, he grinned, shaking his head with sheer wonder that she was here, that she loved him, that a love that had lived in his heart for fourteen years had finally been requited by the woman he'd always wanted.

"Hey," he murmured, resting his forehead against hers. "Why don't you marry me, Mad?"

She gasped with surprise, leaning away from him just enough to catch his eyes, but her smile was made of pure delight. "How many times does a girl have to say yes?" When he blinked at her in shock, she chuckled. "I wasn't asleep that night, Cort. I *already* said yes."

"You already said yes," he whispered with a heart so full of gratitude, he was already flying by the time the plane lifted off the ground.

As he pulled her as close as the seats would allow and started a make-out session that would last until London, a final verse took shape in his head, and he smiled as he kissed her, because it was the perfect final verse to her song:

I said, "Marry me, Mad."
She said, "Yes," and I'm glad.
We'll belong to each other for life.
That bright golden band
She'll wear on her hand,
Means Madeleine Ambler's my wife.

THE END

The Rousseaus continues with . . .

J.C. AND THE BIJOUX JOLIS

THE ROUSSEAUS, BOOK #3

THE ROUSSEAUS
(Part III of the Blueberry Lane Series)

Jonquils for Jax
Marry Me Mad
J.C. and the Bijoux Jolis

Turn the page for a sneak peek of *J.C. and the Bijoux Jolis*!

PROLOGUE

August 1939
Marseilles, France

"You are . . . exquisite," sighed Monsieur Montferrat, peeking at her from one side of the canvas before hiding behind it once again. "*Magnifique.*"

"*Merci,*" said eighteen-year-old Camille Trigére softly, wishing she could flex her arms and roll her neck to get the kinks out.

A bead of sweat that started at the nape of her neck swerved around her collarbone to rest precariously on the tip of her left nipple. It was hot this summer. *Merde,* but it was hot.

Still, to be immortalized by a famous painter like Pierre Montferrat was an honor for a very new and inexperienced portrait model like Camille. A hundred years from now, when she was long gone, this portrait, which Monsieur had titled *Les Bijoux Jolis*, would hang on someone's wall, some-where in the world.

Immortalité.

It was worth a moment's discomfort to live forever.

"Do not move. Not even an inch," said Monsieur Mont-ferrat, pulling at the gray goatee on his chin as he stood to admire her, a glass of muddy-gray water in his hand. "I must refresh the water."

She watched until he had left the small studio, then stretched her arms over her head eagerly, massaging the feeling back into her hands. For over four hours, she'd held the same pose of "young nude wearing emerald necklace," and she was tired, damn it.

Casting her eyes toward the open doors that led to a small terrace, she wondered if her old friend and new lover, Gilles Lévy, was already waiting downstairs to walk her home. The sun was quite low. It must be after four.

Camille and Gilles had known each other forever, grow-ing up in the same neighborhood and attending the same synagogue throughout their shared childhood. Lately, the France of their early years was shifting, however, with con-servatives and socialists whom Camille's father had once considered mainstream now speaking out against the Jews of Marseilles and aligning their politics with worrisome new ideas filtering into France from Germany.

The shift was subtle—Camille saw it in the way that Monsieur Ragout had stopped taking Jewish piano stu-dents this summer, too busy for one more student, though very little lesson music wafted down from his third-floor studio on Rue Saint Dominique. In Camille's own life, the shift had been slightly less subtle and infinitely more per-sonal: Monsieur Montferrat, upon meeting her in July, had commented, "How curious! You don't have the *look* of a Jewess."

His initial inspection had made her uncomfortable enough to reconsider the monthlong modeling job, but she'd accepted despite misgivings. Although her father would skin her alive if he found out what she'd been doing every day, she hoped to make enough money to run away to Paris with Gilles this fall. He had a second cousin willing to share his deux-piéces with the young lovers. Struggling artist Gilles said they'd find work at a local café during the day, and every night he would paint her in the moonlight before sweeping her off to bed to make love until dawn.

When Monsieur Montferrat slipped back into the room, Camille's arms and hands were perfectly in place, though her smile may have been a bit more dreamy.

"It's almost five," he said, flicking a glance at the terrace doors regretfully. "I suppose you have to go soon."

"*Oui*, Monsieur. Gilles will be here at five. How much longer today?" asked Camille politely as the artist stood at his canvas, surveying his work.

After several long moments of staring at the portrait, he looked up at her and sighed. "We're finished."

Camille sat up immediately, grabbing her chemise and panties from under the divan and wiggling into them, always self-conscious of her naked form when Monsieur Montferrat was finished painting. She shrugged her light-blue cotton dress over her head, smoothing the clothing back into place, relieved that she was fully covered once again.

"Shall I come again tomorrow?"

Monsieur Montferrat raised an eyebrow as he smiled sadly at her, slipping around his painting carefully to take his place behind her. Gathering her black hair in her hands, Camille lifted it off the back of her neck and stood still, waiting for him to unclasp the necklace so she could go.

His rough fingers rested on the damp skin of her neck. "Do you know what's happening in the world, *belle* Camille?"

"Monsieur?" she murmured, surprised by the distressed tone of his voice.

"Madness," he cursed softly. "The world is going mad, *petite*."

Camille liked Monsieur Montferrat.

He was gray and wrinkled like her grandfather, but he had been kind to the young model: respectful, not leering; patient as she learned how to maintain a pose for hours on end; and always kind to her, talking of art and music during their long afternoons together. But his outburst made her uncomfortable and eager to leave.

"Monsieur," she said gently, "my friend will be most anxious."

She felt his fingers working the clasp of the ornate emerald necklace. She'd worn it every day for twenty-nine days while her parents believed she was minding Gilles' twin nieces on the other side of town.

The heavy jewels slipped into the crevice of her breasts as Monsieur Montferrat lifted the two sides from around her neck, then raised them over her head. Camille breathed a sigh of relief as he stepped away, and she reached down to tug on her shoes, quickly buckling them.

"You needn't come back, Mademoiselle Trigére," said the artist, crossing the room and placing the priceless necklace back in a black velvet box, which he locked in the bottom drawer of a desk.

"Monsieur?" she whispered, fearing that she had displeased him in some way.

Turning to face her, his smile was rueful. "The portrait is finished."

He beckoned her to stand beside him, and she stepped around the easel to look at the canvas she'd never been permitted to peek at before now.

Her painted body, pale and pink, was stark on the dark-green velvet divan on which she had posed, but she quickly realized that she was merely a palette for the necklace around her throat. The gems caught the afternoon light, facets gleaming, white-gold settings shiny and bright. The centerpiece of the painting was the necklace, and Camille had a sense of disappointment as she realized that her immortality would be forever overshadowed by the jewels she'd worn around her neck. Yet still . . .

"It's beautiful," she said softly.

He collected an envelope full of francs from the shelf at the bottom of his easel, holding it between them, searching her eyes with his. When he finally spoke, his voice was urgent. "Don't go to Paris, *petite*. Go to London. Or better, New York. *Oui, belle* Camille, go to America. *Maintenant.* Now. Promise me."

"America?"

"*Oui.* As soon as possible."

Troubled by the wild look in his eyes and ever more eager to leave, she took the envelope from his fingers. "You have been kind to me. *Merci.*"

"Promise me," he begged her in a whisper, "that you will have a good life."

She stepped forward to press her lips against his papery cheek. "*Adieu*, Monsieur."

Her footsteps echoed down the metal stairs of the tiny apartment building, and she flung herself into Gilles' arms, heady with freedom, as soon as she reached the sidewalk.

"*C'est fine!*" she told him with a beaming smile, offering him the envelope of money that would secure the next step of their shared future.

"Paris, here we come!" he cried, covering her mouth with a lusty kiss.

From the lonely terrace of his apartment, Monsieur Montferrat watched them link hands and scurry joyfully away, wondering just for a moment what would become of the young Jewish girl in the painting . . . the beautiful young woman in his final portrait, *Les Bijoux Jolis*.

Chapter 1

If the best man and maid of honor are both single, thought J.C. Rousseau, taking another peek at Kate English's best friend, Libitz Feingold, *it's practically an unwritten rule that they should pork.*

And if anyone on earth looked to be in dire need of a good, hard, thorough fucking, it was Mademoiselle Feingold.

As the priest droned on about the blessing and sanctity of marriage, the groom—J.C.'s younger brother, Étienne—elbowed him subtly in the side, and J.C. straightened, clearing his throat and shifting his glance away from Kate's skinny, tiny, perpetually annoyed-looking friend.

She was definitely, positively *not* his type—she wasn't even breathing the same air as his type—so why had he kept stealing glances at her over Étienne's wedding weekend? Fuck if he knew. There was something intriguing about her, but he couldn't quite . . .

Look for *J.C. and the Bijoux Jolis* at your local bookstore or buy online!

Other Books by Katy Regnery

A MODERN FAIRYTALE
(Stand-alone, full-length, unconnected romances inspired by classic fairy tales.)

The Vixen and the Vet
(inspired by "Beauty and the Beast")
2014

Never Let You Go
(inspired by "Hansel and Gretel")
2015

Ginger's Heart
(inspired by "Little Red Riding Hood")
2016

Dark Sexy Knight
(inspired by "The Legend of Camelot")
2016

Don't Speak
(inspired by "The Little Mermaid")
2017

Swan Song
(inspired by "The Ugly Duckling")
2018

ABOUT THE AUTHOR

New York Times and *USA Today* bestselling author Katy Regnery started her writing career by enrolling in a short story class in January 2012. One year later, she signed her first contract and Katy's first novel was published in September 2013.

Twenty-five books later, Katy claims authorship of the multi-titled, *New York Times* and *USA Today* bestselling Blueberry Lane Series, which follows the English, Winslow, Rousseau, Story, and Ambler families of Philadelphia; the six-book, bestselling A Modern Fairytale series; and several other standalone novels and novellas.

Katy's first modern fairytale romance, *The Vixen and the Vet*, was nominated for a RITA® in 2015 and won the 2015 Kindle Book Award for romance. Katy's boxed set, *The English Brothers Boxed Set*, Books #1–4, hit the *USA Today* bestseller list in 2015, and her Christmas story, *Marrying Mr. English*, appeared on the list a week later. In May 2016, Katy's Blueberry Lane collection, *The Winslow Brothers Boxed Set*, Books #1–4, became a *New York Times* E-Book bestseller.

In 2016, Katy signed an agreement with Spencer Hill Press. As a result, her Blueberry Lane paperback books will now be distributed to brick-and-mortar bookstores all over the United States.

Katy lives in the relative wilds of northern Fairfield County, Connecticut, where her writing room looks out at the woods, and her husband, two young children, two dogs, and one Blue Tonkinese kitten create just enough cheerful chaos to remind her that the very best love stories begin at home.

Sign up for Katy's newsletter today: www.katyregnery.com!

Connect with Katy:

Katy LOVES connecting with her readers and answers every e-mail, message, tweet, and post personally! Connect with Katy!

Katy's Website: http://katyregnery.com
Katy's E-mail: katy@katyregnery.com
Katy's Facebook Page: https://www.facebook.com/KatyRegnery
Katy's Pinterest Page: https://www.pinterest.com/
    katharineregner
Katy's Amazon Profile: http://www.amazon.com/Katy-Regnery/
    e/B00FDZKXYU
Katy's Goodreads Profile: https://www.goodreads.com/author/
    show/7211470.Katy_Regnery

CPSIA information can be obtained
at www.ICGtesting.com
Printed in the USA
LVOW12s0140071216
516098LV00001B/1/P

9 781633 920934